# HELIXANDRA

## A NOVEL

## BY

## JASON M. BUCKLEW

**For Becca Ahern —**

To a great and loyal friend — your encouragement, your
ideas, and your unwavering belief in me helped carry this
book from a dream to a finished world. Thank you for
pushing me forward, lifting me up, and being there
through every step of this journey.

Cover design by Jason M. Bucklew

Printed in the United States

First Edition

# Chapter 1 The Graduation

The ocean air had a crisp bite that morning, the kind that carried the scent of salt and faint cry of distant seagulls. Viremoor University sat perched above the Pacific, its red-brick buildings framed by fluttering green-and-gold banners. The quad had been transformed into neat rows of folding chairs facing a wooden stage draped in the school's colors, the polished wood gleaming under the early sun.

Matthew Fisher adjusted the collar of his gown as he joined the slow procession toward the seating area. The black fabric clung lightly to his lean frame, and the tassel on his mortarboard brushed against his cheek with each gust. Dark, unruly hair framed a face marked by faint freckles—a face that spoke of countless hours outdoors. His fingers found the short, inch-long beard along his jaw, tugging at it the way he always did when his mind was already somewhere ahead.

Somewhere behind him, a voice rang out over the crowd. "Hey, Matt!"

He turned to see Adam Nolan weaving between clusters of guests. No cap or gown—just jeans, a T-shirt, and a camera slung around his neck like an extra limb. "You better smile when you walk up there," Adam said. "I'm not wasting film on you looking like someone stole your bike."

Matthew smirked. "You know this isn't film, right?"

"Doesn't matter. Same rules apply." Adam gave a mock salute before disappearing back into the current of people.

As Matthew found his seat among the graduates, he spotted Shayne Wood lounging in the back row with the other guests, long hair tucked behind one ear as he scrolled lazily on his phone. Shayne looked up, caught Matthew's eye, and gave a two-fingered salute— somehow managed to be both lazy and sincere.

Near the front, Kaia Bennett stood out like a beacon. Her curly auburn hair caught the light, burning copper in the sun, and the green sash of the biology department cut across her gown. She stood with quiet confidence, her sharp eyes scanning the crowd as though nothing escaped her. When she spotted Matthew, she waved, her smile carrying the warmth of a shared secret.

The ceremony began with the march of faculty across the stage; the air filled with polite applause and the murmur of parents whispering from the sidelines. Speeches followed—the kind graduates listened to with half an ear, already thinking about what came next. When Matthew's name was called, he strode forward into the sunlight, shook hands, accepted his degree, and slipped back into the sea of black gowns.

It wasn't until after the final cheer that Professor Jeremiah Clark approached.

Clark moved with deliberate ease, silver threading through his dark hair, his charcoal suit tailored to perfection. His sharp, charismatic features softened into warmth when he smiled.

"Matthew Fisher," Clark said, clasping his hand. "Environmental Science, top of your class. You've done me proud."

Matthew grinned. "Thanks, Professor. Couldn't have done it without you."

Clark's gazed lingered a heartbeat too long— thoughtful, measuring. "I'm taking a small group on a voyage along the Pacific to celebrate. I'd like you and Miss Bennett to join us."

Matthew blinked. "Seriously? That sounds incredible."

"You've earned it,"

Matthew hesitated for only a moment. "Could I bring my cousin Adam and my friend Shayne? We've been through a lot together, and—"

"Of course," Clark said smoothly. "The more the merrier."

Later that afternoon, the ceremony buzz still clung to them when Matthew, Kaia, Adam, and Shayne found themselves at the café across from campus, crammed into a booth that had seen better days. The place smelled of coffee and cinnamon rolls, the hum of conversation around them a far cry from the formal applause in the auditorium.

Megan had arrived in a swirl of perfume and big sunglasses, plopping down beside Kaia with a grin. "So, she said, propping her chin on her hand, "we're going on a yacht? Like... actual rich-people yacht?"

"Looks that way," Matthew said, sipping his coffee. "Clark says it's a 'celebration of potential.'"

"Fancy way of saying free trip," Shayne muttered.

Megan grinned wider. "As long as there's Wi-Fi and cocktails with little umbrellas, I'm in."

Kaia nudged her. "What about sunscreen?"

"Please. I don't burn," Megan said, then leaned toward Adam. "Do you burn?"

Adam nearly choked on his muffin. "Uh— sometimes?"

Shayne smirked. "Translation: he's about to buy SPF 50 tomorrow."

Megan's laugh cut through the chatter of the café. "Good. I don't sit next to lobster people."

—

Outside the café, the late-afternoon sun glinted off the hoods of parked cars. A few students crossed the street with to-go cups, laughing, their voices fading into the city noise.

Leaning against a dark sedan half a block down, a bald man with a faint scar across his cheek watched the group through the café's wide front window. He lit a cigarette with slow precision, the flame briefly illuminating a calm, unreadable expression.

Matthew, Kaia, Adam, Shayne, and Megan laughed over something none of them would remember later. Grent exhaled a thin ribbon of smoke and let it curl away on the breeze; his gaze fixed on them until they stood to leave. Only then did he drop the cigarette, grind it under his boot, and step into the flow of the crowd.

# Chapter 2  The Invitation

The late-afternoon sun slanted through the tall windows of Professor Jeremiah Clark's office, gliding the rows of bookshelves and the neat stacks of paper on his desk. The light turned the dust motes into slow-drifting flecks of gold, disturbed only by the faint hum of the overhead fan. The scent of polished wood and old paper lingered—a smell Dr. Emilia Varn had always associated with conversations that mattered.

Clark rose from behind his desk as she stepped inside, moving with that same unhurried precision that made every gesture seem deliberate. His tailored suit looked effortless, but not accidental.

"Emilia," he said warmly, as if greeting an old friend rather than a colleague. "You've been avoiding me."

She set her bag on the armchair by the door, smiling faintly. "I've been buried in the conference preparations. Avoiding you would require more energy than I have to spare."

He chuckled, gesturing toward the leather chair opposite his desk. "Then I'm glad I caught you before the semester slips away. I'm putting together a small... celebration. A yacht voyage. A few bright young minds—Matthew Fisher among them. I'd like you to come along."

Her brows lifted. "A pleasure trip?"

"Not entirely." He steepled his fingers, leaning back slightly. "Consider it a field opportunity. Observe Matthew, see how he responds to new challenges. Quietly, of course. I value your eye for... potential."

She studied him for a beat. Emilia had known Clark for years, admired his sharpness and control, but there was something in the way he said *potential*—like it was less about talent and more about destiny. "Why him?"

Clark's smile didn't falter. "Because he's the kind of person who changes things."

The words landed between them with weight, neither casual nor fully explained.

She crossed one leg over the other, folding her hands. "And what am I observing him for?"

"You'll know when you see it."

The finality in his tone was polite but immovable. She had the sense she could press him, but he'd only answer in circles.

They spoke a while longer about logistics—departure time, passenger list, the promise of calm seas and good company. Clark's tone remained light, but his eyes flicked to the clock twice in as many minutes, like a man with more than one countdown running in his head.

When Emilia rose to leave, he walked her to the door with that same courteous air he always carried.

It was then she saw it.

On the corner of his desk, half-hidden beneath a leather-bound journal, lay an envelope. Her eyes caught the name typed across it:

**Dr. Ardan Helix**

She slowed. The name meant nothing to her, but the formality of the typeface—made it stand out. Questions began forming before she realized she'd stopped moving.

Clark noticed her glance and, with an easy, practiced motion, slid the journal over it.

"Something on your mind?" he asked lightly, a hint of humor in his tone, but nothing in his eyes to suggest it was a joke.

"No," she said, stepping into the hallway.

The door clicked shut behind her, but the name still echoed in her mind, repeating with each step she took down the quiet corridor.

Dr. Ardan Helix.

A thread she wasn't sure she wanted to pull—but already had her fingers on.

# Chapter 3  The Professor's Day

Professor Jeremiah Clark stood at the edge of the university greenhouse, a steaming mug of dark roast in one hand, the other resting lightly in the pocket of his tweed coat. Morning sunlight filtered through the glass panes, scattering across the dew-beaded leaves of tropical ferns and delicate orchids. The air inside was humid, fragrant with loam and green life—a small, curated jungle thriving far from where nature had intended it to grow.

He wasn't on duty today. The spring semester had ended with the pageantry of graduation, and the campus had exhaled. The walkways were quiet, save for the occasional echo of a custodian's footsteps. It was the kind of stillness Clark favored—where thoughts could move without interruption.

He took a slow sip of coffee, letting the bitter warmth linger on his tongue. Yet for all the calm surrounding him, his mind was anything but.

Memories had been slipping in more often lately—flashes he didn't invite but never fully pushed

away. He thought of himself at Matthew Fisher's
age: brilliant, ambitious, restless. The world had felt
small back then, a puzzle that begged to be solved. Rules
had been more like speed bumps than barriers, things to
slow down for but never stop. Even among his
peers, he'd felt apart, as though everyone else was bound
by invisible walls he could already see beyond.

He remembered the first real lab, the sterile chill
of it, the hum of refrigeration units, the sharp scent of
ethanol. He remembered the applause that came after the
first breakthrough, the kind that made you believe you
were destined for more. And the long nights, pushing
beyond safe limits because safe limits were for lesser
minds. Genius, they had called it. He'd learned that genius,
unchecked, could spiral in any direction—and sometimes
it spun toward places no one else was willing to follow.

His hand brushed over the leaves of
a rare bioluminescent vine as he walked past. It pulsed
faintly under his fingertips, like a heartbeat you could
almost feel. A faint smile tugged at his mouth. Even here,
there were species that thrived when taken out of their
proper place.

Loss drifted through his mind then—brief, sharp,
unwelcome. He let it pass without unpacking it. The past
was only useful when it served the future.

And the future was approaching fast. The
yacht. The carefully selected crew. The even more carefully
selected passengers. Matthew Fisher among them. That
boy carried the same spark Clark had once seen in the
mirror.

Back in his office, he set the empty mug aside and
lowered himself into his leather chair. The room smelled
faintly of paper, wood polish, and the trace of the
greenhouse clinging to his clothes. Classical music drifted

softly from the old bookshelf speaker, soft strings filling
the corners. On the desk, books in genetics,
paleobiology, and mythology lay stacked neatly, a manila
folder resting on top.

Inside the folder were profiles. Notes written in
his own precise hand.

**Fisher.**

**Bennett.**

**Varn.**

And others—each one a piece on the board, each
one meant to be moved in the right order.

He tapped the folder once, a metronome to the
rhythm of his thoughts. Soon, they would all be far from
here. Off the grid. Out of reach of
conventional oversight. In a place that still obeyed older
laws.

Leaning back, he closed his eyes. He could almost
hear the yacht's engines. Almost hear the ocean closing
in around them.

* * *

Later that evening, the campus had gone
still again, the last streaks of sunlight bleeding away behind
the faculty buildings. The lamplight along the walkways
glowed amber in the mist rising from the grass.

Clark returned to his office after dinner, moving
without hurry. He turned on the desk lamp, the warm glow
catching the dust in the air, and crossed to the filing
cabinet. From the second drawer, he withdrew a thick
envelope and laid it on the desk.

The type on its face was bold, clean, absolute:

**Dr. Ardan Helix**

**CONFIDENTIAL**

He regarded it for a long moment. Then, with the same calm he'd shown all day, he sealed it and slid it into the top drawer.

The greenhouse had been his morning's work. This—this was the work that mattered.

# Chapter 4  The Last Normal Night

Adam Nolan's basement smelled faintly of microwaved popcorn and worn carpet—the comfortable, lived-in scent of too many weekends spent here. The glow of the flat screen painted the three of them in shifting colors as the game blared on.

Matthew Fisher leaned forward on the couch, thumb hammering the controller's trigger. "You can't just camp in the corner, Shayne. That's cowardly."

Shayne Wood, long hair falling into his face, didn't look up from the screen. "It's called strategy. Learn it."

Adam snorted, sprawled sideways in the recliner, legs dangling over on armrest. "No, it's called being a pain in the ass."

The match ended with Shayne's triumphant cry and Matthew's groan. Adam tossed him a soda can, the hiss of carbonation cutting through their laughter.

"So," Adam said, popping the tab on his own drink, "this trip Clark invited you to... we're really going?"

"Yacht's leaving in two days," Matthew said, taking a swig. "Pacific coast, maybe farther. Kaia's coming too."

Adam smirked. "Kaia, huh?"

"Don't start," Matthew said, though his half-smile gave him away.

Shayne grinned, leaning back. "Count me in. Open water, free food, no responsibilities—what's not to like?"

Matthew hesitated for a second, glancing between them. "I asked Clark if you two could come. He didn't even blink. Just said the more the merrier."

Adam frowned slightly. "That's... generous."

Matthew shrugged it off, turning back to the game. "it'll be fun. We could use a break."

As Shayne launched another grenade on screen, Matthew's phone buzzed. He picked it up to see a group chat lighting up—*Kaia Bennett* added *Megan Truss.*

**Kaia**: So... Matthew are you and the two nerds ready to go?

**Megan**: Is this the trip group chat??

**Shayne**: Yes. Prepare yourself for memes.

**Adam**: And for Megan complaining about no cell signal.

**Megan**: Lies. I can survive without it. Probably. Maybe.

Shayne chuckled. "She's gonna last about an hour without Instagram."

Adam smirked. "Bet she'll ask the captain for the Wi-Fi password before we leave the dock."

Matthew shook his head but couldn't help smiling as another message popped up.

**Megan**: What should I pack besides sunscreen and sarcasm?

They played until the controller batteries died and the conversation shifted to old stories—botched camping trips, high school disasters, the time Shayne swore he saw a ghost in Adam's attic. The night felt easy, familiar, like the kind of memory you didn't know was your last until it was too late.

* * *

The motel room smelled faintly of stale smoke and rain. Silas Grent sat on the edge of the bed, the flicker of the television crawling over the scar on his cheek. A half-burned cigarette rested in the ashtray, its smoke curling lazily toward the ceiling.

He answered the phone on the second ring.

"Yeah," he said.

The voice on the other end spoke quietly, efficiently. Grent listened without interrupting, eyes narrowing slightly.

"Understood," he said finally, and hung up.

He crushed out the cigarette with slow, deliberate pressure, then lit another.

Two days.

That was all the time he needs.

# Chapter 5  The Voyage Begins

The morning air carried the tang of salt and the rhythmic clink of rigging against masts. The yacht waited at the pier, sleek and gleaming against the backdrop of a calm, glassy sea. Crew members moved briskly, stowing luggage and checking lines.

Matthew Fisher stood at the foot of the gangway, hands in his pockets, watching the others arrive. Shayne emerged from the parking lot with his long hair pulled back in a loose tie, carrying a backpack slung over one shoulder. Adam followed, tossing his duffel to a waiting crewman with an easy grin.

Then came Megan Truss and Kaia Bennett, side by side but moving at very different paces. Kaia's eyes swept the length of the yacht, quietly taking in every detail, while Megan kept her attention locked on her phone, thumbs flying as she sent a rapid-fire string of texts. She was dressed in layered bracelets, sunglasses perched in her blonde hair, and shoes far too stylish for a dock.

"You ever been on one of these before?" Megan asked, not looking up from her screen.

Kaia shook her head. "Closest I've been to this much water is a ferry ride."

That earned Kaia a quick glance from Megan, followed by a smirk. "And here I thought you were the adventurous one. Guess we'll see who gets seasick first."

Kaia smiled faintly. "I'm not worried."

"Oh, of course you're not. Not with *him* around." Megan nodded toward Matthew, who was busy helping Shayne lift a cooler aboard.

Kaia's brow furrowed. "What does that mean?"

Megan finally slid her phone into her bag and grinned. "Come on. You two practically orbit each other. You ever gonna make a move, or are you waiting for the tides to align?"

Kaia rolled her eyes. "We're friends."

"Uh-huh. And I'm a morning person." Megan slung her bag higher on her shoulder. "Mark my words— by the time this trip's over, you'll have kissed him. Or at least thought about it."

Kaia tried not to smile. "You're ridiculous."

"Ridiculously right."

Up ahead, Captain Lee Cartwright—broad-shouldered, weathered, and standing with military posture—greeted each passenger with a firm handshake. "Welcome aboard," he said, voice deep and steady.

Behind Cartwright, three more students waited to board.

•**Bryce Calder**, tousled sandy hair, wiry and athletic, his baseball cap pulled low. "Hope this thing's faster than it looks," he muttered.

•**Tarek Loomis**, stoner smile plastered on his face, hair unkempt, hoodie sleeves half-pulled over his hands. "Someone said there's an open bar? Tell me there's an open bar."

•**Jules Fenwick**, already sweating in his perfectly tucked button-down, clutched a satchel so overstuffed it looked ready to burst. "I read the yacht's specs online," he began, only for Bryce to cut in—" Nobody cares, Jules."

Professor Jeremiah Clark emerged from the deck above, silvering hair untouched by the breeze, his presence drawing everyone's attention. He moved through the small crowd with a host's practiced warmth, shaking hands and exchanging brief words with each passenger.

Off to the side, Silas Grent leaned against the railing, cigarette between his fingers, watching them board without a word.

Captain Cartwright clapped the rail once. "Quick tour before we shove off." He led them along the warm boards of the main deck. "Galleys below. Cabins to port. Observation decks up the ladder. Helm is off-limits unless I say otherwise."

They passed the dining area, lemon polish and varnish giving the air a clean bite. Megan drifted to the windows with Kaia, phone hovering, then lowered it to take in the view for real. "This is nicer than my apartment," she whispered, grinning.

Adam paused at the observation glass, the city already shrinking behind them. "Feels... different out here."

"It's the seas," Cartwright said. "She's bigger than you think."

He tipped his chin toward a closed corridor. "Crew's quarters stay shut. If you need a hand, you ask a crewman or me." As they swung back toward mid-deck, Grent remained a few paces behind the group, cigarette unit now, twirling slow between his fingers as if he had all the time in the world.

Once the last bag was loaded, Clark gathered them mid-deck. "To new horizons," he said, raising a glass. They echoed the toast, voices mingling with the call of gulls.

The yacht eased from the dock, the city shrinking behind them. Megan leaned on the railing, snapping a quick selfie with Kaia in the background before returning to her messages.

Grent ground his cigarette under his heel, muttering to himself, "Off we go," before disappearing below deck.

# Chapter 6  The Gathering Storm

The following day the sun set high when the morning turned to noon, and by midafternoon the sea stretched endlessly in every direction. Hours passed in an odd rhythm—conversations sparked and faded, naps were taken in shaded corners, and the hum of the yacht's engines became a constant, soothing backdrop.

Matthew leaned on the railing, watching sunlight scatter across the waves, when Dr. Emilia Varn stepped up beside him.

"Enjoying the trip so far?" she asked, her tone light but eyes always watchful.

Matthew shrugged. "Yeah. It's... nice. Feels strange, though. I've never been this far out."

Varn studied him, arms folded, hair pulled into a practical ponytail that swayed in the breeze. "Professor Clark thinks very highly of you."

Matthew raised a brow. "He does?"

"He talks about you often. Says you have... potential."

Matthew felt a flicker of discomfort at her phrasing but pushed it down. "He's been a great mentor. If it weren't for him, I don't think I'd be here."

Varn nodded slowly, her eyes flicking briefly to Clark across the deck, laughing politely with Bryce and Jules. "I imagine you're right," she murmured—and Matthew couldn't help but feel she was weighing him for something he couldn't name.

* * *

Shayne sprawled across one of the benches near the stern, long hair wind-tangled, flipping through an old, dog-eared book of tribal phrases.

Adam sat across from him, drumming his fingers on the table, eyes wandering toward Megan, who sat nearby with her phone held high for another selfie.

"She's not going to notice you staring like that," Shayne said without looking up.

Adam's ears went red. "I wasn't staring."

"You were staring." Shayne smirked. "She's out of your league anyway."

Adam scowled. "Says who?"

"Common sense. Look at her, Adam. She's the kind of girl who thinks camping is room service delayed by five minutes."

Adam ignored him, sitting up straighter when Megan stood, stretching. He cleared his throat. "Hey, Megan. Uh... want a drink?"

She lowered her phone, giving him a once-over. "What kind?"

Adam froze, glancing at the cooler. "Uh... water?"

Megan rolled her eyes but accepted it, her necklace catching the sun as she took the bottle. "Thanks," she said, half-smiling before looking back at her phone.

Shayne smirked wider. "Smooth," he whispered.

* * *

As Matthew leaned on the railing with Kaia, Megan's voice carried over the deck, She was holding her phone like a news reporter's microphone, filming herself against the open sea. "Day two, and still no sign of the Kraken. Will report back," she said, then waved Adam over.

He hesitated but stepped into frame. "This is Adam," Megan announced, grinning. "He's my survival buddy. If anything happens, blame him." Adam groaned. "Delete that." "Not a chance," she said, winking before turning the camera on herself again.

Megan lowered her phone for a moment, leaning into the railing with a content sigh. "Okay, I'll admit it—not hating this trip."

"Not hating?" Adam asked, coming up beside her with two bottles of water. "That's practically a glowing review."

She took one, smirking. "Don't let it go to your head."

Kaia joined them, brushing a curl from her eyes. "You'll be eating those words when we're all sunburned tomorrow."

"Speak for yourself. SPF 50 is my religion," Megan said, tugging a small sunscreen bottle from her bag and tossing it to Kaia.

From the benches, Shayne called out, "You could fry and egg on this deck right now, and she's worried about UV rays."

"Eggs don't get wrinkles," Megan shot back without looking.

Matthew glanced their way, catching the sparkle in her expression. It was easy to see why Adam was hooked already. But when his gaze shifted toward the stern, he noticed Grent there—half in shadow, cigarette smoke curling upward, his eyes fixed on the group with an intensity that didn't match the relaxed afternoon.

* * *

Evening came softly, a pink-orange glow stretching across the sea as the yacht's deck lights flickered on. Professor Clark called everyone to the dining area below deck—the table long and polished, glasses catching the candlelight.

"Everyone, sit, sit," Clark said with his easy, charming smile. "This is a celebration, after all"

As plates of seafood and wine were passed around, Clark rose with his glass.

"To all of you," he said warmly, eyes sweeping the table, "and to the journeys that bring us together. To curiosity. To discovery."

Clark's words hung in the air for a moment before Megan raised her glass, grinning. "And to hoping this ship has Wi-Fi-," she said, earning a round of groans and a few laughs. Tarek leaned over. "You'd never survive without Instagram, would you?" Megan rolled her eyes. "I survived my freshman year roommate stealing all my clothes. I can survive this." Kaia smirked from across the table. "Barely." Megan pointed at her. "Barely is still surviving."

The students raised their glasses, murmuring their own toasts.

"And Matthew," Clark added, gaze lingering on him. "For embodying the kind of drive and integrity the world needs more of. You remind me that this generation still has hope."

Matthew shifted awkwardly under the praise but smiled, lifting his glass in return.

There was a chorus of "cheers" around the table, laughter ringing—but at the far end, Silas Grent's phone buzzed against the wood.

He glanced at the screen, expression unreadable, then pushed back his chair. "Need some air," he muttered.

* * *

Grent stepped into the cool night air, lighting a cigarette. The flame flared briefly, casting sharp shadows across his scar.

He walked slowly toward the helm, nodding casually to two crew members on deck. "Captain wanted to see you down below. Said he needed help with the mainline," he lied with smooth, casual tone.

The crew exchanged glances and left.

Grent's expression hardened the moment they were gone. He crushed the cigarette under his boot and slipped into the navigation room. Fingers tapped across dials and keys with practiced calm. The screen flickered. The course change.

He stepped back out minutes later, face unreadable, smoke still curling from his lips.

* * *

Hours passed. Night fell fully, and the mood on deck shifted.

Captain Cartwright stood at the helm, brow furrowed, his compass trembling slightly in his hand. "That's... odd," he muttered.

Matthew approached. "Something wrong, Captain?"

Cartwright didn't look up. "Compass is off. Dead off. And none of these readings match the maps."

Fog had begun to gather on the horizon, slow and heavy, swallowing starlight. Phones started losing service one by one—first Megan's, then Adam's, then Bryce's.

"Great," Megan muttered. "Now we're really cut off."

The students began talking among themselves, voices low and uneasy.

Kaia stood close to Matthew, whispering, "Something doesn't feel right."

Matthew nodded, staring at the creeping fog.

Cartwright adjusted the wheel, jaw tightening. "Where are we?" he muttered under his breath, half to himself. "None of this... none of this is matching up."

The yacht pushed forward into the mist, the sea suddenly darker, quieter.

Somewhere in the distance, a low, unplaceable rumble rolled across the water.

No one laughed.

# Chapter 7 The Crash

The fog closed heavy, smothering the night like a curtain. The yacht groaned as it cut through the still water, the engines a low hum underfoot.

Then the first thunderclap cracked the sky.

It didn't sound right—too deep, too resonant, like the earth itself had spoken. A second later, the water bucked, a wave rising from nowhere and slamming against the hull with enough force to make everyone grab for the nearest rail.

Captain Cartwright cursed under his breath, hands tight on the wheel. "Storm's coming in fast," he barked to no one in particular.

Another BOOM!

A flicker of green-blue light pulsed in the fog, shimmering against the clouds—not lightning, not anything anyone could name.

The ocean turned restless. Waves slammed against the yacht, harder each time, until the deck tilted and the sea spray became constant, cold, and biting.

———

**Panic spread like fire.**

A wave crashed over the bow, knocking two crew members off their feet. Megan screamed as water drenched her hair and clothes, scrambling for balance in her soaked heels.

"SECURE THE LINES!" Cartwright roared.

Ropes flew, metal clanged, the deck became chaos. A crew member tried to fasten a line to the railing but was thrown sideways by a wave, tumbling overboard with a shout.

"MAN OVERBOARD!" another yelled, but the storm swallowed the call—and the man—whole.

———

Kaia shrieked as another wave hit, knocking her backward. She skidded across the slick deck, arms flailing as she neared the rail.

"KAIA!"

Matthew lunged, grabbing her just as her feet slipped over the edge. She clung to him, nails digging into his jacket.

"I'VE GOT YOU!" he grunted, hauling her back to safety, both of them gasping, soaked to the bone.

———

Near the stern, a loose support pole swung like a battering ram.

Megan staggered as the deck tilted beneath her, heels slipping on the soaked wood. "Of course I wore these," she muttered. "Why would I wear sneakers during a tropical storm?" She caught the railing, hair whipping into her face—just as the swinging pole came toward her.

Adam spotted it as it swept toward Megan.

"LOOK OUT!"

He shoved her out of the way, the pole missing her by inches—but smashing into *him* with a sharp crack.

Adam flipped over the railing with a grunt of pain, one hand catching a dangling rope by sheer luck.

"ADAM!" Megan screamed, rushing to the rail.

His legs flailed above the raging water, knuckles white around the slick rope.

Shayne appeared like lightning, grabbing the rope and leaning out over the edge.

"DON'T YOU DARE LET GO!" Shayne shouted, teeth clenched as he hauled Adam back. Adam's body slammed against the yacht, bruising his ribs, but Shayne dragged him up and over, dumping him onto the deck.

Shayne grinned through the rain, breathless. "Can't lose you just yet. I wanna see how this goes with Megan."

Adam groaned but managed a smirk. Megan went and grabbed his arm, knuckles white. "Adam! Oh my God—you—" Her voice caught. "You could've been killed." Adam gave a crooked grin, still breathless. "Guess I like living dangerously." She released him reluctantly, eyes still wide with shock as the storm roared on.

Megan stayed close to Adam, her hand still gripping his arm as if afraid he might vanish again. "Don't scare me like that," she said over the roar of wind. Adam tried to laugh but coughed instead. "Hey... if I'm gonna be tossed into the ocean, at least I got to save the prettiest girl on the yacht first." She shook her head, water dripping from her hair. "You're ridiculous." But her lips curved despite herself. Shayne came up behind them, clapping Adam on the shoulder. "If you two are done flirting, we've still got a storm to survive." Megan rolled her eyes but didn't let go of Adam's arm.

—

On the far side of the ship, one of the crew fought to secure a whipping line.

He didn't hear the footsteps behind him.

Didn't see Silas Grent raise a piece of broken pipe in his hand.

*THUD*

The blow landed with brutal precision. The man crumpled instantly.

Grent's face didn't change as he shoved the limp body overboard. The sea took him in silence.

No one saw.

—

The storm went mad.

The fog thickened into a wall. Rain lashed sideways, sharp as glass, drenching everyone. Strange flashes lit the sky—bursts of eerie green-blue that rippled across the clouds like living things.

The yacht rocked violently, throwing Bryce into a table hard enough to split the wood. He groaned, clutching his ribs as Jules screamed, tumbling across the deck and clawing at the railing.

Dr. Varn clung to a post, her ponytail plastered against her neck, glasses gone, sharp eyes darting across the chaos.

Professor Clark stood near the stairwell, one hand on the rail, watching with that same unreadable expression—calm, almost curious, as if measuring the storm rather than fearing it.

Another flash of light illuminated his face for an instant—something calculating behind those eyes.

—

The yacht jolted violently, throwing everyone to the deck.

A sound like tearing metal screamed through the night.

"BRACE!" Captain Cartwright roared—but the sea didn't give them time.

The hull slammed into something unseen. The impact ripped through the yacht like a cannon blast.

Screams echoed as the yacht lurched onto its side. Waves poured across the deck, dragging ropes, barrels, chairs—and people.

Another wave struck—and the hull cracked. Wood splintered, glass shattered, and water surged below deck with a deafening roar.

"ABANDON SHIP!" Cartwright bellowed, his voice ragged. "SHE'S DONE!"

Another impact—harder, final.

The yacht split.

One half groaned, tilted, and sank beneath the black water. The other twisted, cracked, and followed.

Bodies scrambled for debris, for air. The storm howled—then suddenly, impossibly...

**Silence.**

The thunder ceased. The flashes died. The rain stopped.

The fog remained.

Floating debris bobbed on a now eerily still sea, the wreckage of the yacht spread like broken bones across the water.

Only the soft drip of water and the distant cry of some unseen bird broke the quiet.

The ship—and the last bit of safety it had represented—was gone.

# Chapter 8  The Aftermath

Water slapped across Matthew Fisher's face. He blinked, and the dream dissolved.

One moment he was sitting across from Kaia Bennett at a little restaurant back home—wood tables, soft music, her auburn hair curled around her shoulders. She smiled shyly when he told her she looked incredible. They ordered water. The waitress came back with their drinks, smiling, and then—

"Here's your water, sir," she said, and threw it in his face.

Matthew gasped, jerking upright. The restaurant vanished. The world was sharp and bright. Sand clung to his lips; salt stung his eyes. The ocean's tide hissed around him. He coughed, rolling onto his side, and spotted Kaia lying across a chunk of yacht debris, still and pale.

"KAIA!"

He crawled to her, shaking her shoulder. For one terrifying moment she didn't respond. Then she coughed, choking up water, and turned to him, eyes dazed.

"Matt...?"

Relief washed over him.

"You're okay. You're okay."

Kaia winced, sitting up slowly. "What... what happened?"

Matthew looked around, heart pounding. Wreckage dotted the beach—planks, luggage, smashed coolers. The yacht was gone.

—

Shayne Wood was the next to stir. He hacked up seawater, sand sticking to his long-wet hair. "Well," he croaked, "that was a hell of a party."

Adam Nolan stumbled out of the surf behind him, face pale but alive. "Shut up, Shayne," he snapped, though his voice cracked with relief.

All along the shoreline, survivors dragged themselves awake.

Megan Truss crawled up the sand, gasping, staring in horror at her ruined phone. "My phone's dead," she muttered, shaking it like it might wake up. Then, catching sight of Kaia and Adam, she pushed herself upright, water dripping from her hair. She crossed to Kaia first.

"Are you okay? Can you breathe?" She asked, brushing damp hair back from Kaia's forehead. Spotting Adam rubbing his ribs, she frowned. "And you—sit down before you fall over." Her phone dangled from her other hand, forgotten for the moment. "Right," she muttered after a beat, "I'll cry about this later."

Captain Lee Cartwright, chest heaving, staggered toward a piece of broken railing and used it to pull himself upright. His sharp eyes scanned the shore—soldier instincts kicking in—counting heads. Bryce Calder groaned as he limped toward the group, clutching his ribs, while Jules Fenwick sat on a rock complaining about the "unbearable humidity."

And there was Silas Grent. He was already standing, strangely calm, helping Jules Fenwick to his feet. His bald head glistened in the sun, a cigarette dangling unlit from his fingers.

"Where's Clark?" Bryce asked, voice trembling.

Everyone froze.

Matthew's eyes darted around the beach. "Professor Clark?"

There was no sign of him.

Captain Cartwright's jaw tightened. "Forget him for now. My crew—" He stopped, scanning the wreckage and the empty horizon. "They're gone."

The weight of it hit like another wave.

Megan wrapped her arms around herself. "Gone? Like... drowned?" Adam came and wrapped his arms around her "Don't think about it."

Cartwright didn't answer, but his silence said enough.

—

The survivors began to search. The sun was already punishing, reflecting off the wet sand in blinding flashes. Every step sank into the soft shore, the grit grinding into skin and cuts.

Megan splashed through the shallows, her hair plastered to her face, gathering stray bottles and anything that looked remotely useful. She passed a warped metal tray to Kaia, who took it without comment.

"You're... really into this whole scavenger thing," Megan said, breathing hard but grinning.

"Better than starving," Kaia replied, tucking the tray into a makeshift pile.

Adam stumbled up the beach with a tangled fishing net slung over his shoulder. "Look what I found— seafood delivery service."

Megan tilted her head. "You realize that's probably been sitting in the ocean for years, right?"

"Adds flavor," Adam said with a shrug.

A wave surged up unexpectedly, soaking their legs again. The water was warmer than it should have been, and Matthew caught himself staring out at the horizon. No land. No Ships. Just the endless, shimmering line where the ocean met the sky—and something about it made the air feel heavier.

"We need anything that floated up," Matthew said. "Food. Water. Anything."

They fanned dragging broken coolers, rope, and bottles into a pile. The salt-stiff rope burned Matthew's palms. Shayne cracked a joke—" First rule of survival: snacks first, panic later"—but no one laughed.

Matthew pried open a half-buried crate and found smashed glass vials and a rusted metal panel stamped with a faint double helix logo. He turned it over, frowning, but said nothing.

Nearby, Megan muttered under her breath about her ruined shoes as she picked through debris. Jules griped that they should "just stay put" because a rescue team would come "any minute," earning an eye-roll from Bryce.

Adam finally sank onto a piece of driftwood, wringing seawater from his shirt. His arms ached from dragging debris and bodies out of the surf, but he didn't want to sit idle for long.

Megan dropped onto the driftwood beside him, brushing her hair from her face. "Hey," she said softly.

Adam glanced over. "Hey. You, okay?"

Megan nodded, then shook her head. "Not really." She took a breath, looking down at her scraped knees before meeting his eyes. "I... just wanted to say thank you."

"For what?"

"For saving me back on the yacht. When that pole swung down—you shoved me from certain death. I know if it had hit me, I wouldn't be here now."

Adam shrugged, trying to sound casual. "You were right there. Anyone would've done it."

"No." She touched his arm—just briefly, but enough to make him freeze. "You didn't think. You just moved. You saved me.

A beat passed before she added, "You're terrible at taking compliments."

Adam smirked faintly. "I'm great at them. I just don't get many."

That earned her first real laugh since the crash, warm and quick. "Well, you're getting one now, so deal with it." She nudged his shoulder. "I'm glad you're here, Adam."

For a second, neither of them spoke. The fire crackled in the distance.

Adam cleared his throat. "Guess I've been hanging around Matt too much. Hero complex must be contagious."

Megan laughed—a soft, surprised laugh. "Well... it suits you."

Adam blinked. "Suits me?"

She smirked a little, pushing her damp hair back. "Yeah. Don't let it go to your head, Nolan."

"I won't," he said, but he couldn't keep the corner of his mouth from tugging up in a half-smile.

For the first time since the crash, the night felt just a little less heavy.

—

By the time the sun dipped toward the horizon, a shape of order had formed. Matthew stood near the salvaged supplies. "We need a fire before dark. It'll keep us warm and visible, if there's any chance of a search party spotting smoke."

People listened. They actually listened.

Cartwright gave him a small nod. "Good call, kid."

That nod felt heavier than anything Matthew had ever earned in college.

—

Later, the survivors sat around a crackling fire, shadows dancing over their tired faces. The flames painted everyone in amber and black, the night air smelling of smoke and salt. Some whispered about the storm—how the compass readings had gone haywire, how their phones had all died at once.

"It was like the Bermuda Triangle," Tarek muttered.

"Or worse," Megan said.

Shayne poked at the fire with a stick. "Whatever it was, we're not in Kansas anymore."

A few weak laughs broke the tension, but the fire didn't chase away the unease.

When most had drifted into uneasy sleep, Grent wandered from the firelight. He stood at the shoreline, cigarette glowing in the dark.

Adam, still awake, glanced over—and froze.

Grent wasn't just staring at the water.

He was turning something metallic in his hand, the moonlight catching on it in cold flashes. For an instant, the light revealed the faintest smile on his scarred face—quiet, knowing, almost please.

A wave hissed against the sand, swallowing the sound as he closed his fist around it.

# Chapter 9  The Man with the Scar

The cigarette ember glowed red in the dark.

Silas Grent stood on the beach, just beyond the reach of the campfire's light. The survivors were huddled by the flames, some asleep, some whispering. Adam Nolan was pretending to sleep but kept stealing glances.

Grent didn't care. He turned the little metallic object in his hand under the moonlight—a broken piece of navigation tech, or maybe something older, stranger—and let his mind drift.

It had been a long time since he'd allowed himself to remember.

Megan was crouched near the wreckage with Kaia, stacking bits of driftwood into a small windbreak to block the breeze from the sleeping survivors. She shot Grent a wary look once before shaking her head and going back to work.

"That guy gives me serial killer vibes," she whispered to Kaia, who gave a quiet, uneasy nod.

* * *

**Years Ago**

He used to be different.

He used to be a husband.

Back then, Silas Grent had hair on his head and no scar across his face. He lived in a cramped but decent house with his wife, Sophie. She laughed easily, cooked dinner with the radio on, and once told him he had a smile that could melt anyone's walls.

But over the years, that smile vanished.

Grent got angrier. The jobs he took—security, shady contract work—hardened him. He came home later and later.

And Sophie noticed.

One night, she stood in their kitchen, hands trembling around a mug of tea.

"I can't do this anymore, Silas," she said. "You scare me now."

Grent froze. "Scare you? I've never hurt you."

"You don't have to hit someone to hurt them," Sophie whispered. Her eyes were wet. "I want a divorce."

The word *divorce* landed like a knife itself.

Grent felt his throat tighten. "No," he said.

"Silas—"

"No." His voice turned sharp, desperate. "We can fix this. We *will* fix this."

She shook her head. "I already tried. You don't listen."

The shouting started—words blurred, bitter, ugly.

* * *

**The Fight**

It happened fast.

Sophie grabbed a kitchen knife when he slammed his hand on the counter.

"Stay back!" she snapped, shaking but defiant.

Grent reached for her, to stop her—he told himself—but her hand shot out and the knife flashed.

Pain ripped across his cheek.

He staggered, touching his face, and when he pulled his hand back it was covered in blood.

The cut ran diagonally across his cheek—the scar he would carry forever.

He stared at Sophie, stunned, and something inside him snapped.

"You cut me," he rasped.

"Silas, I—"

He lunged.

It was brutal. Messy.

When it was over, Sophie lay still on the kitchen floor.

The knife clattered to the tiles, slick with blood.

Grent stood over her, chest heaving, his own cheek burning.

* * *

**Aftermath**

He didn't cry. Didn't call anyone. Just... cleaned.

He wrapped her body in a sheet. He scrubbed the blood from the counter. He buried Sophie where no one would find her.

And no one ever did.

* * *

**The Drifter**
After Sophie, Grent didn't go back to being a man.

He became something else.

He drifted from job to job—private security, "protection work," things that blurred into intimidation and worse.

People whispered about him: *The guy you call when you need something handled. The guy who doesn't ask questions.*

It wasn't a life. It was just motion.

* * *

**Helixis**
Then one day, someone *did* come calling.

A man in a gray suit slid into the bar booth across from him.

"We've heard about you, Mr. Grent," the man said smoothly. "We represent a research company. Helixis Corporation. We're looking for men like you."

"Men like me?"

"Men who don't mind... cleaning up problems."

* * *

**Meeting Dr. Helix**
Months later, Grent found himself in a gleaming white conference room, face still scarred, wearing a borrowed suit.

Across the table sat a man with silvering hair and sharp, charismatic eyes—**Dr. Ardan Helix.**

Helix studied him like a specimen.

"You've done... questionable things before, haven't you, Mr. Grent?"

Grent leaned back. "Only when I had to."

Helix's smile was almost fatherly.

"That's what I like to hear."

The two men shook hands.

It wasn't a job offer. It was a pact.

* * *

**Present Day**

The memory faded as the waves hissed against the sand.

Grent flicked his cigarette into the surf, the last ember dying in the dark.

He looked back at the fire, at the survivors sleeping around it.

"Always the cleanup man..." he muttered.

His eyes lingered on Adam Nolan, who was still pretending to sleep.

Grent smiled—faint, but real.

*He wondered which of them would need cleaning up first.*

# Chapter 10  The Morning After

The sun was already high when Matthew Fisher stirred awake, the heat pressing down like a weight. His skin burned, his back ached, and sand clung stubbornly to every inch of him. For the briefest second, waking up felt like an ordinary summer day at the coast—until memory rushed back. The storm. The yacht. The screaming.

The tang of salt clung to his lips, each breath drawing the sour rot of seaweed into his nose. His skin felt tight and grainy, baked by the early sun. Somewhere beyond the crash site, seabirds cried—sharp, distant notes that made the silence between them feel even heavier.

Beside him, Kaia stirred, brushing grains of sand from her auburn curls. She squinted at the blazing sky, voice hoarse: *"The nightmare didn't end."*

Matthew sat up, stretching his shoulders. "No," he murmured, "it didn't."

A few feet away, Shayne lay sprawled face-down in the sand, his hair half covering his face. He groaned like a dying man. *"If anyone's got sunscreen and a beer, I'll trade my soul."*

Kaia cracked a small laugh—short, but welcome in the stillness.

Dr. Emilia Varn sat cross-legged a few yards away, hair tied in a messy knot, her glasses smudged. She was scribbling in a small, weathered notebook she'd salvaged, eyes flicking between the survivors like she was quietly cataloging their reactions.

"Already taking notes?" Shayne muttered, lifting his head.

Varn didn't look up. "Observation keeps me focused," she replied, her voice even. "Panic helps no one."

Adam Nolan sat apart from them, knees drawn up, staring toward Grent. The scarred man was already awake, cigarette between his fingers, smoke curling upward as he stared out at the sea like he was waiting for something.

Matthew caught Adam's expression—his jaw tight, brows furrowed.

"You, okay?" Matthew asked, brushing sand from his arms.

Adam leaned closer, voice low. *"It's him. Grent. Something's off."*

Matthew frowned. "Off how?"

Adam's eyes darted back toward Grent. "He's to calm. Everyone else looks wrecked, but he's just standing there, smoking like this is a Sunday stroll. And last night..." He hesitated, then added, "I saw him pocket something from the wreckage. Didn't show anyone. Didn't say a word."

Matthew looked at Grent—still as stone, cigarette glowing. "Maybe it was something useful."

"Or maybe," Adam muttered, "he doesn't want us to know what it was."

Matthew held his cousin's gaze. "Keep it between us for now. But watch him. I will too."

Adam nodded once, but his eyes stayed locked on Grent.

* * *

By mid-morning, the heat had turned cruel. The survivors moved slowly across the beach, scavenging what little the tide had coughed up.

Captain Lee Cartwright trudged back from the wreckage; his military frame stooped under exhaustion. He carried a few finds—two half-full water bottles and three soggy snack bars.

"That's it?" Shayne said, shielding his eyes against the sun.

Cartwright dropped the bottle onto a tarp. "That's it. Unless you want to drink seawater and puke yourself dry."

Kaia frowned, sweat glistening on her forehead. "We'll need more water. Real water."

Cartwright nodded. *"Only one way to get it. We'll have to go inland. There'll be streams, maybe a spring... but we won't find it standing here."* His eyes lingered on the jungle wall just beyond the sand, dark and dense.

Megan Truss sat on a smooth rock, shoes dangling from her fingers, her face twisted into a scowl. *"I can't believe my shoes are ruined."*

Kaia crouched beside her, smirking faintly. "Your toes are still painted, though. And in good shape, considering we survived a shipwreck."

Megan wiggled her toes and, despite herself, laughed under her breath. "Guess that's something."

While the others searched, Dr. Varn quietly moved among the survivors, handing out what little water Cartwright had found, her tone measured and calm. She made eye contact with each person she passed, offering quiet words: "*Sip slowly. Don't drink it all.*"

Matthew stayed near the crates, helping Kaia sort scraps of rope and twisted metal. He noticed Adam stop mid-step—his body stiff.

Adam's eyes were on Grent again.

Grent crouched by another pile of wreckage. For a second, Matthew saw it—Grent's hand slipping something small and metallic into his pocket before straightening, face unreadable.

Adam leaned close, voice low. "See? He's hiding things."

Matthew's jaw tightened. He didn't answer right away, just studied Grent as he lit another cigarette, smoke rising into the relentless sky.

Finally, Matthew muttered, "We'll figure out what he's up to."

Adam stared, jaw clenched. "We better."

The sun climbed higher, turning the sand into something close to molten. The survivors clustered beneath a makeshift shade—a torn sail stretched between two broken rails—trying to escape the heat.

Matthew crouched over the pitiful supplies they'd salvaged, arranging them neatly: two bottles of water, some damp crackers, a tangle of rope. "We'll ration," he said firmly. "A sip at a time, and we stick close to shore. If a plane or ship passes by, this is the best place to spot them."

Kaia nodded faintly, wiping sweat from her forehead. Shayne offered a half-hearted salute.

Then Grent spoke up. His voice was steady, measured—too measured. "Or we could stop pretending this beach is gonna save us," he said, cigarette burning low between his fingers. "We need to move
inland. That's where the water will be. Food. Maybe shelter."

Matthew's head snapped up. "It's not safe inland," he countered. "We don't know what's in there. Her, at least, we've got open sightlines. We can signal for help."

Grent's scar tugged into something almost like a smile, though there was no humor in it.
"Sightlines won't matter when you're dead from thirst.
You want to sit here until we're sunbaked skeletons?
Fine. But the jungle's the only way we make it longer than two days."

Captain Cartwright crossed his arms. "The kid has a point about staying visible," he said, voice gruff but even. "But he's not wrong either —we'll need water soon."

Grent let the words hang, watching Fisher. His tone stayed calm, almost reasonable—but it carried weight. "Then let's not wait until we're too weak to walk."

Matthew felt his chest tighten, the subtle push-and-pull of who the group would follow.

The remains of last night's fire were nothing but a dead ring of ashes. Around it, tempers simmered under the relentless sun.

—

A lull settled over the group, the sound of the surf filling the space where arguments had been.

Shayne wandered a little farther down the beach, kicking at the sand. "Hey... you guys see this?" he called.

Matthew walked over and followed Shayne's gaze to a half-rotted log resting crookedly near the tree line. Its surface wasn't weathered smooth like driftwood. It was torn—deep, jagged furrows raked into the grain, as if a set of claws had tried to peel it apart.

"Those aren't from a storm," Cartwright said as he joined them. His tone was low, deliberate.

Kaia stepped closer to get a better look, but the captain's arm shot out, blocking her path. "No closer. Whatever made those might still be watching."

As if on cue, a sound drifted from the shadows beyond the tree line—not quite a growl, not quite a scream. It rose and fell with a metallic rasp, like bone scraping steel.

Megan shivered and hugged herself. "That's... not a monkey."

They didn't argue. As they turned away, Matthew glanced back one last time at the shredded wood, the claw marks so deep he could have fit his whole hand inside them.

Whatever left them wasn't just big. It was hunting.

Megan sat barefoot on a log, arms folded. "This is insane. We should have been rescued by now. Someone *has* to be looking for us."

Jules, hunched on the sand, muttered, "Or maybe no one even knows, where we are. Maybe we're just—"

"Maybe you should shut up," Megan snapped, glaring. "Your whining isn't helping anyone."

Jules flushed red. "I'm being *realistic.*"

"You're being obnoxious," Megan shot back. "If you think you can do better, Jules, go build us a resort!"

The argument sparked uneasy glances. Dr. Varn paused in her notebook, eyes sharp behind her glasses—quietly watching the way panic chipped at patience.

Jules leaned closer to Grent, lowering his voice. "This whole thing is falling apart. That Fisher kid... he doesn't know what he's doing."

Grent didn't look at him—just stared at the jungle wall like he was seeing something the others couldn't. "Maybe," Grent murmured. "Or maybe he just needs the right... direction."

Jules blinked, unsure what he meant. But Adam heard the exchange, his teeth clenching, his body inching closer to Matthew's side.

Meanwhile, Matthew kept scanning the tree line. He wanted to believe they could stay on the beach, that rescue might come. But every word Grent spoke—calm, persuasive, deliberate—pressed like a thumb on the scale, nudging the group toward the dark wall of trees.

By late afternoon, the heat had become punishing. Every breath felt heavy, and every movement seemed to drain what little strength remained.

Captain Cartwright squatted beside the wreckage, staring at the dwindling stash of water. He finally stood, wiping sweat from his brow. "We'll last another day at most if we keep this up," he said flatly. "Two if we're lucky. After that..." He didn't finish the sentence. He didn't have to.

Matthew glanced toward the ocean, its horizon painfully empty. He wanted to believe a ship might appear, or a plane might pass overhead. But silence stretched on, heavy and absolute.

Grent stood near the tree line, cigarette in one hand, eyes fixed on the wall of green. "You all see it don't you?" he said calmly. "The jungle isn't just danger. It's life. Food. Water. You think sitting here will save you?"

Matthew straightened. "If we move inland too soon, we lose our best chance of staying alive."

The words hung there.

Kaia stepped closer to Matthew, her hand brushing his arm in a quiet gesture of support. "Matt," she said softly, "he's not wrong about the water."

Shayne piped up from his spot in the sand, voice lighter but still serious. "I mean, as much as I'd love to die looking fabulous on a beach, I kind of like living more."

Cartwright nodded once. "If we're going in, we do it soon. Before the heat burns us out."

Matthew hesitated, then finally exhaled, the decision settling on him like a weight. "Tomorrow morning," he said. "We move inland."

Grent's eyes lingered on him for a long moment, that thin smile flickering again—like he'd just won something.

As the group began gathering what few supplies they had for tomorrow's move, Kaia knelt near a pile of wreckage and tugged out something half-buried in the sand—a pair of battered canvas sneakers, faded but intact.

She walked over to where Megan sat cross-legged on a log, rubbing her bare feet.

"Found you something," Kaia said, holding them out.

Megan's face lit up for a half a second—then she wrinkled her nose. "No socks?"

Kaia raised an eyebrow. "It's a shipwreck, not a department store."

Megan eyed the shoes again, hesitant.
"I can't wear them without socks. I'll get blisters."

Kaia smirked. "You'd rather walk barefoot into the jungle?"

Megan crossed her arms. "Blisters are worse than barefoot."

Kaia gave a laugh and sat down next to her. "That's not true. You'll step on something sharp or— I don't know—a snake. You'll wish for a blister."

Megan groaned dramatically, taking one of the shoes and holding it up like it was some foreign artifact. "I'm just saying," she muttered, "fashion and survival should not have to clash."

Kaia grinned. "Oh, right. Because the jungle is going to care if your shoes match your outfit."

Megan laughed despite herself and finally slipped one shoe on, wiggling her toes. "Fine. But if I get a blister, I'm blaming you."

Kaia smirked. "Blame me all you want—at least your toes will still be attached."

The evening brought a sliver of relief, the sky bleeding orange as the sun dipped low. The group moved slowly, packing up what little they had—the cracked water bottles, the scraps of food, the rope.

Adam kept his eyes on Grent, noticing how he barely helped—just stood there, staring at the tree line, cigarette ember glowing in the dusk.

Grent flicked the cigarette into the sand and muttered under his breath, just loud enough for Adam to hear: "Tomorrow we see what this island's really made of."

Adam felt a chill, but before he could say anything, Matthew's voice carried across the camp.

"Tomorrow," Matthew said firmly, looking inland, "we move."

The group fell silent, their eyes following his gaze toward the jungle. The wall of green loomed, dark and alive, whispering promises and threats none of them could name.

Later, after the others drifted into uneasy sleep...

Matthew stood near the remains of the fire pit, staring into the coals. Kaia, Adam, and Cartwright gathered quietly around him, their voices low.

Cartwright was the first to break the silence, his voice blunt. "Grent. He's trouble."

Matthew glanced toward where Grent sat in the shadows, Jules and Bryce close by their silhouettes lit by the faint glow of another cigarette. "I know," Matthew said. "Adam saw him pocket something earlier. And he's pushing hard for us to go inland."

Adam folded his arms tightly. "He's getting into their heads, too. Jules hangs on his every word. Even Bryce is starting to nod along. Tarek's not sharp enough to see through him—he'll follow whoever sounds the toughest."

Kaia's voice cut in, quieter but sharper. "And we don't know what's in there." She nodded toward the black line of jungle. "Snakes. Wild animals. Worse. Whatever's behind those trees might make the other night's storm feel like nothing."

Matthew's jaw tightened. "We don't have a choice about moving. But we do have a choice about how we move."

Cartwright stepped closer, his voice a gravelly whisper. "Then we keep eyes open. You, me, Kaia, Adam. We watch the others. We watch Grent."

Kaia nodded, her hand brushing Matthew's arm in a steadying touch. "If we don't, he'll divide us before we even take the first step."

Adam's eyes stayed on Grent across the fire, his face hard. "Then we make sure that doesn't happen."

The conversation wound down, but the unease didn't fade. As the others drifted toward the firelight, Matthew stayed back, glancing toward the tree line.

Grent was there, half-hidden in shadow, a faint curl of smoke rising from between his fingers. His eyes were locked on Matthew—not the group, not the camp— just him.

Somewhere deep in the jungle, a low, guttural cry echoed, and every head turned toward the sound. No one spoke.

# Chapter 11  Into the Green

Matthew Fisher stood on the beach, but it wasn't the same beach he had collapsed on the night before.

The sand was pristine—no wreckage, no footprints, no sign anyone had ever been there. The sea was flat and black, the horizon blurred by a pale mist that clung to everything. There was no sound but the faint hiss of the tide.

"Hello?" His own voice sounded swallowed, thin.

No one answered.

He turned—Kaia wasn't there. Neither was Adam. Shayne. Cartwright. Everyone was simply gone.

A line of footprints appeared in the sand ahead of him, leading toward the jungle's edge.

They weren't his—the stride was longer, steadier.

Matthew followed.

The mist thickened as he reached the tree line. That's when he saw him.

Professor Clark stood just beyond the mist, hands folded behind his back, the same calm, composed smile Matthew had seen so many times at the university.

"Matthew," Clark said, his voice smooth, familiar, almost warm. "I wondered when you'd find me."

Matthew's throat felt dry. "Where is everyone? Where are *you?*"

Clark didn't answer directly. Instead, he stepped closer, looking him over like a proud teacher eyeing his best student. "You've done well," Clark said gently. "They're already looking to you."

Matthew shook his head. "I don't feel like I'm doing well. I don't even know if I'm leading them right."

Clark smiled—not a smirk, not a grin, just a reassuring curve of his lips. "Leadership is never about having all the answers, Matthew. It's about trusting your instincts."

Matthew stared at the misty ground. "What if I make the wrong call?

Clark stepped closer, his voice lowering to something almost fatherly. "Then you'll learn and make a better one. That's what leaders do."

His hand rested briefly on Matthew's shoulder—surprisingly solid for a dream. "You have something the others don't. A steadiness. They need that."

Matthew blinked, uneasy. "The others... they trust me. But I don't even know what we're doing. Or why we're here."

Clark's expression softened, though his eyes carried something deeper, something harder to read.

"Trust yourself. And trust the island—it's here for a reason. *You're* here for a reason."

Matthew's brow furrowed. "The island? What do you mean?"

Clark tilted his head slightly, the mist curling around him. "You'll understand when it's time. For now... keep them moving. They're safer with you."

Matthew hesitated. "Am I... doing the right thing?"

Clark's voice was softer now, almost a whisper. "You're doing great, Matthew. Better than you think."

Clark turned, beginning to walk into the fog.

Matthew tried to follow, but the mist thickened, his legs suddenly heavy, the footprints vanishing in front of him.

"Wait!" he called out.

Clark didn't turn back, his voice drifting through the fog one last time: *"Trust yourself..."*

Matthew's eyes snapped open.

He was lying on the beach again, the smell of salt and smoke filling his lungs. The mist was gone, replaced by harsh sunlight and the chatter of waking survivors. Kaia was already up, talking softly to Cartwright by the firepit.

Matthew sat up slowly, the echo of Clark's voice still clinging to him like the mist.

* * *

The survivors moved like shadows as dawn burned away the cool night. The sun hadn't climbed far yet, but its heat was already heavy on their shoulders.

Matthew stretched the stiffness out of his arms and started organizing supplies: rope, scraps of food, the two battered water bottles they'd saved. "Pack light," he said, voice steady. "We'll need to move fast."

Shayne yawned, dragging his feet. "Fast, huh? You're lucky I didn't have my morning coffee."

Grent was already awake, standing off to the side with his arms folded, cigarette dangling from his fingers. "Where are you putting me?" he asked smoothly. "Front or back?"

Matthew glanced up. "We'll keep it tight. Cartwright and I will lead. You can—"

"—I'll take the front," Grent interrupted, his tone calm but deliberate. "You don't want me in the back. Might miss something."

Matthew didn't argue—but Adam's eyes narrowed. He watched Grent casually pluck a small knife from a supply bundle, twirl it once in his hand, and slip it into his belt without asking.

Adam muttered to Matthew, just loud enough for him to hear. "Did you see that?"

Matthew nodded slightly. "I saw it."

The group crossed the line where sand met the dense wall of green.

The jungle swallowed them whole.

The air changed instantly—heavy and humid, smelling of earth and rot. Insects buzzed relentlessly, and shafts of sunlight cut through gaps in the canopy like broken glass.

The deeper they pushed into the green, the more the jungle seemed alive in ways Matthew couldn't explain. Every so often, a low, distant rumble passed through the ground—not thunder, but something heavy moving far away. The canopy groaned in the windless heat, and the air had a taste to it, faintly metallic, as if the whole forest was breathing with them.

Kaia glanced up at the swaying branches, her voice barely above a whisper. "It's like it's watching us."

Matthew didn't answer, but the thought followed him.

"Feels like we just stepped into someone's mouth," Shayne muttered, swatting a mosquito off his arm.

Megan wrinkled her nose. "This is disgusting. It's like breathing soup. You owe me a spa day after this. And not one of those cheap ones where they just stick your feet in fish water." Kaia chuckled, "You mean a pedicure?" "Whatever it's called, it better come with champagne."

Jules groaned and slapped at his neck. "Why does everything here want to bite us?"

"Stay close," Matthew said firmly. "Don't wander off. The jungle's easy to get lost in."

Dr. Emilia Varn walked near the back, notebook tucked under her arm, her eyes flicking from person to person, studying who was tense and who was quietly panicking.

They pushed along a narrow trail, vines snagging at their arms and legs.

Matthew called out, "Watch your footing—"

"Relax, Boy Scout," Grent interrupted with a lazy smirk. "We'll live."

Adam shot him a look. "Don't talk to him like that."

Grent's smirk widened slightly. "What? I'm just saying, he doesn't have to hold our hands."

Jules chuckled under his breath, siding with Grent. Adam's jaw clenched.

"Cool it," Cartwright barked, stepping between them. "We're not even an hour in and you're already snapping at each other."

The tension didn't vanish—it just simmered, quieter, as they kept moving.

The terrain grew rougher. Roots and vines reached like traps across the ground, and mud sucked at their shoes.

Megan tripped on a root and yelped, stumbling to her knees. Matthew immediately helped her up.

Grent didn't miss the moment. "Dead weight slows everyone," he muttered just loud enough for Adam to hear.

Adam turned sharply. "Shut up!"

Grent just smiled faintly—the kind of smile that wasn't friendly, wasn't warm. It was a smile designed to get under Adam's skin.

By midday, sweat slicked every face and shirt.

A sudden crash in the brush froze everyone in place.

The group went silent—even the air seemed to hold its breath.

Something moved through the leaves, big enough to make the branches tremble.

Shayne whispered, "That wasn't a squirrel."

The brush split—and a strange birdlike creature darted through the clearing. It was about the size of a turkey, with a long, narrow beak and bright, startled eyes.

The creature bolted into the trees and was gone.

Everyone exhaled at once.

Megan whispered, "What the hell was *that*?"

Cartwright shook his head. "Doesn't matter. It won't be the last thig we'll see."

By evening, the jungle spat them into a small clearing. The group dumped their loads and
Slumped down, exhausted.

Megan collapsed onto a flat rock, pulling off her borrowed sneakers with a dramatic groan. "My feet are *dying*," she muttered. "And I *hate* you, Kaia, for making me wear these awful shoes."

Kaia smirked faintly, crouching near the fire pit they were scraping together. "You'd hate me more if you stepped on a snake barefoot."

"Still not forgiven," Megan shot back, wiggling her toes in the open air.

Adam shook his head and dropped down next to her. "Come here," he said, holding out his hands. "I'll give you a foot rub before you whine us all to death."

Megan hesitated—then handed over one foot, smirking despite herself. "Fine. But if you make it weird, I'll kick you."

Adam snorted. "Yeah, yeah. I'll keep it strictly medical."

As Adam worked at the knots in her arches, Megan leaned back on her elbows, looking up at the canopy where the last rays of sunlight broke through. "You know," she murmured, "if you keep this up, I might actually miss you if we ever get off this island." Adam grinned. "Might?" "Don't push it."

Megan winced as he started working at her arches, but her voice softened. "Okay... maybe you're slightly less useless than I thought."

A few feet away, Matthew sat with Kaia and Cartwright, going over what little they'd seen.

Adam leaned in briefly, voice low. "He's pushing us, Matt. All day. I see what he's doing."

Kaia glanced toward where Grent sat alone, sharpening the knife he'd taken that morning. Jules and Bryce sat near him, listening more than they should.

"He's already pulling them in," Kaia whispered. "Jules, Bryce... maybe even Tarek. He's making them his."

Across the clearing, Grent said something low to Jules that made him laugh—really laugh, like they were old friends. Bryce leaned in too, nodding at whatever Grent was saying. It wasn't loud enough for Matthew to hear, but the way the three of them glanced over at him made the back of his neck prickle.

Cartwright's voice was steady, but there was iron under it. "Then we watch him. Day and night."

Matthew nodded slowly, the firelight flickering across his face.

Kaia turned to him suddenly, her expression softening. She slipped an arm around him in a brief, firm hug. "I'm so glad you're here," she murmured.

Matthew met her eyes, something unspoken passing between them—then his gaze drifted past her, over the firelight.

Across the clearing, Grent looked up.

Their eyes locked.

Grent smiled faintly, the knife still glinting in his hand.

# Chapter 12 The Devil's Handshake



**Present Day**

The jungle was asleep, or pretending to be.

Grent sat apart from the others, small ember of firelight flickering over his face. The scar that ran diagonally across his cheek caught the glow, turning it into something almost ceremonial—a dark brand carved into his skin.

He didn't seem to notice the mosquitos orbiting his head or the suffocating humidity pressing against his chest.

The blade in his hand caught the fire's glow as he drew a whetstone across it, slow and deliberate. *Shhhht. Shhhht.* Each pass made a violence being prepared.

Across the clearing, the others slept fitfully, their shapes bundled in makeshift bedding. Matthew Fisher lay on his back; one arm draped over his chest. Grent's eyes locked on him—not with rage, not even contempt, but with a strange, cold calculation.

He rose slowly, almost without sound, and took a step toward the sleeping young man. Fisher murmured something in his dreams, shifting slightly. Grent's fingers flexed against the knife hilt. For a moment, the jungle's silence seemed to close in tight around them, waiting. Then, with a faint shake of his head, Grent turned away and settled back into his spot. Some things weren't meant to happen yet.

He spoke softly, as if sharing a secret with the knife itself. "Helix saw something in you," he muttered, voice low enough to be swallowed by the night. "I see it too."

The words hung there, half a promise, half a threat.

A soft rustle. Megan turned over in her sleep and blinked toward the fire, bleary. She noticed Grent awake, the steady motion of his arm, the whisper of stone on steel.

"You ever sleep?" she whispered, just loud enough to carry.

Grent didn't look up. "Sometimes," he said. "When there's nothing to watch."

She squinted, as if weighing whether the remark was a joke. "Creepy answer," she breathed, then tugged her blanket up and rolled away, closer to Kaia and Adam.

From the shadow just beyond the firelight, Adam's voice came, guarded. "Put the blade down, Grent. It's the middle of the night."

Grent's mouth curved—something
that wasn't quite a smile. He slipped the knife into its
sheath with a slow, audible click.

"Happy?" he asked.

"No," Adam said. "But it'll do."

Grent flicked his cigarette lighter, the brief flame
dancing against his face. He didn't light anything—he just
stared at the fire, lips curling into something
that wasn't quite a smile.

The jungle was silent. But Grent's mind wasn't.

* * *

**Flashback: Recruitment**

The world was different then.

Grent remembered sitting at a cracked Formica
table in a nameless diner, the kind where the coffee was
always burnt and the air always smelled like grease. His
scar was fresh in those days, still an angry red slash instead
of the faded welt it had become.

He'd been drifting since Sophie. Drifting was
the kind word—rotting was more accurate. He took jobs
no one else wanted: collections for loan sharks, "security
work" where you didn't guard things, you got rid of them.
His hands weren't clean, but they'd been dirty so
long he'd forgotten what clean felt like.

A man in a gray suit slid into the booth across
from him. He didn't say his name, didn't have to. He wore
that smooth, practiced smile that said *I know everything about
you already.* He set down a porcelain cup, stirred the coffee
three times clockwise, tapped the spoon twice on the
saucer, and didn't drink. A ritual. A tell.

"Silas Grent," the man said, tasting the name. "You've been useful to some people. Rough around the edges, but useful."

Grent watched the spoon. Tap. Tap. "If you're selling something, I'm not buying."

The man adjusted his tie by a millimeter. "I'm offering something. There's someone who'd like to meet you. A man with... vision. When he asks for things, he expects them done. Quiet."

Grent looked up, eyes narrowing. "And why me?"

The man smiled wider. "Because you don't flinch."

He slid a folded business card across the table. In embossed silver letters, it read:

**Dr. Ardan Helix.**

* * *

**The First Meeting**

The house wasn't what Grent expected.

It wasn't a mansion on a hill or some fortress behind gates—it was a modest, modern home in a quiet neighborhood. Too quiet. The kind of quiet that felt intentional.

The man in the gray suit led him through a front door that clicked shut too softly. Inside, the air smelled of polished wood and old paper.

And then he was there.

**Dr. Ardan Helix**

He wasn't what Grent pictured, either. No mad scientist in a stained lab coat, no eccentric recluse muttering to himself. Helix was poised, silver at his temples, his face all sharp lines and calm, controlled charisma.

"Mr. Grent," Helix said, voice smooth as glass. "I'm please you came."

Grent said nothing. He just took in the room—the shelves lined with books on evolution, genetics, philosophy. The framed photo of a younger Helix shaking hands with some nameless politician; a small display box on a pedestal holding a carved wooden totem—human and animal shapes braided together—old and worn in a way that didn't belong to this tidy house. Against one wall, an aquarium glowed dimly, not with fish, but with pale, translucent things that pulsed and folded in the water like strange flowers.

Somewhere deeper in the house: a faint mechanical hum. The sound of a secret.

Helix crossed the room with unhurried grace, poured two fingers of amber liquid into a pair of crystal tumblers. He handed one to Grent.

"You've been doing... difficult work," Helix said, studying him with those pale, unreadable eyes. "Work most men couldn't live with."

Grent took the glass, didn't drink. "It pays."

Helix's mouth curved into the slightest smile. "It does. But you strike me as a man who isn't in it for the money."

Grent didn't respond.

Helix stepped closer, looking him dead in the eye. "I need someone who doesn't hesitate. Someone who can keep... complications from becoming catastrophes."

He extended his hand.

It was an ordinary gesture—polite, even. But it felt like something more.

Grent stared at it for a long moment. He could feel the weight in the room change, as if the house itself was holding its breath. He set the untouched tumbler down on a coaster he hadn't noticed before. Then he took Helix's hand.

The grip was firm, cool, confident. And in that handshake, the deal was made—unspoken but ironclad.

"I think," Helix said softly, releasing his hand, "we'll be very good for each other."

Across the room, the carved totem seemed to watch, its worn faces unreadable.

* * *

**The Devil's Work**

Time blurred after that handshake.

Grent remembered it in flashes, fragments— moments stitched together like scars.

• A dark alley behind a lab. Rain hammered the pavement. A man in a lab coat lay crumpled against a dumpster, begging. "I didn't mean to leak anything," the man pleaded, voice shaking. Grent's shadow stretched over him, long and sharp under the streetlight. "You did," Grent said simply, and the alley went quiet.

• A warehouse fire on the edge of the city. Grent watched the flames rise, the air thick with the stench of melting plastic and scorched paper. Helix stood beside him, hands folded behind his back, as calm as if they are watching a sunset. "No evidence left?" Helix asked without looking at him. Grent took one last drag from his cigarette, flicked it into the fire. "Not a scrap."

• An office at night. Grent sat across from a trembling investor, the kind of man who thought he was untouchable until tonight. "You don't get to back out,"

Grent said, his tone almost conversational. "Not without consequences." The investor slid the paper back across the desk with a shaking hand. Grent smiled faintly. "Good choice."

•A job he never forgot. The cage rattled in the truck bed, the metal groaning against something inside. Grent didn't look in—Helix's orders were clear. He drove to the docks, met a man with no name, and watched the cage vanish onto a freighter bound for coordinates he never saw. Whatever was inside didn't make a sound after that.

• Helix's quiet house again. The aquarium's pale things folded and unfurled in blue light. Helix poured another drink. "You've been indispensable, Mr. Grent," he said, almost warmly. "Some things can't be done in the light. I'm glad you... understand that."
Grent didn't answer. He didn't need to.

• A corridor lit by a single flickering bulb. A crate at Grent's feet stamped with the Helixis Corporation logo. Heavy. What was inside wasn't moving anymore. He didn't look long. He just slid it into the waiting truck and shut the door.

* * *

**The Island Before the Crash**

There was a job before the yacht. Quiet. Off the books.

A helicopter door yawning open to gray sky and a green knot of land below. The pilot didn't talk. No markings on the fuselage. Grent's headset hissed with static as jungle rushed up to meet them.

On the ground, a small team in unmarked gear. "Two klicks," one of them said, pointing through the trees. "We don't stay long."

The air was different here—heavy, metallic, alive. Grent moved through the brush with the team, listening to the forest breathe. A distant call rolled across the canopy, low and alien. Not a bird. Not anything he had a name for.

They stopped at a ridge. In the valley below: a fenced perimeter, floodlights off, a cluster of low buildings half-swallowed by green. A logo he knew, faint on a rust-edged sign: **HELIXIS**

"Recon only," the team lead said. "Confirm condition. No engagement."

But Grent had already knelt, fingers brushing the mud where something huge had passed. Three-toed. Deep. The edges of the print were wet, still surrendering water.

He looked out over the valley and felt a rare thing: not fear. Anticipation.

Back at the landing zone, the pilot never took off his sunglasses "Well?" he asked over the engine's rising whine.

Grent buckled in, the rotor wash tearing at the leaves below. "It's ready," he said. "He'll want it soon."

The helicopter lifted, and the island tilted away, as if it were closing its eye.

* * *

**Present Day Return**

The fire in the clearing popped softly, waking a few crickets.

Grent sat where he had been all along, whetstone and knife in hand, though now the blade gleamed sharper, meaner.

He looked across the fire at Matthew Fisher again, the young man tossing in his sleep, muttering something... Kais's name.

Grent's face was unreadable.

He leaned forward slightly, murmuring under his breath, voice a rasp the night barely carried. "Helix wanted you for a reason... and I'll make damn sure you are delivered."

He stood without sound, every movement unhurried. At the edge of the clearing, he paused, turned his head toward the tree line like he was listening for an answer only he could hear. One hand slipped into his pocket and drew out a small, black rectangle—no signal, just a dead screen. He checked it anyway, out of habit. Out of ritual.

The lighter clicked again. A moth drifted close to the sudden bloom of flame, wings powdering the night air. It circled once, twice, then blundered into the heat. The tiny body flared and was gone.

Grent closed the lighter and walked into the jungle, swallowed by the dark, leaving only the insects' chorus and the faint, rhythmic whisper of steel on stone echoing in memory.

# Chapter 13  First Blood

The jungle woke them before the sun did.

Birds—or what *sounded* like birds—screeched from somewhere high in the canopy, a guttural, almost mechanical sound that made it impossible to tell if it was a call or a warning.

Matthew sat up, stiff from the night on the ground, and rubbed the back of his neck. The air was thicker here, almost syrupy, and every breath carried the smell of wet earth and rotting leaves.

Around him, the camp stirred. Shayne yawned dramatically, brushing ants off his arm. "Nothing like sleeping on a pile of roots to make you miss dorm beds," he muttered, voice dry.

Kaia smiled faintly, stretching as she walked over to Matthew. "You didn't sleep much," she said softly, brushing a strand of auburn hair from her face.

Matthew shrugged, scanning the tree line. "Didn't feel like I should."

She crouched beside him, close enough that her should brushed his arm. "You know," she said, voice lighter now, "you could always lean on someone. You don't have to do the whole brooding-hero thing all the time."

Matthew blinked, caught off guard by the teasing glint in her eye. "Brooding-hero?" he echoed, managing a small smile.

Kaia grinned and tilted her head. "Well, you do have the look for it. Unkempt hair, little beard... you'd look good on a book cover."

Matthew shook his head, trying not to laugh, but his ears burned all the same. "Thanks... I think?"

Grent was already awake, crouched by the fire pit, running the flat of his knife against his thumb to check the edge. His movements were slow, deliberate—the kind of calm that wasn't comforting.

"You keep waiting for rescue, we're gonna rot here," Grent said without looking up. "We should be moving."

Matthew stiffened slightly but didn't bite. "We will," he said, trying to keep his voice even. "But we move smart. The jungle's thick—we rush, we get lost."

Grent smirked like he'd expected that answer.

Across the clearing, Megan muttered, wiggling her toes. "I hate wearing shoes with no socks. My feet feel like they're dying in here."

Adam walked over, crouching in front of her. "You're surviving in the jungle," he said gently, "I'd say you're doing pretty damn good."

Megan gave a short laugh despite herself, brushing hair from her face. "Yeah, well, my toes don't agree."

Adam smirked and reached for one of her shoes, loosening the laces a bit. "Better?"

Megan blinked, surprised by the small gesture, then nodded. "Yeah... thanks. You didn't have to."

Adam shrugged, grinning softly. "If I didn't, who would?"

That earned him a real smile—small, but real.

Shayne, leaning against a tree, muttered, "Adam Nolan: jungle foot therapist. Book your appointment now."

"Shut up," Adam shot back, but he was grinning too.

Bryce chuckled quietly. Jules muttered something about "not wasting daylight," echoing Grent like a shadow.

Matthew stood, brushing dirt from his jeans, feeling Kaia's gaze on him again.

"Alright," he said, forcing his voice steady. "Pack what you need. Stay close. Watch your footing. We move inland—carefully."

Kaia lingered near him as the others got ready, leaning in just enough for her voice to be for him alone. "I meant what I said," she murmured, a small smile playing at her lips. "You don't have to carry this by yourself."

For just a moment, Matthew let the words sink in before looking back at her.

"I'm glad you're here," he admitted quietly.

Her smile widened—subtle, but enough.

Grent slid his knife back into its sheath, his smirk lingering like a shadow. "Careful," he muttered under his breath, lighting a cigarette as they started gathering their things. "Yeah. We'll see how long that lasts."

* * *

The jungle swallowed them whole.

Within minutes of leaving the clearing, the world behind them was gone—the campfire embers, the open patch of sky—all replaced by a living wall of green. Vines hung low like ropes, ferns brushed their legs, and every few steps, someone swatted at something crawling on their skin.

The path wasn't a path at all, just the occasional break in the foliage. Matthew led them, machete in hand, which he found when scavenging the wreckage. He hacked away at vines when he had to, Kaia close behind him.

"This place feels... wrong," Bryce muttered, swiping a fat mosquito from his neck.

"It's a jungle," Shayne replied, but his voice lacked its usual bite. "Jungles are *supposed* to feel wrong."

Grent smirked at that, cigarette tucked behind his ear as he casually shoved branches aside. "You're jumpy, kid."

Bryce didn't answer, just glared at his back.

Every few minutes, they'd hear it—something distant, too heavy to be a bird, too deliberate to be wind. A branch snapping. Leaves rustling. Once, a low, guttural growl that stopped everyone mid-step.

"What was that?" Megan whispered, clutching Adam's arm.

Adam squeezed her shoulder. "Probably nothing. Just stay close."

Cartwright scanned the tree line, his military instincts bristling. "We're being watched."

"By what?" Jules asked, voice cracking slightly.

Cartwright didn't answer.

Grent took a drag from his cigarette and exhaled slowly, too calm for anyone's comfort. "Doesn't matter," he said, "as long as it keeps its distance."

They pressed on, but the air felt thicker, heavier—as if the jungle itself was holding its breath.

* * *

The jungle was too quiet.

Every crunch of a footstep felt like it carried for miles. Even the bugs had gone still, as if they, too, were waiting for something.

Megan muttered under her breath, adjusting her sneaker for the fifth time. "These things are chewing my heels up," she complained softly, wincing as she stepped on a rock.

Adam slowed his pace, letting the others pass until he was walking beside her. "You'll get used to it," he said quietly, offering her an encouraging smile.

Megan sighed dramatically. "I'm not cut out for this."

Adam nudged her lightly with his elbow. "You're doing better than half of us. You've made it this far in the jungle wearing shoes you hate and no socks. That's tougher than half of us."

That pulled a reluctant laugh out of her. "You think so?"

Adam grinned, leaning just close enough that his voice softened. "I know so."

For a moment, her complaints stopped, and she smiled at him—a real smile that reached her eyes.

"Gross," Tarek muttered loudly from up ahead, turning to grin over his should. "Are we doing jungle dating now? Should I go find somcone to hold hands with?"

Shayne rolled his eyes. "Maybe focus on now tripping over your own feet first."

Cartwright barked "Quiet," he knew they weren't alone.

Tarek snorted and kicked a fallen branch out of his way. "Seriously, you guys are wound too tight. Thee's nothing out here. It's just trees and bugs and—"

"WATCH OUT!" Cartwright's voice bellowed like a gunshot.

The bushes to their left exploded

A mass of feathers and claws hurtled out of the green—a terror bird, taller than a man, its eyes black and unblinking, its beak jagged and lethal.

It hit Tarek before he even had time to scream.

The impact slammed him into the dirt, the bird's talons pinning him like iron stakes. He flailed, kicking wildly, his voice cracking into a high-pitched panic.

Then the beak came down.

It pierced his throat with a wet, tearing crunch, and his scream cut off in a horrible gurgle. Blood sprayed across the leaves as the terror bird yanked its head back, ripping a chunk of flesh free. The metallic stench hit them at once, mingling with the sharp, wet heat of the jungle air.

"TAKE COVER!" Cartwright roared, but everyone was already scattering, shrieking, diving behind trees and roots.

The bird raised it head, feathers bristling, ready to lunge again—

BANG!

The gunshot cracked through the jungle like lightning.

The bird shrieked, its head snapping up, and bolted into the foliage, vanishing as suddenly as it came.

The echo rattled in their chests, lingering long after the creature was gone.

Everyone turned—and saw Grent, calm as stone, lowering the pistol in his hand.

No one had known he had a gun.

For a moment, the only sound was the hiss of leaves swaying from the bird's exit.

Then Bryce stumbled forward, falling to his knees beside Tarek. "Oh God—Tarek—"

But Tarek wasn't there anymore. Not really. His eyes were glassy, his body slack, his throat a shredded ruin.

Bryce's voice cracked as he whispered, "He's gone..."

Megan buried her face into Adam's chest, trembling. Shayne stood frozen, mouth open, for once without a joke to give.

Matthew's hands curled into fists as his gaze shifted from Tarek's body—to the dark tree line—to the pistol still in Grent's hand.

Grent slid it into his waistband, casual as if he'd just swatted a fly.

The jungle seemed to hold its breath.

The only sound was Bryce kneeling in the mud, his breath coming in broken gasps as he stared at Tarek's body. Blood pooled beneath the head, dark and sticky, already drawing flies.

"Jesus Christ," Shayne whispered, hands clamped on top of his head. "That thing—it just—"

"Ripped him apart," Bryce choked out, his voice cracking. "I couldn't even—" He turned, doubling over and vomiting into the ferns.

Kaia's hand trembled against Matthew's arm. He turned slightly, seeing her eyes wet—not just with fear, but with the kind of helpless sorrow he couldn't fix. H wanted to tell her it would be alright, but the lie stuck in his throat.

"We have to move the body," she said finally, her voice thin but steady.

"No," Grent said flatly, sliding the pistol into his waistband like he'd been carrying it openly all along. "Leave him. The smell will just draw more of them."

Everyone froze at the sight of the weapon.

"You—you had a gun?" Adam's voice cut through the silence, sharp and accusing. "Since when?"

Grent didn't even flinch. "Since before we got here."

"You didn't think to mention that?" Shayne snapped, taking a step forward. "We've been walking blind through this place and you—"

"—and I just saved your asses," Grent interrupted, his tone cool and measured. "You'd rather I let the bird finish?"

Shayne's jaw clenched, but he didn't answer.

Dr. Emilia Varn had been standing just off to the side, quiet, her notebook clutched to her chest like a shield. Her sharp eyes moved between the survivors—lingering on Matthew's clenched fists, Adam's protective hold on Megan, Bryce's shaking hands, and finally Grent, who seemed unbothered, almost too calm. Her pen moved methodically—names, reactions, posture. She wasn't just documenting shock; she was taking inventory of who would break first.

"This group just saw someone torn apart," she said softly, her voice even but cutting through the tension.

"Everyone is in shock. That needs to be acknowledged before we start pointing fingers."

Cartwright stepped closer, his voice low and edged with steel. "What needs to be acknowledged," he growled, "is that he kept a gun from us."

Grent smirked faintly, striking a match to relight his cigarette. The hiss of the flame sounded loud in the heavy silence.

Megan pressed her face against Adam, clinging to him like anchor. He wrapped his arms around her protectively, glaring over her shoulder at Grent.

Matthew crouched next to Bryce, his hand on the young man's shoulder. "Bryce," he said softly. "I'm sorry, but we need to keep moving."

Bryce shook his head, his hands slick with Tarek's blood. "We can't just leave him like this. We can't—"

"We don't have a choice," Matthew said, his voice heavy.

For a moment, nobody moved.

Then Grent exhaled a thin stream of smoke, his voice breaking the silence like a knife. "One down," he muttered, almost to himself. "More will follow."

Everyone turned to look at him, horror and suspicion mixing in their eyes.

Dr. Varn's brow furrowed slightly, her pen moving almost unconsciously, scribbling a single note in the margin of her notebook as she whispered under her breath—not meant for anyone, but audible enough for the jungle to keep.

*"And there's the crack in the mask."*

# Chapter 14  A Fragile Victory

Matthew stood in the jungle clearing—or what he *thought* was the jungle clearing.

The air was still, too still. The leaves didn't move, not even when he brushed his hand across them. The ground beneath his boots felt firm, unreal, like it had been painted there.

And then he heard the voice.

"Matthew."

He turned, and there he was—Professor Clark.

Clark wasn't ragged like the survivors. He wasn't mud-stained or sweating. He stood tall, coat crisp, that same warm, practiced smile on his face.

"You're doing better than you realize," Clark said, stepping forward. "Better than anyone could've hoped for."

Matthew blinked, disoriented. "I... I don't know if I am."

Clark's hand landed on his shoulder—firm, reassuring. "You are. You're leading them. You're protecting them. You were made for this."

Matthew's brows furrowed. "Made for this?"

Clark's smile widened, almost fatherly. "Some people are just born to step up. You are one of them."

The words sank in, warm and heavy at the same time.

"But," Clark added softly, leaning in slightly, "you have to trust yourself. Trust your instincts. Don't let doubt slow you down. Doubt will get them all killed."

Matthew felt the world sway—the trees rippling like water—and then he blinked.

He woke up, heart pounding.

The fire from last night was ash now. The others were stirring around him.

Kaia was kneeling by her pack, Adam and Megan whispered quietly off to the side, and Grent stood a few feet away, flicking his lighter open and shut with that same unreadable smirk.

The words from the dream clung to him like mist. **Trust your instincts. You were made for this.**

---

Matthew sat up, breathing deep, and looked around the group.

They were tired. Scared.

And they were looking at him.

Matthew sat there for a long moment after waking, Clark's words still hanging in his mind like mist. *Trust your instincts. You were made for this.*

He rubbed his eyes, sat up, and looked around the clearing.

The group was scattered in little clusters—Kaia rolling up her blanket, Bryce sitting with his back against a log staring into the dirt, Adam checking over Megan's sneakers while she teased him lightly, Shayne trying to joke with Cartwright and not getting much back, and Grent... Grent was just standing there, cigarette between his fingers, the faintest smirk on his face as if he knew something the rest of them didn't.

Matthew's chest tightened.

They'd lost Tarek yesterday. The shock still hung over the camp like smoke. If something didn't change, the grief would rot into despair—and despair would kill them faster than any terror bird.

He stood, brushing dirt from his jeans. "We need to find water," he said, his voice firm enough that the group actually looked up. "Food, too. Something to keep us moving."

Cartwright nodded once, his ex-military bluntness cutting through. "Good call. Can't keep people together if they're starving."

Grent exhaled a stream of smoke and muttered, "There's water everywhere out here. Question is, which of it won't kill you."

Matthew ignored the jab and kept his eyes on the others. "We don't sit here waiting for help that might never come. We move, we search, we *find something good* to give us a reason to keep pushing, I know I was hesitant a couple days ago about leaving the beach, but after what has transpired yesterday, we need to survive, which is why we need to keep pushing forward."

Kaia stepped closer, brushing a leaf from her hair. "Where do we even start?"

Matthew glanced back toward the thicker jungle, the place that felt the least welcoming—and yet somehow right.

"My gut says inland. Thicker brush means more water." he admitted.

"Your gut," Grent repeated with a smirk, flicking his lighter shut. "That's the plan?"

Cartwright stepped toward him, the quiet weight in his voice sharper than a shout. "You got a better one?"

Grent didn't answer.

Matthew straightened, feeling every eye on him again. "Pack what you need," he said. "We head out in ten minutes. If there's clean water out there, we'll find it."

No one argued. Even Grent just gave a slow, lazy smirk before stubbing his cigarette into the dirt.

For the first time, Matthew felt something new behind their looks—not just expectation.

**Trust.**

* * *

The trek started slow.

The jungle seemed thicker today, the vines heavier, the branches lower. Every step was a tangle of roots and mud, and yet Matthew felt strangely clearheaded. Clark's words still echoed softly in his mind, like a distant voice keeping him upright.

*Trust your instincts. You were made for this.*

He followed his gut, cutting through the brush where it felt right, even when there wasn't an obvious trail. Kaia stayed close behind, occasionally brushing against his arm, her steady presence grounding him.

"Sure, this is the way?" Shayne asked from the back, trying to sound light, though his voice carried tension.

Matthew nodded. "Yeah. Feels like it."

Grent snorted, cigarette dangling from his lips. "Feels like it," he echoed, rolling the words in mockery, but he didn't try to take the lead.

They pushed through another wall of foliage—and then the jungle opened.

At the edge of a small clearing, the ground was churned up. Deep furrows in the mud, almost like talon marks, led from one side of the clearing to the other. A heavy branch had been snapped clean in half, hanging like a broken limb. Cartwright saw it too and gave a small shake of his head. Neither said a word to the others. They just kept moving.

—

They pushed through another wall of foliage—and then the jungle opened.

A stream cut through the earth like a ribbon of glass, glinting in a shaft of sunlight. The gentle rush over smooth stones filled the clearing, the sound crisp and clean after days of jungle silence.

"Oh my God," Megan gasped, immediately dropping to her knees by the bank. She dipped her hands in, splashing her face with a laugh that sounded like a tiny bell after days of tension. The water was shockingly cold against sunburned skin, sending a shiver down her spine.

"It's fresh," Cartwright said, crouching to inspect it. He cupped some in his hand and drank, nodding firmly. "Safe, too."

The mood shifted instantly.

Shayne crouched beside Megan, flicking water at her with a grin. "We're saved. Forget terror birds—death by dehydration is off the table!"

Kaia turned to Matthew, her eyes bright. "You *found* this."

Matthew shrugged, a little embarrassed. "We all did."

"No," Kaia said softly, "you did. You got us here."

She lingered near him as the others drank, lowering her voice. "You keep doing this—making me feel like we might actually get out of here."

For a second, Matthew didn't know what to say. He just smiled faintly, and she gave his arm a quick squeeze before moving back toward the group.

Bryce grabbed a handful of water and poured it over his head, laughing for the first time in what felt like days. Even Adam cracked a smile, tossing some fruit he found to Shayne, who barely caught it and muttered, "Guess we're not starving either."

Dr. Varn crouched by the stream, her notebook out, jotting something quickly before tucking it away and watching Matthew for a moment—as if cataloguing this shift in him.

Grent stayed a few paces back, arms crossed, cigarette smoldering. He didn't look impressed. "Water won't keep you alive forever," he muttered.

But for everyone else, it felt like the first real **victory** since the crash.

—

Kaia splashed Matthew lightly with water, her laugh carrying in the clearing. "Not bad, Fisher," she teased. "Not bad at all."

And for the first time, Matthew allowed himself to smile.

For a little while, the clearing felt lighter. The group drank, washed, and even laughed. The stream's water ran over their hands and faces, cool and clean, rinsing away more than just dirt. It rinsed away some of the fear.

But the moment couldn't hold forever.

Grent sat on a flat rock, cigarette hanging between his fingers, eyes never leaving Matthew. His smirk was there, faint but constant, as if he was amused by the sudden joy.

"You all act like you just struck gold," he said, voice dry. "It's water. That's all."

Adam's head snapped toward him, irritation flashing. "Yeah, water—the thing we *need* to live. Maybe try not sneering at the first good thing we've found?"

Grent's smirk only widened. "Enjoy it. Won't last."

Adam muttered something under his breath and turned away, but his eyes lingered on the gun tucked at Grent's waistband.

Kaia knelt by the stream, wringing water from her hair, and glanced back at Matthew. "Don't let him get to you," she murmured quietly.

Matthew nodded, but he felt the weight of the glance. Grent wasn't just another survivor—he was an unpredictable element; one Matthew couldn't quite pin down.

Dr. Varn sat cross-legged on the ground, notebook balanced on her knee. She watched the exchange carefully, jotting something before tucking the pen behind her ear. "It's interesting," she said softly, "how hope makes everyone louder—and how doubt cuts sharper in the middle of it."

Cartwright took a long drink from his canteen and spoke up, his voice steady and grounding. "Kid found us water. That's what matters. He made the call, and it was the right one."

Kaia smiled softly at Matthew.
"Exactly. We're still here because of you."

For a moment, Matthew let the praise settle, feeling something shift—not pride, but responsibility.

Behind him, Grent flicked ash into the stream. The tiny gray specks swirled in the water, carried away.

———

The group slowly settled as the sun dipped lower, the golden light turning the stream into a band of fire through the trees.

Megan slipped away from the water's edge, glancing over her shoulder. "Adam," she called softly.

He looked up from where he was repacking some of their salvaged supplies. "Yeah?"

"Walk with me," she said, her voice quieter than usual.

Adam hesitated for a second—then followed.

They wandered a few dozen yards from the others, far enough that the campfire chatter faded into the hum of the jungle. Megan stopped near a tree, leaning against the trunk.

Her sneakers—the ones she'd complained about all day—were scuffed and dirty, her hair a bit tangled from the humidity. But when she looked at him, her usual sarcasm was gone.

"Adam," she said softly, "yesterday... we watched Tarek die. Just like that."

Adam's jaw tightened. "Yeah. I can't stop seeing it."

She stepped closer. "Life's too short to wait around, you know?

He blinked, caught off guard. "What do you mean?"

She didn't answer with words. She just reached up, cupped his face with both hands, and kissed him.

It started soft—hesitant—then deepened as Adam's arms slid around her waist, pulling her closer.

When she pulled back just enough to breathe, her voice was barely above a whisper. "I don't want to waste time pretending I don't like you. Not here. Not after..."

Adam kissed her again, harder this time, his hands pressing against the small of her back.

She laughed breathlessly against his lips. "Took you long enough."

They moved together, almost without thought, deeper into the trees where the shadows grew thicker.

There, away from the others, they shed the weight of fear for a little while. The world shrank to the press of their hands, the heat of their skin, the quiet gasps muffled by the jungle.

For a few fleeting minutes, the island and its horrors didn't exist—only they did. For Adam, it was the first moment since the crash that felt untouched by fear or loss.

Grent's gaze flicked briefly in their direction, noticing the way Megan's hand lingered on Adam's arm when they returned later. His smirk deepened, but he said nothing.

—

The jungle night wrapped around them like a blanket, thick and heavy, but the fire they'd built cut a warm circle of light into the darkness.

They sat scattered around the flames—Bryce hunched over, poking at the fire with a stick; Shayne leaning back on his elbows, humming some half-remembered tune; Cartwright sitting upright like he was still on duty; Dr. Varn cross-legged with her notebook resting on her lap, though she wasn't writing now.

Matthew sat near the edge of the light, staring at the fire as if answers might flicker there.

Kaia stood.

At first, she didn't say anything—she just looked around at all of them, her gaze settling on Matthew.

"He did this," she said finally, her voice clear, cutting through the crackle of the fire.

Matthew blinked, looking up. "What?"

Kaia stepped closer to the firelight. "He found this place. He got us water. He gave us something we didn't have yesterday—hope."

Matthew started to protest, but Cartwright spoke before he could.

"She's right," the captain said, voice gruff but sincere. "The kid's got steel. He didn't hesitate, and that's what we needed."

Dr. Varn nodded, closing her notebook. "Leadership isn't about who shouts the loudest. It's about who steadies the group when it starts to fall apart. And that's what you've been doing, Matthew."

Matthew shifted uncomfortably under their words. "I'm just—"

"—keeping us alive," Kaia interrupted, a soft smile on her lips.

Shayne grinned and threw his arms wide. "I mean, I *did* help, but yeah, Matt's the guy."

Laughter rippled through the group—small, but real.

Adam and Megan had slipped back into the circle quietly; Megan's cheeks were faintly flushed, Adam's hair a little mussed. Megan squeezed Matthew's shoulder. "Kaia's right. You've been holding us together when the rest of us... couldn't."

Adam nodded. "We're behind you, man. All the way."

Matthew's throat tightened. He glanced around— at Kaia's proud smile. Shayne's playful smirk, Cartwright's steady nod, Dr. Varn's measured but approving gaze, Megan and Adam's quiet support.

The fire crackled louder in the silence that followed, the weight of their trust settling on him like a mantle.

He managed a faint smile. "Alright," he said, his voice low but steady. "Then I won't let you down."

From the far edge of the firelight, Grent sat on a log, cigarette glowing in the dark, his eyes fixed on Matthew.

He muttered softly, almost too quiet to hear: "Wins don't last long out here."

And with that, he took a slow drag, the ember flaring like an omen in the dark.

# Chapter 15 The Shattered Path

The morning broke with the kind of light that made you forget where you were for a moment.

Matthew Fisher stirred awake to the warmth of sunlight cutting through the jungle canopy. The fire from last night had burned down to a soft ember glow, smoke curling lazily into the air. For once, the camp didn't feel like a desperate, temporary pit stop—it felt almost... safe.

Kaia was already awake, crouched by the water's edge rinsing a small pot they'd used for boiling. Her auburn curls caught the morning light, and she smiled faintly when she noticed Matthew stirring. "You actually slept," she teased.

"First time in days,' he admitted, stretching the stiffness from his shoulders. It was true—last night had been their best night so far. They'd found a safe clearing, fresh water, and even a few edible fruits. The fire had kept the predators away. For the first time since the crash, everyone had gone to sleep without fear gnawing at them.

Not everyone had woken up in the same mood, though.

"These shoes are a nightmare," Megan muttered, sitting cross-legged with her legs stretched out in front of her. She stared down at the thin pair of beat-up sneakers that Kaia gave her days ago—the cheap material was splitting at the sides, and the backs were rubbed raw from walking.

"My feet are literally bleeding," she grumbled, kicking them off with a sharp flick. One landed in the dirt, the other by the firepit. "Forget it. I'm going barefoot. These aren't helping anymore."

Adam smirked from where he sat sharpening a stick. "Good call. I was wondering how long it would take before those things gave up."

Megan shot him a look. "Oh, shut up, Adam. Like you've been walking on sunshine this whole time."

From across the clearing, Grent watched the exchange, cigarette dangling between two fingers. He took a slow drag before muttering just loud enough to be heard, "Barefoot in this jungle? Smart. Real smart."

Adam's head snapped up, already irritated. "What's that supposed to mean?"

Grent didn't look at him. He exhaled smoke, squinting into the trees. "Just means this place will chew up anyone who doesn't think ahead." His tone was flat, but it hung heavy, a reminder that even in this morning calm, Grent's presence was a shadow.

Matthew caught the tension but let it pass. The morning *felt good*—almost normal—and he wanted to keep it that way for as long as he could.

Kaia crossed back to him, handing over a piece of fruit. "Eat," she said softly. "You'll need the energy."

Matthew looked around the clearing one more time. For now, the world was quiet, and for a brief flicker of time, it almost felt like they'd found a fragile rhythm to survival.

But he knew better than to trust calm for too long.

* * *

The decision to send out a scout party came easily that morning.

"We should see what's around us," Cartwright said, standing with his hands on his hips, scanning the tree line. "If we're gonna stay here a few days, we need to know what we're dealing with."

Matthew nodded, already sliding his pack over his shoulder. "I'll go."

It ended up being him, Cartwright, Grent, Bryce, and Dr. Varn—the rest would stay behind to tend the fire, watch the supplies, and keep camp intact.

"Don't go too far," Kaia called as Matthew tightened the strap on his pack.

He gave her a reassuring smile. "We'll be back before dark."

Grent simply muttered, "Let's get moving," the cigarette he'd been holding snuffed out and flicked into the dirt.

They entered the jungle, with no idea what waited inside.

Small birds darted through the canopy, flashes of yellow and green. Something small and quick—a mammal with long ears and a tail like a whip, something they'd never seen before—scurried out of sight as the group stepped over a fallen log.

Bryce, walking just behind Matthew, grinned at the sight. "Well, at least the local wildlife isn't all teeth and claws."

"Don't get too comfortable," Cartwright replied, his voice low. "If there's little ones like that, there's big ones too."

He was right. Every so often they saw signs of something larger—a massive footprint sunk deep in the mud, a snapped tree branch at shoulder height. Once, they even heard a distant guttural roar that made the group freeze for a long moment before quietly pressing on.

They moved slow, quiet, careful not to disturb more than they had to.

After nearly an hour of walking, they reached a clearing.

It looked out of place—a small patch of overgrown ground surrounded by vines and old roots, as if nature had reclaimed it from something man-made.

Matthew stepped forward first, his eyes narrowing. "What... is this?"

Half-buried under moss and dirt was a piece of old tech—a rusted control panel, a cracked monitor, wires snaking out like dead vines. The double helix logo was still faintly visible, stamped into the metal like a forgotten signature. The panel gave off a faint metallic tang, the sun-warmed metal hot under Varn's fingers.

Dr. Varn crouched down, brushing dirt away with the back of her hand. She didn't say anything at first, just stared at the logo for a long second.

Her brow furrowed. *Helix...*

Cartwright joined her, squinting at the device. "Old tech. Been here a long while."

"Long enough for the jungle to eat it," Matthew said.

Bryce called them over to a nearby tree. "Guys. Look at this."

On the bark were markings—carved lines, shapes, and swirls. They weren't random; there was intent behind them.

More carvings appeared on a rock nearby, faint under moss.

"Tribal?" Cartwright guessed, leaning closer.

"Looks like it," Matthew said, tracing one faint groove with his fingertips. He couldn't make sense of any of it.

"We'll need Shayne," he decided. "He might recognize something."

The moment was still and heavy—until a sharp *CRACK!* Shattered it.

A gunshot.

Everyone spun toward the sound.

Grent stood a few feet away, his pistol raised, smoke curling from the barrel. At his feet, a small wild pig twitched once before going still.

"Jesus Christ," Cartwright snapped, his voice exploding like the gunshot. "What the hell are you doing?"

Grent holstered the weapon, completely unbothered. "Getting us dinner."

Cartwright strode over, eyes burning. "We talked about this. You don't fire unless you must. You don't make noise we don't need to make."

Grent just smirked, kneeling to life the pig by its hind legs. "Relax, Captain. The shot was clean. And now we don't have to eat boiled roots again."

Cartwright's jaw clenched, but he turned away, muttering a curse under his breath.

Matthew glanced at Varn—she was still crouched near the marked tree, staring at the helix logo, her lips pressed together in thought.

"Let's head back," he said, his voice measured.

No one argued.

Grent swung the pig over his shoulder as if it weighed nothing. "Let's not keep them waiting."

And with that, they turned back toward camp— the jungle swallowing the sound of their footsteps, leaving only the faint smell of gunpowder behind.

* * *

The camp felt strangely homey after just one night.

Kaia sat by the firepit, nudging embers with a stick and adding pieces of driftwood. Smoke curled into the canopy, fragrant with the faint sweetness of the fruit peels they'd burned the night before.

Adam emerged from the trees with an armful of kindling. He tossed it into the pile, brushing his hands off. "If I keep hauling wood like this, I expect a trophy or something," he said, smirking.

"Your trophy is survival," Shayne replied from where he sat on a log, lazily carving a stick into what might eventually become a spear. "Congratulations. You're alive another day."

Adam rolled his eyes. "Thanks, sensei."

Megan was sitting cross-legged nearby; her bare feet stretched toward the warmth of the fire. She was absentmindedly spinning her necklace between her fingers—the thin chain catching the light.

Adam noticed. "That thing really means something to you, doesn't it?"

Megan looked up, a little caught off guard. "Yeah. It was given to me by my grandmother."

Her voice softened in a way it rarely did. "She gave it to me when I was younger, told me it would be good luck. Ever since then I have never taken it off."

Adam nodded, sitting beside her. "Guess she was right."

Megan let out a small laugh. "Guess so."

There was a beat of quiet between them, more comfortable than awkward.

Adam smirked. "Don't worry, I won't let anyone take it off you."

Megan arched an eyebrow. "Oh, so you're my bodyguard now?"

"Guess so," he said, that same sarcastic smirk softening into something warmer.

Across the fire, Jules ruined the moment.

"You two planning on making a Hallmark card out of this?" he muttered, fussing with his pack. "Or do you two want to flirt while the rest of us actually keep this camp from burning down?"

Kaia groaned, tossing a stick into the fire harder than she needed to. "Jules, if you correct me one more time about how I stack wood—"

Shayne didn't even look up from his carving. "He's right, Kaia. You're totally doing it wrong."

She shot him a glare. "Don't start."

Jules smirked, delighted to be irritating. "Hey, just trying to keep us alive."

"You're keeping us annoyed," Shayne muttered under his breath, which made Kaia chuckle.

The sound of rustling came from the trees.

Everyone tensed for a second—but then Matthew, Cartwright, Grent, Bryce, and Dr. Varn stepped into the clearing.

"Scouts return," Shayne announced with mock dram, tossing his half-finished spear onto the ground.

Grent swung something heavy off his should and tossed it near the fire. A small wild pig landed with a soft thud.

"Dinner," Grent said simply.

For a second, the entire camp just stared—then the mood shifted.

"Holy crap," Shayne grinned. "We're eating real food tonight."

Even Jules forgot to complain, his eyes lighting up.

Within minutes, the fire was stoked high, the pig being prepared. Laughter bubbled up—real laughter—as the smoke carried the scent of cooking meat through the clearing.

For the first time since the crash, the camp felt like a camp, not just a place to survive another night.

* * *

The smell of roasting meat drifted through the clearing, thick and warm, mixing with woodsmoke. For the first time since the crash, the scent wasn't just of survival—it smelled like comfort.

The group sat around the fire, the pig turning slowly on a spit cobbled together from scavenged branches. It sizzled and cracked, grease dripping into the flames with quiet pops. The smoke curled up through the canopy, carrying the savory scent into the night like a beacon.

"God, that smells amazing," Bryce said, leaning back on his hands.

"Better than roots and fruit," Shayne added, grinning. "Man, I think I'd trade my college diploma for a sandwich right now. But this'll do."

"Your diploma isn't worth much anyway," Adam quipped, tossing a stick at him.

Shayne caught it, feigned a gasp, and tossed it back. "Hey, tribal languages major—you'll see how valuable I am soon enough."

The laughter that followed wasn't forced this time.

Kaia sat next to Matthew, her knees pulled up, firelight painting her auburn curls gold. She nudged him gently.

"You're doing good," she said softly, her voice low enough that only he could hear.

Matthew looked at her, brow furrowing slightly. "Doing good?"

She smiled, a little crooked, a little tired. "Leading. Keeping everyone together. This—"

She gestured to the fire, to the meal, to the group laughing— "we needed this."

For a moment, the weight on his shoulders felt lighter.

Across the fire, Grent sat slightly apart, chewing on a piece of fruit, silent but watchful.
He hadn't stirred trouble tonight. He hadn't needed to.

The quiet smirk that occasionally crossed his face was enough reminder of his presence—and of the fact that the peace they felt might not last.

By the time the pig was carved and shared, everyone was full for the first time in days.

Megan leaned back against a log, hands on her stomach. "I could die happy right now."

"Don't say that" Adam muttered, but he was smiling.

Shayne wiped his greasy fingers on his shirt and stretched. "Man, if this place had Wi-Fi, I might just stay."

That got another laugh, even from Cartwright.

The fire burned lower, the voices softened, and one by one, the group drifted toward sleep—some curling up by the warmth of the flames, others making small nests of leaves and spare clothing.

Matthew stayed up a little longer, staring into the embers.

The jungle beyond their little camp was silent, unnervingly so—but for tonight, it felt like a good silence.

For the first time since the yacht went down, they felt safe enough to close their eyes without fear scratching at the edges of their thoughts.

Matthew let himself believe it, just for a moment.

*For the first time since the crash, Fisher let his guard down—not knowing how short-lived this peace would be.*

# Chapter 16  Signs in the Trees

The jungle woke slowly.

A thin mist clung to the treetops, curling in ribbons of pale gray above the survivors' makeshift camp. The last embers of last night's fire glowed faintly, sending up a crooked line of smoke that hung still in the humid air. For once, there was no storm, no roar of the ocean—only the quiet shuffle of leaves and the distant cries of unseen birds.

Matthew Fisher stirred first. His back ached from the hard ground, but the scent of woodsmoke and the low crackle of the dying fire grounded him. He sat up, stretching, rubbing grit from his eyes. Around him, the others were still sprawled in awkward shapes, their sleeping arrangements little more than blankets over roots and damp soil.

Kaia was awake a moment later, sitting up and tucking her hair behind her ears. She smiled faintly at him, her voice low.

"Morning."

Matthew smiled back, though it was tired, and muttered, "Morning," before leaning to poke at the coals with a stick.

Behind them, Megan groaned dramatically and rolled over. "Ugh. My neck feels like I slept on a rock."

"That's because you did," Kaia teased, arching a brow. "Still worth it for those pink toenails though, right?"

Megan shot her a glare and wiggled her feet out from her blanket. The polish was chipped but visible—an oddly cheerful splash of color against the mud.

"Don't start with me," Megan said, pushing her hair back into place. "Just because I refuse to go feral doesn't mean I can't survive out here."

Kaia laughed under her breath, and even Matthew cracked a smile.

A few feet away, Dr. Emilia Varn sat cross-legged with a journal balanced on her knees. She'd been up longer than the others, quietly jotting notes as the camp stirred. Her glasses caught the light as she looked over the pages, then at Matthew, studying the way he leaned over the fire.

He hadn't noticed how naturally he was taking charge—poking the fire back to life, passing out the few water bottles they had left, murmuring, "Let's get this warmed up for breakfast."

Varn made a note in the margin of her journal before snapping it shut, a small smile playing at the corner of her mouth.

Another day on the island had begun—and for the first time since the crash, the morning felt very calm.

By the time the camp was fully awake, the fire had been coaxed back to life, sending up a small curl of warmth against the damp morning air. A few of the leftover scraps of pig from last night sizzled in the pan Cartwright had rigged out of bent metal and rope.

Cartwright crouched near the fire, poking the sizzling meat with a stick. "We need to decide what we're doing today," he said, his voice steady but edged with the weight of command. "We can't just sit around waiting for rescue that's not coming."

Matthew nodded, crouching opposite him. "Those markings we saw yesterday—" He looked at Dr. Varn. "They weren't random. Someone made them."

"They were deliberate," Varn agreed, flipping open her journal and turning it toward them. She'd sketched a rough copy of the carved symbols and the way they wrapped around the trees. "This wasn't graffiti. It felt... organized. Almost ceremonial."

Cartwright frowned, rubbing his jaw. "Could be warnings. Could be territory lines. Either way, I don't like it."

Matthew's gaze drifted to Shayne, who was still sprawled under a blanket a few feet away, face buried in his arm. "Shayne's the one who'd know if these are warnings or something else."

Matthew picked up a pebble and tossed it lightly at him.

Shayne groaned, shifting. "Ow. What was that for?"

"You're coming with us today," Matthew said.

Shayne cracked one eye open. "Coming where?"

"We are taking you to a tar pit to leave you in." Matthew chuckled.

"Haha very funny," Shayne responded.

"We are taking you to those markings we found," Matthew replied. "You've read more about indigenous cultures than anyone else here. We need you."

Shayne sat up slowly, rubbing his face. His hair was sticking in every direction. "Great. I survive a shipwreck, a storm, and a dinosaur, and now I'm the designated anthropologist."

Kaia smirked from her spot by the fire. "What, are you saying you don't want to be Indiana Jones?"

Shayne gave her a flat look. "I don't even get the hat."

The humor cut through the tension like sunlight, and a few chuckles went around the circle. Even Cartwright cracked the faintest hint of a smile before leaning back over the fire.

"Hat or no hat," Cartwright said, "we'll head out after breakfast. See what we're dealing with."

Matthew nodded. "We'll take the scout group except Bryce, need you to stay here. Everyone else stays here."

The plan hung in the air for a moment. It felt... official, like they were finally organizing into something more than just shipwreck survivors.

Shayne muttered, "Guess I'm going on a field trip," and reached for the water bottle Kaia passed him.

* * *

The jungle swallowed them whole as they left camp behind., the morning sun barely piercing the thick canopy. The air was heavy with moisture, each breath damp and warm. Cartwright led the way, machete in hand, cutting through the stubborn brush that blocked the faint trail from the day before. Matthew followed just a few paces behind, with Shayne and Varn in the middle, while Grent trailed at the rear, scanning the shadows. Matthew stayed alert, his eyes scanning for movement, while Shayne scribbled mental notes, murmuring under his breath as he studied every etched surface they passed.

"This feels wrong," Shayne muttered, crouching to examine a tree trunk marked with crude, deliberate symbols. The grooves were deep, freshly carved. "These aren't scratches from animals. This is language."

Matthew leaned closer, squinting. "Can you read it?"

Shayne shook his head slowly, brushing the dirt off one mark. "Not fully. But the patterns... they mean something. Warnings maybe."

Dr. Varn, keeping a deliberate few paces behind, knelt and snapped a photo with her phone out of habit, forgetting the dead screen. She frowned. "It's methodical. Whatever this is, someone took the time to leave these here."

Grent stood a few feet away, arms crossed, eyes on the shadows rather than the markings. "Or to scare us." His voice was flat, the edge of a smirk curling his lip.

Cartwright glanced back at him sharply. "We don't assume hostility. Not yet."

They pressed on, moving deeper into the undergrowth. The trail widened slightly before opening into a small clearing—and that's when Varn's breath caught.

At the base of a toppled tree sat the old tech they saw just the day before. Now with tribal markings all over it.

"What the hell is that?" Cartwright muttered, crouching.

"The old tech from yesterday, but now with fresh markings. Shayne what do you think?"

Shayne's eyes lingered on the markings longer than anyone else's. "This is amazing, let me see if I can decipher it."

A branch cracked somewhere beyond the clearing.

Everyone froze.

From the corner of Matthew's vision, something moved between the trees—fast, deliberate, and gone just as quickly.

"You saw that, right?" Matthew whispered.

Cartwright raised his machete slightly. "Eyes sharp. We're not alone."

Shayne scanned the markings again, his voice dropping low. "Whatever lives here... it knows we're here too."

Grent stayed calm, unsettlingly calm. He raised his pistol, eyes fixed on the tree line, and said flatly, "if they're out there, they'll show themselves. Eventually."

* * *

The trek back to camp felt heavier than the walk out. The silence between the group wasn't just exhaustion—it was tension, thick and unspoken. Cartwright led the way again, jaw tight, his machete swinging low.

Grent was the only one who seemed unbothered. He had slung a freshly killed wild pig over his shoulder, blood dripping down its side, leaving a trail behind them.

Matthew finally broke the silence. "You didn't need to shoot that thing."

Grent didn't look at him. "It's food," he said simply.

Shayne shook his head, muttering, "Yeah, and it's also loud. That shot carried for miles. Whatever saw us out there now knows where we're camped."

Cartwright stopped walking, turning on his heel to face Grent. His voice was sharp, the military edge unmistakable.

"You fire that thing off again without clearing it, we'll have bigger problems than dinner. We're not here to announce ourselves."

Grent's response was a half-smile and a shrug. "Relax. I just got us dinner."

No one laughed.

When they broke through the tree line into camp, the smell of smoke from the fire still hung in the humid air. The others looked up as the scouting party returned. Eyes went straight to the pig dangling from Grent's grip.

"Holy crap," Bryce said, standing. "You got another one!"

"Yeah, maybe more than just food." Shayne spoke under his breath, tossing his pack to the ground.

Megan wrinkled her nose at the dripping blood but didn't complain. "Well... gross or not, at least we'll have more fresh meat tonight."

Matthew glanced around camp, noticing how quickly Grent had become the center of attention simply for bringing food. His jaw clenched. Something about the man's calm, calculated smile as he tossed the pig beside the fire unsettled him.

Grent caught his stare and held it for a beat too long before kneeling down, pulling a knife, and calmly beginning to gut the pig.

* * *

Night felt heavy and thick over the camp. The pig was cooked, the smell clinging to everyone's skin, and for a brief moment there was comfort—the group laughing softly, sharing bites, pretending the world wasn't hostile and strange.

That's when the **first arrow hit.**

It came from the darkness with a sharp hiss, burying itself in the sand inches from the fire. Everyone froze.

A second arrow flew, this one not missing.

"AHHH!" Bryce screamed as it buried itself deep in his thigh, sending him sprawling, clutching his leg as blood seeped between his fingers.

"Down!" Cartwright barked, dropping low and grabbing his machete.

**Chaos exploded.**

More arrows whistled through the trees, thudding into the ground, the fire, the pig they'd been eating. The sound of shouting—not English, but guttural, fierce calls—came from the tree line. Figures moved in the shadows.

Matthew sprang to Bryce, Kaia already at this side.

"He's hit bad," gasped, gripping under Bryce's arms.

"Up—come on!" Matthew grunted, hauling Bryce to his feet. Bryce face twisted in pain, teeth gritted as they half-dragged him away from the fire.

"MOVE!" Cartwright bellowed, swatting an arrow away with machete.

Shayne grabbed the fire's edge with his bare hands and kicked burning logs into the darkness, sparks erupting like angry fireflies.

It didn't matter.

The arrows kept coming. Somewhere in the dark, bowstrings thrummed in rapid bursts, each snap sending another shaft hissing past. The acrid smell of burning wood from their scattered fire hung in the air.

"Who the hell is that?!" Adam yelled, his voice cracking as another arrow sliced past his head.

"Doesn't matter—RUN!" Cartwright ordered.

**The camp dissolved.**

People scattered—some grabbing who they could, others just bolting blindly.

Matthew clutched Bryce's arm with Kaia's help dragging him as fast as his injured leg would allow. Dr. Varn stayed with them, shielding Bryce's other side.

Shayne stayed with Cartwright, the two ducking into the brush.

Adam grabbed Megan's wrist, pulling her into the dark—only to see Grent already there, moving fast, unnervingly calm, pistol in hand.

Through the panic, Jules's voice could be heard shouting once... then gone. It came from somewhere off to the left—then cut short, swallowed by the jungle. The silence that followed was worse than the shouting.

No one saw which way he ran. No one saw him after that.

The firelight behind them faded, replaced by black jungle and frantic breathing.

By the time the shouting stopped, three groups had formed without even realizing it... and Jules was simply gone.

In the darkness, Grent walked almost leisurely, while Adam half-dragged Megan through the vines, his voice cracking as he yelled, "Megan! This way—keep moving!"

Grent's mouth curled into the faintest smirk as he glanced into the black trees and muttered under his breath, *"Now this is where things get fun."*

# Chapter 17 The First Night Apart

The jungle was different at night. It wasn't just dark—it was thick, suffocating. The moon was barely a suggestion behind the canopy, casting the world in shadow. Every step felt too loud, every broken branch like an alarm to whatever might be listening.

Matthew pushed forward, one arm hooked under Bryce's shoulders, helping him hobble over roots and uneven ground. Kaia was on Bryce's other side, steadying him with her smaller frame, her auburn hair plastered to her forehead from sweat.

Bryce's leg dragged, his breath coming in sharp, uneven bursts. The arrow wound in his thigh oozed dark blood that had already soaked through the strip of Kaia's shirt they'd wrapped around it.

"Think we're far enough?" Matthew whispered, glancing back into the black trees.

Kaia shook her head. "Not yet. The drums are still out there."

As if on cue, a faint rhythm pulsed through the jungle—distant, but unmistakable. A slow, hollow *thump-thump-thump* that seemed to vibrate in the ground beneath their feet.

Bryce let out a pained laugh that turned into a grimace. "Well... this is one hell of a graduation trip."

Matthew glanced at him, managing a tight smile despite the tension. "You're gonna be okay. We'll get you fixed up."

"Good," Bryce muttered, teeth gritted. "Because limping around the jungle with an arrow in my leg in not how I pictured going out."

Kaia tightened her grip around him as they stepped over a fallen log. "You're not going out. Not here."

Bryce went quiet, but Matthew felt the weight of the words. They all did.

Behind them, Dr. Varn walked in silence, scanning the darkness with sharp, thoughtful eyes. She carried a stick sharpened into a crude spear—more for comfort than defense—but she didn't look afraid.

Instead, she studied Matthew, watching how he adjusted his pace for Bryce, how he glanced over his shoulder every few seconds.

"You're holding up well," she said quietly, almost to herself.

Matthew didn't respond—he didn't feel like a leader, just someone doing what he had to do.

They moved on in silence for several minutes, the jungle swallowing their footsteps. The air was heavy, humid, pressing down on them. Somewhere far off, a night bird shrieked, making Bryce jump despite himself.

"You know what's really messed up?" Bryce panted. "I'd kill for a cheeseburger right now."

Kaia actually laughed—a soft, genuine sound. "If you keep talking about food, we're all going to starve faster."

It was a brief moment of levity, a flicker of warmth in the cold dark. But the drums came again, close now, thudding through the night like the heartbeat of the island.

The group froze.

Matthew's grip on Bryce tightened. He turned to Kaia and Dr. Varn, his voice low but firm. "We keep moving. Quietly."

And they did—slipping further into the jungle, every step slower, every breath quieter, the darkness closing in like a tide.

* * *

The jungle swallowed sound differently here. Shayne noticed it first—how every word, every snapped twig seemed to echo for a heartbeat and then vanish, like the air itself was eating the noise.

He tightened his grip on the heavy branch he'd fashioned into a crude club and glanced at Cartwright, who strode ahead with military precision, machete in hand.

"Do you always walk this quietly?" Shayne whispered, "or is that comfort thing, or—"

Cartwright didn't look back. "It's a survival thing."

Shayne smirked, though his voice wavered. "Guess I missed that day in college."

A branch cracked somewhere to their right.

Both men froze.

Cartwright's head tilted just slightly, eyes scanning the tree line. He didn't speak—didn't need to. Shayne saw it in his body language: **they weren't alone.**

Another sound—lighter this time, like a footstep on wet leaves. Then silence.

"Okay," Shayne murmured, "I'm officially not loving this."

Cartwright crouched, his hand up for quiet. "Someone's following us. Close."

Shayne investigated the dark, trying to joke through the unease. "Could be squirrels. Really, really big squirrels."

No response. Cartwright's jaw tightened, his hand firmly gripped to the machete, preparing for any attack that comes forth.

He stood slowly, voice low. "Whoever it is, they know how to move."

Shayne swallowed. "Which means they're either friendly... or not."

Cartwright didn't blink. "Doesn't matter. Keep moving."

They started forward again, quieter now, steps deliberate, ears straining for every rustle.

Somewhere behind them, a shadow shifted between the trees—quick, fluid and gone in an instant.

Shayne felt the hairs on his neck rise.

Cartwright muttered just loud enough for Shayne to hear: "We're being tracked."

* * *

The jungle floor was cruel. Every root, every jagged rock seemed to find Megan's bare feet. She stumbled again, hissing as she scraped her heel against a stone, and clutched Adam's arm for balance.

"Sorry," she muttered, wincing. "I think I've stepped on every sharp thing this island had to offer."

Adam looked at her feet in the dim light—they were already raw, streaked with dirt and small cuts. "You should've kept the sneakers you had," he said softly.

"They were two sizes too small and smelled like death," Megan replied, then forced a weak smile. "Guess I should've kept them anyway, huh?"

Adam slowed his pace a little, glancing behind them. "Want me to carry you for a while?"

Megan blinked at him, then actually laughed—tired, but genuine. "Adam, if you try to carry me, you'll face-plant into the nearest bush. But... thanks for offering."

Behind them, Grent moved like a shadow, pistol loose in his grip, eyes scanning the tree line with that same unnerving calm. His voice cut through the night: "Less talking. More walking."

Adam turned slightly, jaw tight. "She's hurt. She can't just—"

Grent stopped walking for the first time and looked at him, expression blank but dangerous. "Then she'll have to deal with it. We all do."

The words hung there, sharp and cold.

Megan let go of Adam's arm and stepped forward on her own, even though every step clearly hurt. "It's fine," she whispered, more to Adam than to Grent. "I can walk."

Adam frowned but didn't push it.

They moved on in silence for a few minutes, the only sounds Megan's occasional sharp inhale when her foot caught something and the distant hum of insects.

Finally, Megan broke the tension. "You know… when we get off this island, I'm never wearing shoes again."

Adam glanced at her. "Really?"

"Yeah," she said with a crooked smile. "Shoes are overrated. They just make you take walking for granted."

It was a small moment, but it softened the edges of her pain. Adam smiled, and even Grent's silence seemed a little less suffocating—though he still scanned the jungle, pistol at his side, calm in a way that wasn't comforting at all.

* * *

The jungle was quiet here—too quiet.

A thin mist clung low to the ground, curling between twisted roots and ferns. The moonlight broke through the canopy in silvers, catching on something in the mud: **a single shoeprint.**

It was Jules's.

The impression was fresh, the edges still wet. A few feet away, a broken branch hung at an odd angle, as if someone had shoved through the brush in a hurry.

The camera (if this were a movie) would linger here, in this strange emptiness, as if waiting for him to appear.

Somewhere in the distance, a faint sound—almost like a laugh—drifted through the trees, carried on the wind.

Then silence.

No sign of Jules.

No voice calling for help.

Just the single footprint in the mud... and the suggestion that he had vanished into the island itself.

* * *

By the time Matthew's group found shelter, their bodies ached from exhaustion. The jungle seemed endless, every turn looking the same—but finally, they stumbled onto a shallow rock overhang, barely wide enough for four people to huddle under.

"Here," Matthew said, voice low, "we'll stop here for the night."

He eased Bryce down against the stone wall. The younger man groaned, clutching at his leg. The makeshift bandage Kaia had tied earlier was already soaked through.

"Easy," Kaia murmured, crouching beside him. "Let me take a look."

She peeled the fabric back. The wound was angry and swollen, the flesh around the arrow's entry point red and hot.

"Not good," Dr. Varn muttered, studying it carefully. "We need to clean it. Properly. Soon."

Matthew sat on his heels, eyes darting over the wound, over Bryce's pale face. "He'll make it," he said firmly, almost to convince himself.

Bryce forced a crooked smile through the pain. "You're terrible at lying, Fisher."

Kaia swatted at his shoulder gently, her face tight. "Don't talk like that. You're going to be fine."

For a moment, the four of them sat in silence, the jungle pressing in on every side. The distant drums they'd been hearing all night thudded again— low and ominous, carrying on the still air like a heartbeat.

Matthew moved closer to the edge of the overhang, scanning the black wall of trees. His voice was low but steady.

"We'll find the others. No matter what."

Kaia placed her hand lightly on his arm, grounding him, He didn't look at her, but the weight of her touch settled the storm in his chest—if only for a moment.

The fireless night stretched before them, the darkness heavy with unseen eyes, and relentless, somewhere deep in the jungle.

# Chapter 18 Shadows and Whispers

Matthew wasn't on the island anymore.

He stood in a quiet, empty Viremoor University classroom—the old linoleum floor shining faintly, the smell of chalk and stale coffee hanging in the air. The sunlight through the windows was golden, almost too perfect, like a memory that had been polished and softened.

At the front of the room, Professor Clark leaned casually against his desk. His sleeves were rolled up, his tie loose like it always was after long lectures. He looked calm. Fatherly. Like the chaos of the island couldn't touch him here.

"Matthew," Clark said, his voice warm. "You've been leading them well."

Matthew's brow furrowed. "What is this? Why do I keep seeing you?"

Clark smiled faintly. "Because you need me to. The island is testing you, and you're rising to it. You're stronger than you think."

Matthew felt the praise sink in, but it didn't settle right. "What do you mean the island is testing me?"

Clark stepped closer, his shoes echoing softly against the floor. "It can make you who you're meant to be... if you let it."

Matthew swallowed, uneasy. "And if I don't?"

For the briefest moment, Clark's smile faltered. Something in his eyes—sharp, calculating—flickered before smoothing over again.

"Then," he said softly, "the island will shape you anyway."

The words rang in Matthew's ears, louder than they should have been.

Suddenly the classroom dimmed, the golden light turning gray. The chalkboard behind Clark filled with strange symbols—the same shapes Matthew had seen carved into trees.

"Why am I seeing this?" Matthew demanded.

Clark tilted his head, as if the question amused him. "Because, Matthew..."—his voice was calm, almost soothing— *"you're not just surviving the island. You're becoming it."*

Matthew's breath hitched—

—and he woke up, heart pounding, the jungle heat pressing down like a weight.

Matthew sat up, chest heaving. His heart was still thudding from the strangest dream, one that left him with more questions than answers. The classroom's golden light and Clark's voice clung to him like mist, even as the reality of the jungle replaced them—damp earth, insect hum, and the faint ache in his back from sleeping on stone.

Under the low overhang, Bryce stirred, a fever sheen on his forehead. Kaia crouched next to him, wringing out a strip of cloth she'd used to clean his wound. Dr. Varn sat cross-legged nearby, her eyes half-closed, as though she hadn't slept at all.

Matthew rubbed his face, then broke the silence. "I saw him again," he said.

Kaia looked up. "Clark?"

Matthew nodded, uneasy. "In another dream. Or a vision. Whatever it is, he's there, and he's talking to me. He keeps praising me, saying I'm doing well—but..." He hesitated, then shook his head. "There's something off about it. Like there's more he's not saying."

Dr. Varn's gaze sharpened behind her glasses. "What does he say?"

"He tells me I'm becoming who I'm 'meant to be.' That the island is testing me," Matthew said quietly. "But it doesn't feel like a test. It feels like he's trying to pull me somewhere."

The jungle hummed around them for a beat before Varn spoke again—slower, more deliberate this time. "Matthew... I need to tell you something."

Both Matthew and Kaia looked at her.

"When Clark invited me on this trip, it wasn't just for company," she continued. "He asked me to observe you. Quietly. To see how you reacted under stress."

Matthew blinked, the words hitting like a cold splash. "He what?"

"He said you had... potential," Varn said, her voice steady, though there was regret in it. "I thought he meant as a leader. That's all he told me. But I never trusted him completely. But since Clark didn't make it, none of what I'm here for matters anymore, only survival."

Kaia's jaw tightened, her hands gripping the damp cloth she held.

"So, you were studying me?" Matthew asked, his voice sharper now.

Varn shook her head quickly. "Not like a lab rat. I wouldn't have come if it felt like that. Yes. I agreed to watch you, but only because I wanted to understand what Clark was really after."

Bryce groaned softly from where he lay, his voice thin. "Man... even the doc didn't trust that guy. And he's showing up in your dreams?"

Matthew didn't answer. The weight of Varn's words pressed into his chest. Clark wasn't just guiding him in visions—he'd been planning this long before the island.

* * *

The jungle felt different when you stepped into it alone.

Matthew tightened the strap of his pack over his shoulder, glancing back at the makeshift shelter. Kaia was kneeling beside Bryce, changing the soaked bandage on his leg, and Dr. Varn was quietly organizing their dwindling supplies.

"I won't go far." Matthew said, adjusting the stick he'd sharpened into a crude spear. "Just need to see what's ahead. We can't keep sitting here."

Kaia straightened, frowning. "We shouldn't split again."

"I'm not leaving," Matthew said gently. "I just need to see what's nearby—water, shelter, anything."

Kaia hesitated, then nodded reluctantly. "Come back before it's dark."

Matthew gave her a small smile, one that didn't quite reach his eyes. "I will."

The jungle swallowed him quickly, each step muffled by moss and fallen leaves. Alone, the sounds were louder—the rustle of branches, the distant shriek of a bird, the hum of insects like static in his ears.

He moved cautiously, eyes sweeping over every tree, every patch of brush.

That's when he saw it:

An arrow, wedged deep into the trunk of a leaning tree, its shaft decorated with rough red markings. The wood was dark with age, but the paint was fresh.

Matthew ran his fingers over the grooves. Tribal. Recent.

He stepped carefully around a patch of vines and froze again. Hanging from a low branch was something stranger—a **talisman,** woven from twigs and dried leaves, tied together with sinew. A crude figure, almost human-shaped, its "head" marked with black streaks.

It swayed lightly in the breeze. Watching.

Matthew's chest tightened.

A little farther ahead, the mud gave way to footprints. Human. Barefoot. And not just one set—small and large. Side by side. A family.

They weren't old.

Matthew's breath was steady, but his knuckles whitened on his spear. Whoever left these prints could be anywhere.

He stared down the narrow path ahead—the footprints led deeper into the trees, the direction pulling at him.

For a long moment, he considered following them.

But the drums he'd been hearing since last night thudded again, close now, and a distant voice—or maybe an animal cry—echoed through the canopy.

Matthew backed away, forcing himself to stop. Not yet.

He turned, heading back toward the overhang. Every step back felt heavier, like the jungle itself didn't want to let him go.

* * *

Back at the overhang, the air felt still and heavy.

Kaia sat cross-legged next to Bryce, dipping the blood-stained bandage in a shallow pot of water and wringing it out. Bryce winced as she pressed the cloth back against his swollen leg, but he didn't complain.

"You ever gonna stop looking like you're about to cry?" Bryce teased weakly, his voice strained but playful.

Kaia glanced at him, half a smile tugging at her lips. "You've got an arrow wound, Bryce. Excuse me for looking concerned."

Bryce smirked, sweat streaking his forehead. "Nah, not about me. You've been staring into the trees like Fisher's about to come back wearing a crown and save the day."

Kaia rolled her eyes, but there was no bite in it. "You don't know what you're talking about."

"Oh, I do," Bryce said, coughing out a laugh. "Girl, I might be half delirious, but I'm not blind."

Dr. Varn, quietly repacking their few medical supplies, looked over with interest but didn't say a word.

Kaia hesitated, her hands pausing over the bandage. "It's not like that," she said softly, but her voice lacked conviction.

Bryce raised an eyebrow. "Not like what?"

Kaia sighed, looking down at the bloodied strip of fabric in her hands. "I don't even know when it happened. I just... trust him. More than anyone."

She swallowed, forcing the words out before she could stop herself. "When he's here, it feels like maybe we'll actually get through this."

Bryce gave her a tired grin, eyes drooping slightly. "Knew it."

Kaia's face flushed faintly, but she didn't backpedal.

"Don't tell him." She murmured, half to Bryce, half to Varn, whose gaze lingered on her with unreadable weight.

Bryce chuckled, coughing once as the sound faded. "Wouldn't dream of it."

Varn finally spoke, her tone calm but slightly amused. "Secrets don't stay buried forever, Kaia. Not here."

Kaia didn't answer. She just tied off the bandage again and stared at her hands, the admission lingering in the air like smoke.

With the sky bruising into twilight, Matthew finally pushed back through the brush. Dirt streaked his arms, sweat plastered his shirt to his back, and his grip on the sharpened spear was tight.

Kaia was the first to see him. She stood quickly, the relief plain in her eyes. "You're back."

Matthew nodded, setting the spear aside and holding up what he'd found—the crude **talisman,** still swaying slightly from his hand. "They're out there," he said quietly. "The tribe. I saw arrows, footprints... signs everywhere."

Dr. Varn leaned forward, her voice sharp but steady. "How close?"

"Close," Matthew replied. He crouched near Bryce, who lay against the rock, eyes half-lidded and flushed with fever. "We need to move soon. If they find us sitting here..." He didn't finish.

Kaia took the talisman from his hand, holding it delicately like it might burn her. "What does it mean?"

Matthew stared at the crude figure. "I don't know. But it wasn't made to welcome us."

Bryce groaned softly, trying to grin despite his pallor. "You didn't see anyone?" No shadowy jungle kings?"

Matthew nearly smiled at the joke but couldn't quite manage it. "No. Just proof they're close.

The small overhang suddenly felt smaller. The jungle around them hummed with the sounds of insects and distant birds, but under it all was something heavier— the drums, faint but present, beating like the pulse of the island.

Matthew sat down beside the fire pit they hadn't dared light, looking at the talisman again. "They know we're here," he said.

No one disagreed.

* * *

Meanwhile the jungle felt different for Shayne and Cartwright—quieter, tighter, like the trees themselves were listening.

Cartwright led, machete low, his movements careful and deliberate. Shayne followed close behind, muttering softly to himself like the words might keep the darkness at bay.

"We should've found water by now," Shayne whispered, his voice almost too loud in the stillness.

Cartwright didn't answer. He stopped so abruptly Shayne nearly bumped into him.

"What—?"

Then Shayne saw it.

Jammed into a tree ahead of them was a spear.

Its shaft rough, stripped of bark, and the tip was crudely sharpened stone bound in sinew. Red paint streaked down its length, smeared into symbols Shayne couldn't read.

The sight made his stomach twist.

Cartwright crouched, his fingers brushing the shaft but not polling it free. He studied the marks, his jaw tight, eyes scanning the surrounding jungle.

"They're not hunting animals," he muttered, voice low, certain.

Shayne swallowed, his throat suddenly dry. "Then who are they hunting?"

Cartwright's eyes flicked to the tree line, scanning the shadows.

"They're hunting us," he said.

At that exact moment, the jungle answered—not with words, but with the sharp crack of a branch snapping somewhere beyond the trees.

The drums thudded again, louder now. Closer.

# Chapter 19 The Splintered Paths

The jungle woke them with sound instead of light—insects clicking, birds screaming somewhere in the canopy, a distant howl that didn't belong to any animal Matthew Fisher had ever studied. He sat up slowly, his neck stiff from sleeping on damp ground, and brushed a layer of leaves from his shirt.

The small fire they'd finally decided to make out of pure survival had dwindled to embers. Kaia crouched next to it, stirring the ashes with a stick, her curly auburn hair tangled and heavy with humidity. Dr. Varn sat nearby, her knees pulled close to her chest, watching the tree line like she expected something to step out of it.

But it was Bryce who made Matthew's stomach tighten.

He was lying on his side, pale and slick with sweat, clutching his leg just below the makeshift bandage they'd tied days ago. The wound looked worse this morning—angry red streaks crawling outward from the wound.

"Morning, champ," Bryce rasped, voice dry as paper. He attempted a smile, but it twisted into a grimace. "How's the five-star resort treating you?"

Matthew crouched beside him, heart sinking at the heat radiating off Bryce's skin. "We need to clean this again," he said, trying to sound steady, like he knew what to do.

Kaia moved closer, her green sash from graduation now filthy and tied around her waist like a utility belt. "He's burning up," she whispered, eyes searching Matthew's face for reassurance she wasn't going to find.

Bryce chuckled weakly, though it came out more like a cough. "Feels like I'm on fire from the inside. Pretty sure I'm just... evolving into a superhero. Fever powers, it's a thing, right?"

The joke hung in the air, brittle.

Dr. Varn shifted, tucking a stray strand of hair behind her glasses. "Matthew, if we don't get him to cleaner water—or find herbs, medicine, anything—this infection is going to spread."

Matthew stood and glanced at the dense wall of green beyond their little clearing. He felt the weight of it—not just the jungle, but the responsibility, the expectation that he would fix this. His vision of Clark from the night before whispered at the back of his mind: *Every leader has doubts—but doubt is what keeps you from becoming a tyrant.*

He swallowed. "I'll find something," he said, almost to himself.

Kaia frowned, standing as well. "You're not going out there alone—"

"I'll move faster on my own," Matthew said firmly, grabbing his bag. "If there's fresh water, edible plants, anything... I'll find it. Stay here. Take care of him."

Bryce raised a shaky hand, flashing him a faint thumbs-up. "Go on, Fisher. Save the day. I'll keep my seat warm."

Kaia squeezed Matthew's arm before he left, her voice softer now. "Just come back, okay? Don't make us wait for you."

Matthew nodded, gave one last look at Bryce's painted but hopeful face, and pushed into the jungle—the vines swallowing him whole.

Matthew pushed through the jungle alone, the damp air heavy in his lungs. Every step made the world feel larger—vines draped from the canopy like hanging nooses, and the ground seemed to swallow his boots with every step.

He told himself not to think of Bryce's fevered face, but it kept flashing in his mind with every step.

He didn't go far at first, only a few hundred yards from camp, but when he found nothing—no water, no fruit—he pressed further.

The jungle seemed endless.

He hacked through a wall of low branches with a stick, muttering to himself as sweat dripped from his forehead. "Water. Just water. That's all I need."

A rustle made him freeze.

Matthew crouched, heart pounding. The jungle here was too quiet.

Something darted between trees—fast, low to the ground. His mind whispered raptor, but the shadow was too human-shaped. He stayed still until the movement faded, then kept walking.

After nearly an hour of climbing, he reached a rise in the terrain—a rocky slope cutting up through the jungle. He grabbed roots and branches, hauling himself up until he broke through a line of ferns at the top... and froze.

In the distance, through the shifting green, he saw smoke.

At first it was just a thin gray thread rising between the trees. Then his eyes adjusted, and he saw **structures**—low huts built from wood and leaves, their walls ringed by torches. Figures moved among them, small and distant, but undeniably **human.**

Matthew's breath caught.

A **village**.

He crouched low, afraid to be seen, and watched. He could hear faint sounds carried on the wind—a drumbeat, soft voices, the hum of a world that had existed long before they'd crashed here.

Part of him felt a surge of hope—civilization— but the other part remembered the attack from days ago. Could this be the same people?

He stayed only a minute longer before backing away, careful not to snap a branch or break the spell.

On the way back down, he found a muddy stream trickling between rocks. He cupped water into his hands and tasted it—clean. A gift.

Nearby, he spotted a patch of wild herbs he recognized from his environmental studies—known for cleaning wounds and soothing fevers.

Matthew filled his pack, his chest tightening. This could save Bryce.

As he headed back toward camp, one thought pulsed in his head, steady and determined:

*Hang on, Bryce. Just hang on.*

* * *

The jungle was thicker here, the air still and hot, every step like wading through soup. Shayne Wood wiped his brow with the back of his hand and squinted up at the canopy.

"You ever notice," he muttered, "how every tree here looks exactly like the one you just passed?"

Cartwright grunted, shifting the pack on his shoulder. "That's called being lost, Wood."

Shayne smirked, though his tone was lighter than his face felt. "I call it déjà vu. Over and over and over..."

Cartwright didn't reply. He was scanning the trees—that soldier's instinct always on edge.

That's when they heard it.

A low growl, deep and wet, coming from the brush ahead.

Cartwright froze, one arm out, signaling Shayne to stop. "Don't move."

Shayne tilted his head, listening. "That's not a dog," he whispered.

The leaves in front of them exploded.

The creature that lunged out looked like something torn from a nightmare—the powerful frame of a saber-toothed tiger, its massive fangs dripping, but its arms and back twisted with raptor-like claws and a whipcord tail. It moved like a cat, but faster, meaner, wrong.

"MOVE!" Cartwright barked, shoving Shayne aside as the creature lunged.

Cartwright went down hard, the beast on top of him, claws raking across his arm. He shoved a forearm against its throat, trying to keep the teeth from snapping down.

Shayne grabbed the thickest branch he could find and swung it with a wild yell, smacking the creature across the face. It barely flinched—just snarled and whipped its head toward him, eyes glowing an unnatural yellow.

"Not good, not good, not good—" Shayne muttered as he stumbled backward.

And then—

A shadow moved.

A blur of motion cut through the clearing.

A spear slammed through the creature's side with a sound like splitting wood.

When the hybrid creature screeched, Shayne caught a glimpse of its twisted anatomy—saber teeth and raptor claws fused in something that never should have existed. It was wrong, and the wrongness made his stomach lurch.

A mysterious female in tribal cloth.

This tribal female yanked the spear free and drove it again, hard and deliberate, into the creature's neck. One more wrenching twist—and the beast collapsed, twitching once before going still.

Shayne stood frozen, breathless, branch still raised like it mattered.

Cartwright shoved the creature off and sat up, arm bleeding, staring at the woman who had just appeared from nowhere.

She stood over the kill, breathing evenly, her long black hair streaked with beads and sweat, her spear dripping with the creature's blood.

She looked at Shayne and Cartwright, her dark eyes sharp but not unkind.

"I not hurt you," she said, her voice low but certain. "I am here to help."

Shayne blinked, finally lowering his stick. "Uh... hi."

She glanced between the two men, then stepped back from the corpse and planted the butt of her spear into the dirt. She touched her chest lightly.

"Avara," she said simply, voice stronger this time.

* * *

The jungle felt quieter with just the three of them, like it was holding its breath.

Megan Truss walked a few paces ahead of Adam Nolan, now proud to be barefoot, her feet caked in mud...

"Okay," she said, stepping gingerly over a slick root, "I give up. I'm a barefoot goddess now. Someone get me a crown of vines and call it a lifestyle."

Adam smirked despite himself. "You'll regret that when you step on something sharp."

"Already did," she said, lifting one foot briefly to show a streak of dirt on her heel. "But it's fine. I'm going for that rugged, survivor-chic vibe."

She grinned at him—wide, easy, the kind of grin that made her feel alive in a way none of the others quite managed.

Adam looked away, trying to hide the warmth creeping up his face. "You're ridiculous," he muttered.

She laughed, brushing her blonde hair back from her face. "And you love it."

Behind them, Grent moved silently, his boots making barely a sound on the jungle floor. He carried himself like a shadow—hands loose, eyes always moving. But his gaze kept drifting to Megan, and every time it did, Adam's chest tightened.

Megan felt it too, though she hid it behind a grin—his stare was heavy, like he was weighing her rather than watching her. Adam noticed the way her shoulders stiffened each time.

They reached a fallen tree blocking their path. Megan hesitated, unsure where to step.

"Here," Adam said, offering his hand.

She took it, light fingers brushing his as she hopped over the trunk. "Look at you," she teased, "the only gentleman left on this trip."

Adam felt his ears go hot. "Someone's gotta make sure you don't trip and crack your head open."

From behind them, Grent's voice slid in—smooth, low, almost amused. "Sweet," he said, almost under his breath. "Real sweet."

Megan glanced back, unsure if it was a compliment or a warning.

A few minutes later, Megan shifted her pack on her shoulder, the strap slipping. Grent moved closer, his tone light but his eyes sharp.

"Here," he said, "let me help."

Before she could respond, his hand brushed her side, close enough to make her flinch.

Adam stepped in instantly, pulling the strap from Grent's grip. "I got it," Adam said, voice flat.

Grent's eyes met his—cold, unreadable—and then the faintest smirk tugged at his mouth.

"Careful, kid," Grent said softly. "Don't start something you can't finish."

The words slid between them like a blade, and Adam realized for the first time that whatever Frent wanted, it had nothing to do with survival.

Adam didn't look away, jaw tight, hand gripping the strap like he might crush it. Megan looked between them, her earlier smile fading, but she didn't say anything.

The three of them kept moving, the silence now louder than any jungle noise.

* * *

By the time Matthew broke through the last wall of vines, his pack was heavier than he remembered.

Inside it: a skin full of water, a handful or herbs he was sure could treat infection, and the hope that he'd done enough.

The clearing was quiet when he stepped into it.

Too quiet.

Kaia was sitting beside Bryce, her hands folded in her lap, eyes red. Dr. Varn knelt a few feet away, staring at the fire that had burned down to coals.

Matthew felt the weight in his stomach before anyone said a word.

"Kaia?"

She didn't look up at first. When she did, her face told him everything.

Bryce lay on his back, still as stone. His chest didn't rise. The fever sweat had dried on his skin, leaving a pale, waxy sheen.

Matthew's throat close. He dropped the pack and fell to his knees beside his friend.

"No," he whispered. He touched Bryce's should, as if the warmth of his own hand might be enough to spark something back to life. "No, no, no..."

Kaia's voice cracked. "It happened fast. He just... stopped breathing."

The herbs Matthew had carried all this way slipped from his hand into the dirt. For a moment he wanted to scream, but the jungle seemed to smother even that—replacing it with a silence that felt like judgment.

Dr. Varn broke the silence. "There wasn't anything we could do."

Matthew pressed a hand to Bryce's chest—nothing. No heartbeat, no warmth, no chance.

He shut Bryce's eyes gently, his own vision blurring.

For the first time since the crash, he felt like he'd failed.

Kaia rested her hand on his should, her touch soft and trembling. "He wasn't alone. That's something."

Matthew swallowed hard, but the words didn't make it past his throat.

He stayed there, kneeling by Bryce, staring at the herbs he'd carried back too late—and wondering how many more times he would have to feel this before the island was done with him.

* * *

*Matthew had brought water, herbs, hope—but none of it mattered. And for the first time, he wondered how many more he would lose before this island was done testing him.*

# Chapter 20  The Breaking Point

Matthew Fisher was running.

At least, that's how it felt.

The jungle was gone—replaced by the neat, familiar sprawl of Viremoor University's campus. The sun was warm, the grass sharp and green, and he could hear laughter drifting from the quad like it was graduation day all over again.

Except it wasn't.

The students walking past weren't people he recognized. They didn't have faces—not really. They were blurs, silhouettes, voices that didn't belong to anyone he knew.

And there, on a bench beneath the shade of a sycamore tree, sat Professor Clark.

The same calm smile, the same crisp button-down shirt, sleeves rolled just above the elbows. His silvering hair caught the sunlight, his posture easy, inviting.

"Matthew," Clark said, patting the bench beside him. "Come. Sit."

Matthew felt his legs move without question, like a kid again. He sat down, the wood cool under his palms.

Clark studied him for a moment, his eyes kind but sharp, like he could see every thought behind Matthew's.

"You've been through a lot," Clark said softly. "More than most could bear."

Matthew swallowed, his voice heavy. "Bryce..."

Clark nodded, the smile never fading. "Loss is... painful. It should be. But it can also be... enlightening."

Matthew frowned. "Enlightening?"

Clark leaned in just slightly, his tone low, coaxing. "Matthew, every great leader is shaped by loss. Pain chisels away the boy and leaves the man behind. The deaths you carry... they'll make you stronger, if you let them."

Matthew's chest tightened. "Stronger? He was my friend."

"I know," Clark said, placing a hand on his shoulder. The warmth was almost too real. "And he mattered. But sometimes, to become who you're meant to be... you must lose the ones who mattered most."

Matthew stared at him. "That doesn't make it right."

Clark's smile softened, but didn't falter. "Right? Wrong? Those are words for people who don't have to lead. You do. And you can't let this loss break you. Use it. Grow from it."

The campus around them began to fade—the green of the grass dimming, the blue of the sky turning to a washed-out gray.

Clark's hand squeezed his shoulder one last time.

"You're closer than you think, Matthew," he said, voice almost a whisper now. "Don't stop walking forward."

The world peeled away like smoke.

Matthew woke with a start, the sound of the jungle crashing back in. The warmth of Clark's hand still lingered on his shoulder, but it made him shiver instead of comforting him.

He stared at the canopy above, his breath slow and uneven, and wondered for the first time:

**Was Clark really helping him—or shaping him?**

—

He sat up slowly, looking over his shoulder at the others.

Bryce's body lay wrapped in vines and leaves, a makeshift shroud.

Kaia and Dr. Varn were already at work, their hands dirty, digging at the earth with sharp stones and hollowed sticks. The soil here was dark and soft, but it still fought them for every inch.

Matthew moved without a word, grabbing a broken plank of wood from the wreckage of a crate and joining them.

The digging was quiet, except for the scrape of wood against soil and the occasional grunt of effort.

When the hole was deep enough, they lifted Bryce in together. Kaia's hands shook as she tied the last knot in the shroud.

For a moment, none of them spoke.

Kaia crouched, brushing dirt from her palms. She reached into her pocket and pulled out a small seashell she'd found on the beach the first night. She placed it gently on Bryce's chest.

"He said it was good luck," she whispered. "I think... he'd want it with him."

Dr. Varn stood with her hands folded, her glasses smudged, a strand of hair plastered to her cheek. "He had humor until the end," she said softly. "That's more than most manage."

Matthew didn't say anything at first. He looked down at the bundle of vines and leaves, at the body beneath, and felt his throat tighten.

"He saved us," Matthew finally said. His voice wasn't steady. "Out there—that first night— he didn't even hesitate. He jumped in. And I..."

He stopped, swallowing hard.

Kaia touched his arm lightly. "We all tried. You tried."

Matthew's hands curled into fists. "Not hard enough."

He grabbed a handful of earth and dropped it into the hole. The sound was soft, final. Kaia and Varn followed, each taking turns, until the body was gone beneath the soil.

They packed the dirt tight, building a small mound, and then stood there, silent.

The jungle seemed to pause with them, the usual chorus of birds and insects dulling as if the world itself was observing.

Matthew stared at the mound and whispered, almost to himself:

"I won't let this be for nothing."

* * *

The jungle around Adam Nolan felt like a closed fist—humid, heavy, and pressing in from all sides.

Megan didn't seem to mind.

She padded barefoot over roots and leaves, humming some tune Adam didn't recognize, something light and sweet that didn't belong in a place like this.

"This humidity," she said with a laugh, pulling her blonde hair into a messy knot, "is either going to kill me or make me look like some kind of jungle influencer."

Adam glanced at her, the corner of his mouth twitching despite himself. "Pretty sure you'd break the internet."

Megan grinned and twirled once in the mud, nearly slipping. "Look at you—supportive *and* sarcastic. A man of many talents."

Behind them, Grent walked silently, boots crunching over sticks. He didn't laugh, didn't even smirk this time—but his eyes lingered.

They reached a low ravine with a tangle of vines acting like a crude bridge. Megan hesitated, then tested it with one foot.

"Not exactly OSHA-certified," she joked.

Adam stepped closer. "Here, hold on to me."

She gripped his hand, her balance wobbling as she crossed. Her fingers tightened around his, and she shot him a quick smile. "Thanks, Nolan. You might actually be the only gentleman left, not just from the trip, but in the world."

From behind them came Grent's voice—smooth and flat, but with that faint edge.

"Gentleman," he repeated, almost like it was a joke only he understood.

Megan looked back at him, unsure if he was teasing or testing.

On the other side of the vines, her pack slipped on her shoulder. Grent moved forward, silent as a shadow.

"Here," he said, reaching for the strap. "Let me—"

His hand brushed her side.

Megan froze, a flicker of discomfort flashing across her face.

Adam was there instantly, yanking the pack out of Grent's grip. "I got it," he said, voice flat, eyes locked on Grent.

Grent didn't resist. He just looked at Adam, cold and unreadable, and then that faint smirk crept back—the kind that didn't reach his eyes.

Careful, kid," Grent said softly, his voice low enough that Megan might not even hear.
"Remember, don't start something you aren't prepared to finish."

Adam's jaw tightened. He didn't say anything, but you could see Grent is getting to him. The grip on Megan's pack strap turned his knuckles white.

The three of them walked on, but the mood had shifted.

Megan tried to hum again, but her voice was thinner now, and Adam walked closer to her— close enough that Grent noticed.

Grent just smiled that cold smile and lit another cigarette, smoke trailing behind them like a shadow that wouldn't go away.

* * *

The jungle opened into a narrow clearing where Avara walked ahead of them, her spear balanced lightly across her shoulders.

Shayne Wood couldn't stop staring.

It wasn't just that she'd saved him and Cartwright the day before—it was the way she moved. Graceful, but alert. Every step deliberate, every glance scanning the trees as if she knew exactly what to listen for.

Cartwright trailed a few paces behind, his wounded arm freshly wrapped, his military eyes studying her like she was another tactical puzzle.

Shayne finally broke the silence. "So... about that thing yesterday. The... uh, the saber tooth-raptor nightmare you killed."

Avara glanced back at him, dark eyes sharp.

"That wasn't..." Shayne hesitated, then found the word. "...natural, was it?"

She stopped walking for a moment, then spoke, her voice calm but edged with disgust.

"It was not born," she said, her English broken but clear. She tapped the spear against the ground. "It was made."

Shayne blinked, taking that in. "Made? Like... people made it?"

Avara nodded once.

"By who?" Cartwright asked, his voice flat, wary.

Avara's gaze flicked between them, then up to the canopy like the answer lived in the leaves. "Outsiders."

The word carried weight, like it was heavy in her mouth.

She started walking again, her braid swaying behind her.

"More like that?" Shayne asked carefully, stepping around a root.

"Many," Avara said simply. "Some worse."

Cartwright cursed under his breath. Shayne glanced at him, then back to her.

Avara slowed, pointing ahead with the tip of her spear. "We go to my people. You follow. You live."

Shayne studied her for a long moment, then gave a little smile—not a flirty one, but an honest one. "I think I'm okay with that."

For the first time since they'd met her, Avara's lips twitched into the hint of a smile—brief, but there.

Then she turned and kept moving, and Shayne followed, his mind racing with a second thought he didn't voice.

* * *

The day dragged on like wet rope—heavy and slow.

Fisher's group stayed quiet after Bryce's burial. The jungle seemed to honor the silence, the wind low, the birds muted.

Matthew walked a few steps ahead, eyes distant, his pack slung low on his shoulders.

Behind him, Kaia leaned closer to Dr. Varn, her voice barely above a breath.

"Tomorrow," Kaia whispered, her eyes on Matthew's back. "I'm going to tell him."

Varn glanced at her. "Tell him what?"

Kaia hesitated, then smiled softly, almost shy. "That I like him. That I... really like him."

Her voice dropped even lower. "Life's too short not to."

Varn gave the faintest nod, her usual sternness softening for a moment.

Ahead of them, Matthew didn't hear a word—his mind still locked on Bryce, and what he could have done differently.

———

Shayne and Cartwright moved steadily under Avara's lead.

She didn't talk much, but her presence made Shayne feel like, for the first time in days, they weren't wandering blindly.

Shayne fell in step with her, offering occasional jokes—some she ignored, others earned the faintest curve of her lips. Cartwright stayed silent, but there was respect in his eyes when he looked at her.

They were following someone who knew the island better than anyone.

———

Adam's group was different.

Megan's voice was lighter than the air around them, the light singing, laughing about how her hair was a "lost cause."

Adam stayed close to her, protective without saying the word.

And Grent—Grent walked in the back, smoking, watching, the ash of his cigarette glowing every few steps like a warning light.

He didn't say much, but when his eyes met Adam's, it felt like a hand on the back of his neck—a quiet, constant threat.

———

By nightfall, all three groups had stopped moving.

Three fires in three different parts of the island burned low.

**Matthew stared at his fire**. The herbs he'd brought back sat beside him, useless now.

**Shayne stared at Avara's fire**. The woman who had saved him from a monster now sat silent, watching the flames, a spear across her lap.

**Adam stared at Grent's fire**. Megan hummed softly next to him, her voice sweet and small, while Grent sat on the other side of the flames, smoke curling in front of his eyes like it belonged there.

The island seemed to breathe around them, quiet but alive, as if the jungle itself was waiting.

—

*The island felt quieter than it should have—like every creature was waiting for the moment the silence would break.*

# Chapter 21  Venom

The night had left the jungle damp and heavy, the air thick with the smell of wet earth and smoke from the embers of their fire. Morning light filtered through the canopy in pale streaks, not bright enough to be comforting, only enough to remind them they had survived another night.

Matthew sat a few feet from what remained of the grave they had dug, the earth still fresh and dark where they had dug, the earth still fresh and dark where they had laid Bryce to rest. His elbows rested on his knees, hands clasped tight enough that his knuckles had gone white.

Kaia stirred beside him, brushing a few strands of auburn hair out of her face. Her voice was soft, almost hesitant. "Hey," she murmured, easing herself upright. "You didn't sleep, did you?"

Matthew shook his head; eyes still fixed on the mound of dirt. "Someone should've. Just... couldn't."

Kaia shifted closer, knees brushing his.
"You've been holding this together, you know that?"

He glanced at her, eyes tired. "Doesn't feel like it."

"Well, you are." She managed a small smile, but there was sadness behind it. "If it wasn't for you, half of us would've fallen apart already."

Matthew swallowed hard, the weight of her wors settling on him like another stone on his shoulders. "Some leader I've been. As far as we know, there are only three of us left. We don't know what happened to the others."

A few feet away, Dr. Emilia Varn knelt by the firepit, quietly organizing the last of their supplies. Her eyes flicked between Matthew and Kaia, observing without intruding, her expression unreadable.

When she spoke, it was calm, almost clinical. "You need to eat something, Matthew. Both of you."

He gave a half-shrug, not looking away from Bryce's grave. "Not hungry."

Varn didn't push. She only studied him a moment longer, as if measuring the toll this leadership was taking—not just his body, bit his mind.

Kaia's hand brushed his, just for a second. A fleeting touch, but enough. "Bryce wouldn't want you staring at that grave all morning," she whispered. "He'd want you to keep us moving."

Matthew's jaw tightened. She was right. He knew she was right. But for just one more breath, he stayed still, eyes on the grave, before finally standing.

The jungle felt bigger today. And heavier.

* * *

The jungle felt different for Adam Nolan's group—tighter somehow, as if the trees leaned in just a little closer with every step. The canopy above swallowed most of the morning light, casting everything in a green gloom.

Megan. A pro at walking barefoot in a jungle, tossed aside the beaten shoes she'd been given and declared herself "done with them forever." Despite it all, she still managed a smile, nudging Adam with her elbow.

"You realize you basically saved my life back on the ship, right?" she said, her voice light, teasing. "Pulled me out of the way of that swinging pole like some action movie hero."

Adam smirked, glancing at her from the corner of his eye. "Guess all those years of playing pickup basketball paid off. Quick reflexes."

She laughed, genuine and bright, cutting through the oppressive silence of the jungle. For a moment, it felt almost normal—two friends sharing banter on a hike.

Behind them, Silas Grent was silent. Always silent. He trailed just far enough back to make Adam uneasy, hands in his pockets, eyes scanning the trees.

Every so often, Adam would catch him watching Megan. Not just looking—watching. Measuring.

It made Adam's skin crawl.

Megan didn't seem to notice, or maybe she was just good at ignoring things she didn't want to see. She twirled the necklace around her neck absently, the one she was *always* wearing, and joked, "if we get rescued, I'm telling everyone you carried me on your back the whole way."

"Carried you?" Adam raised an eyebrow. "You barely weigh anything. I could carry you and a backpack of coconuts."

That earned another laugh from her, and for a heartbeat, Adam forgot about Grent behind them.

But then the man spoke.

"You two sure have a lot of energy," Grent said, his voice calm, almost lazy. "You should pace yourselves. This island..." He took a slow drag from the cigarette he'd just lit, the smoke curling upward through the trees. "...this island has a way of draining people. Sometimes it's not the island that kills you."

Adam turned slightly. "What's that supposed to mean?"

Grent met his eyes, unflinching, the faintest smile tugging at his scarred cheek.

"Sometimes," he said, flicking the cigarette ash onto the damp earth, "it's each other."

The words hung there, heavy and sharp. Megan's smile faltered, and Adam's hand tightened on the strap of his bag.

For the next mile, no one spoke.

* * *

Meanwhile in a quieter part of the jungle.

Shayne Wood noticed it first, pausing mid-step, his long hair sticking to his face with sweat. "Hear that?" he asked, tilting his head.

Captain Cartwright scanned the trees, his ex-military instincts kicking in. "Hear what?"

"That's the thing." Shayne's brow furrowed. "No birds. No bugs. Nothing. Like the jungle's... holding its breath."

Avara walked ahead of them, bare feet silent against the damp ground, spear balanced casually in her hand. Her dark eyes flicked over her shoulder.

"It is because we are close," she said simply.

"Close to what?" Cartwright pressed, adjusting the strap on his pack.

She didn't answer right away. Instead, she crouched low, touching the ground where faint impressions marked the soil—almost like footprints, but not quite. Shayne crouched next to her, brushing the dirt with his fingertips.

"These are... trails," Shayne said, his voice low. "Human ones. Old."

Avara nodded once. "My people walk here."

Shayne exchanged a glance with Cartwright. "So... we're near your village?"

Avara straightened, her face unreadable. "Near enough."

They pushed forward another few paces until the first signs appeared: a feather tied to a branch, strips of woven grass fluttering faintly in the breeze, a scattering of small stones arranged deliberately in a spiral.

"Definitely signs of civilization," Cartwright muttered.

Avara stopped suddenly and turned to face them, her expression serious now, the warmth in her features replaced with something harder.

"The creature you fought," she said, her accent rolling over the words carefully. "The one with the long teeth."

"The saber-tooth thing?" Shayne asked.

Avara's eyes lingered on him. "It was not born. It was made."

Cartwright's jaw tightened. "Made by who?"

She hesitated—just long enough to make it clear she was choosing her words carefully. "The one we call Helix," she said finally. "And others before you."

The name landed like a stone dropped into still water.

Shayne felt the hairs on his neck rise. "Helix? You mean he—"

But Avara wasn't done. She stepped closer, her gaze sharp, almost warning. "Some of my people... will not want you there."

"Not want us there?" Cartwright asked, frowning. "You mean... hostile?"

She held his stare. "They will see you, and they will see him. And they will remember what was taken."

Shayne opened his mouth, but no words came. The jungle seemed even quieter now, as if it were listening.

Avara turned away and started forward again, but her last words hung between them, heavy and certain.

"They will remember."

* * *

Back at Matthew's group where the jungle seems softer, almost quiet enough to breathe in without choking on fear. Matthew led the way, machete in hand, swatting at stubborn vines that clung to their path.

Behind him, Kaia walked close, their shoulders brushing every now and then—little collisions neither of them mentioned.

For the first time all day, there wasn't a crisis at their heels. The silence between them felt fragile, like if either spoke too loudly it would break.

Kaia finally broke it, her voice tentative. "Matthew..."

He turned slightly, curious. "Yeah?"

She hesitated, brushing her curls behind one ear. "There's... there's something I've been meaning to tell you."

Matthew slowed, giving her his full attention. The weight of her words—and the way she wouldn't meet his eyes—made his pulse quicken.

Kaia's fingers fiddled with the strap of her bag. "After everything we've been through... after Bryce, after the crash... I just—"

A sharp hiss split the air.

Kaia froze.

From the brush, a streak of movement—a snake lunging, fangs flashing in the dim light.

Matthew barely had time to shout her name before it struck.

Kaia screamed as the snake's fangs sank deep into her leg just above the ankle. She stumbled, the confession lost on her lips, pain replacing the words.

Matthew swung the machete down hard, severing the snake's head in one desperate motion.

The jungle went still again—except for Kaia's labored breaths.

She collapsed against him, clutching her leg as the skin around the bite turned a sickly purple.

"Kaia!" Matthew's voice cracked. He dropped to his knees, trying to press against the wound, anything to slow what was already coursing through her veins.

Dr. Varn was suddenly there, yanking a cloth from her pack, tying it above the bite to slow the spread. She leaned in and started to suck venom, spitting it out, doing it again—but after a moment she stopped, her face grim.

"It's not enough," she said, breathless. "This won't stop it."

Matthew's eyes darted between her and Kaia, panic creeping into his voice. "Then what do we do?!"

Varn looked him dead in the eye.

"We need medicine. The kind they might have," she said, jerking her head toward the deep jungle. "The tribe."

Kaia's breathing was already shallow, her skin clammy as she whispered his name, "Matthew..."

He squeezed her hand, voice steady but trembling at the edges. "I'm here. I'm not letting you go."

Kaia's breaths came in uneven gasps; her skin already slick with sweat despite the cooling jungle air. The purplish color creeping up her leg made Matthew's stomach twist.

He held her hand like it was the only thing tethering her here. "Stay with me, Kaia. You hear me?"

Her eyelids fluttered. She tried to smile, but it was weak—fleeting.

Dr. Varn crouched beside them, hands stained with dirt and venom. Her voice was calm, but there was an edge of urgency. "If we don't get her proper treatment soon, she won't last the day."

Matthew's head snapped toward her. "What do we need? Tell me."

Varn met his gaze squarely. "Anti-venom. Herbal remedies. Something strong enough to slow the poison. And there's only one place we might find that here."

Matthew already knew what she was going to say, but he asked anyway. "Where?"

"The tribe," she said. "If anyone has medicine, it's them."

The words felt heavy, heavier than the pack on his back. The tribe—the same people they'd seen traces of, the ones who might see them as enemies.

Matthew looked down at Kaia. She was pale now, trembling faintly, her grip on his hand slackening.

There wasn't a choice.

He adjusted his hold on her, sliding an arm under her shoulders, then under her knees, lifting her carefully. She was lighter than he expected—or maybe he was just running on adrenaline.

"We're going," he said, voice low but firm. "Right now."

Varn nodded, grabbing what supplies they could carry.

Matthew glanced toward the jungle ahead, toward the unknown.

*Toward them.*

Somewhere in the distance, the faint sound of drums carried again—steady, patient, as if the tribe already knew they were coming.

He didn't care anymore if the tribe wanted them there or not. They would save Kaia.

Or he'd die trying.

* * *

*For the first time since the crash, the survivors weren't just walking toward the tribe—they were racing against death itself to reach them.*"

# Chapter 22  Into the Vokari

Matthew's arms burned.

Every step felt heavier than the last, his boots sinking into the soft jungle floor, mud pulling at his feet like hands trying to drag him down. Kaia's weight wasn't much—she'd teased him about being able to "carry her like nothing' on the yacht—but now every ounce of her felt like it was pressing against his bones.

He wasn't letting go. He promised her.

Kaia's head rested against his chest; her hair plastered to her damp forehead. Her lips moved faintly, whispering something too soft to hear. Matthew adjusted his grip, keeping her close, as if holding her tighter could keep her here.

"Keep moving," Dr. Varn urged, walking just ahead, her voice firm but strained. Sweat streaked the sides of her face as she brushed a branch out of the way. "Matthew, every minute matters."

"I know," he said, his voice tight.

Kaia stirred, her hand twitching against his shirt. Her eyes blinked half-open, unfocused. "M-Matthew?"

He looked down, heart pounding. "I'm here. You're okay. Just stay with me."

Her breathing hitched, and she managed a weak smile. "You're... warm."

Matthew's throat tightened. He didn't know if that was good or if the poison was making her delirious.

The jungle around them seemed to close in the deeper they went—the air thicker, the heat pressing against his back. The distant cry of something large echoed through the canopy, but Matthew didn't slow.

Varn glanced back at him, her eyes sharp. "You can't keep carrying her forever. We'll need the tribe soon."

The word hung in the air.

The tribe.

His jaw clenched. He didn't know if they would help, or if walking into their arms meant walking into danger, but none of it mattered—not with Kaia's breath getting shallower, her skin clammy under his hand.

He adjusted her again, whispering, almost like a prayer. "Just hold on. Please. I-I love you Kaia, I can't lose you."

A sudden memory stabbed through him—Kaia on the yacht, hair whipping in the wind as she laughed, teasing him for always worrying too much. That lightness felt like a lifetime ago. Now she was limp in his arms, and he hated how fragile she seemed.

The path narrowed as they pressed deeper into the jungle, until Matthew wondered if it was even a path at all or just an illusion his exhausted mind created.

Kaia shifted faintly in his arms, murmuring something he couldn't make out. Her skin felt hotter now—not the heat of the jungle, but fever heat.

Dr. Varn's voice cut through the thick air. "Look around," she said quietly.

Matthew did—and froze.

The jungle wasn't empty anymore.

Carved totems stood like silent sentinels among the trees: twisted faces etched into wood; feathers tied with animal sinew fluttering faintly in the stagnant air. Skulls— bird, monkey, something larger—hung from vines, swaying ever so slightly, their empty sockets staring.

"These weren't here before," Matthew said under his breath.

"They've been here the whole time," Varn replied, her tone unsettlingly calm. "We just weren't looking."

A faint smell drifted on the air—ash mixed with dried herbs, like incense burned days ago. Matthew's stomach tightened. This was no accident. This was warning.

Matthew felt it before he saw it—the sensation of eyes on him.

Then a flicker of movement above.

He stopped dead, shifting Kaia in his arms as his gaze swept the canopy.

For a heartbeat, there was nothing.

Then a shadow moved between the branches—a figure, gone as quickly as it appeared.

Matthew's pulse spiked.

"Did you see that?"

Varn didn't turn to look; she just kept moving, but her voice was lower now. "They're watching us."

Matthew turned slowly in place, his breath sharp. He thought he saw another flicker, this one to his left—

another shape, high and silent, gone the moment his eyes found it.

He tightened his grip on Kaia, his voice barely above a whisper. "What if they don't want to help?"

Varn didn't look back, didn't even break stride. "Then we'd better pray they don't want to kill us either."

Just then the jungle went quiet.

Not the usual hush of birds scattering or wind dying down—this was a silence that *arrived,* like a blanket thrown over the world.

Matthew stopped moving. Every instinct screamed at him that something was about to happen.

He could hear his own heartbeat pounding in his ears, louder than the forest, louder than Kaia's weak breaths.

And then it did.

Figures stepped out of the green.

They came fast not rushed—but calculated, practiced. Vokari warriors emerged from the trees, first three, then six, then a dozen, their bodies painted in streaks of dark clay and ochre. Some wore feathers woven into their hair; others had scars that spoke of past battles.

They didn't shout. They didn't need to.

The sound of spears lowering was enough.

Matthew shifted Kaia higher in his arms, his heart hammering. Her head lolled against his shoulder, unaware of the ring of warriors forming around them.

Dr. Varn froze, her hands slowly lifting in a gesture of peace. "We're not here to hurt you," she said calmly, her voice steady even as her eyes flicked between the weapons pointed at them.

One warrior stepped forward—taller than the rest, a wide scar cutting across his jaw. His stance was rigid, commanding. Koro.

He spoke a short phrase in the Vokari language, sharp and clipped.

Matthew didn't understand the words, but the meaning was clear: *Stop. Don't move.*

Varn nodded faintly at Matthew. "Do what he says."

Matthew slowly bent his knees and set Kaia down on a patch of moss, his hands raising instinctively—though his eyes never left her face.

Another warrior darted forward, seizing the machete from his belt.

The leader, Koro, barked another command. 'Shai'ten varu vokari!" The circle tightened.

Matthew felt his pulse surge. "She's hurt," he said, gesturing to Kaia, his voice breaking past his own fear. "Snake bite—she needs help!"

Koro's eyes flicked to the wound, then back to Matthew.

He said nothing.

The silence was almost worse than anger.

Varn spoke softly to no one in particular. "They're deciding if we're a threat."

Matthew swallowed hard, his gaze darting between the wall of spears and Kaia's shallow breaths.

And for the first time since the crash, he wasn't sure if carrying her this far had brought her closer to safety—or delivered her into even greater danger.

Matthew dropped to his knees beside Kaia, his hands shaking as he turned her slightly so the warriors could see the swelling bite mark on her leg.

"She's dying!" his voice cracked, raw with desperation. "Please—she was bitten by a snake. You must help her!"

The warriors didn't move.

Their painted faces were unreadable, eyes fixed on Matthew like they were studying an animal caught in a trap.

Dr. Varn stepped forward, careful not to make sudden movements. Her palms stayed open and visible. "She's poisoned," she said slowly, enunciating each word like she hoped they'd understand the tone if not the language. "She needs medicine."

Koro crouched down slightly, not close enough to touch Kaia, but close enough to see the dark discoloration creeping up her leg.

For a fleeting second, something flickered in his eyes—recognition, or memory—but then his face returned to stone.

He said something harsh in the Vokari tongue— short, sharp syllables.

Another warrior responded in the same language, his voice lower, uncertain.

Matthew didn't understand a word, but he understood the *look* in their eyes—it wasn't agreement. They were divided.

One warrior's face softened as he glanced at Kaia, murmuring something that almost sounded like concern.

But another spat on the ground and barked a word Matthew didn't need translated. The venom in the tone told him it wasn't good.

Matthew's throat burned. He leaned over Kaia, clutching her hand, then looked up at the leader.

"She hasn't done anything wrong," he said, voice trembling. "None of us have. Please—help her."

Kaia stirred faintly, whispering his name, "Matthew..." her voice was little more than a breath.

Matthew's chest tightened like someone was crushing it with their fist.

"Please," he said again, his voice cracking now, breaking past pride and fear. "She'll die if you don't."

The warriors exchanged more words, their tones clashing—some sharp, some hesitant.

Koro's face remained still, unreadable, but he finally raised his hand. The circle around them loosened slightly.

Another warrior stepped forward, crouching to examine Kaia's bite without touching her.

He looked up at Koro and spoke a single, decisive word.

The leader gave a curt nod.

The warriors moved with sudden precision.

Two of them stooped, lifting Kaia gently but firmly from the ground, one taking her shoulders, the other her legs. She stirred faintly at their touch, her head rolling to the side, auburn curl falling into her face.

Matthew lunged forward. "Careful—"

A spear pressed lightly against his chest.

Koro stood there, unmoving, eyes steady on him. It wasn't a threat—it was a warning.

Matthew froze, his breath sharp.

Another warrior yanked the pack from Fisher's shoulder, then gestured for Varn to hand over her pack as well. She did so without protest, her expression unreadable as the supplies were confiscated.

Weapons, tools—everything stripped away in a moment.

Matthew's hands clenched into fists, but he didn't fight it. Kaia's safety mattered more than anything else.

The warriors formed into a loose column; Kaia carried at the center.

"Where are they taking her?" Matthew asked, his voice hard.

Varn stepped close enough to murmur, "The village. They'll treat her there—if they choose to."

The jungle swallowed the group as they began to move.

Matthew walked behind the two who carried Kaia, his fists tight, every step heavier. He hated the feeling—not just of helplessness, but of surrender.

He caught a glimpse of Kaia's face as they carried her over a root—her lips parted, a faint breath escaping.

Matthew forced the words out, almost like a vow. "You're going to be okay. I promise."

The warriors didn't look back, didn't answer.

They just kept walking, deeper into the green, where the jungle was giving way to something older—carved totems growing taller, smoke rising faintly from somewhere ahead.

A low drumbeat rolled through the trees now, steady and distant, joined by faint chanting carried on the wind. Each step made it louder, until Matthew realized they weren't just walking into a village—they were walking into judgment.

And for the first time, Matthew wondered if saving Kaia might cost them everything else.

# Chapter 23
## Shadows of the Vokari

The morning had been quieter than it has been in a while, but it wasn't the silence of safety—it was the kind that made Shayne feel like they were being measured with every step.

He swatted a mosquito off his neck and glanced over at Avara, who moved like the vines and roots simply made way for her. Her spear was balanced across her shoulders, her posture steady, graceful, like she belonged here in a way Shayne never would.

"You always walk this fast?" Shayne asked, trying for lightness even as he struggled to keep up. "Or is this just because you're trying to make us look bad?"

Avara turned her head, a single braid falling across her cheek as she looked at him. "I walk as fast as I need to."

Shayne smirked. "So... that's a yes."

She didn't smile, not exactly—but the corner of her mouth lifted for a split second before she looked away.

Cartwright, behind them, muttered something about "kids and their flirting" under his breath, though Shayne pretended not to hear him.

They kept moving, ducking under a low branch. Shayne noticed Avara slowed slightly, letting him catch up so they were side by side instead of always ahead.

"You didn't have to save us," Shayne said, his voice quieter now. "That thing you killed—whatever the hell that saber-tooth lizard-cat was—you could've just... let it finish us off."

Avara's expression didn't change much, but her voice softened. "Some of my people would have."

"Why didn't you?" Shayne asked.

She hesitated, her eyes on the path ahead. "Because you fought back."

Shayne blinked. "Fought back?"

"You didn't run," she said simply. "Most outsiders do. You and the old one—" she glanced at Cartwright, "—you stood your ground."

Shayne grinned a little, even if his throat felt oddly tight. "So, what? That impressed you?"

Avara turned her head, her dark eyes locking on his. "Maybe."

Shayne's smirk faltered into something smaller, more genuine.

They walked in silence for a few paces before he spoke again, his tone lighter to hide the way his pulse had kicked up. "Well... glad I could make a good first impression, you know—being half-eaten and all."

This time, Avara *did* smile, just slightly, shaking her head at him.

Behind them, Cartwright sighed like a man who'd been through too many campaigns to be amused, but he didn't say anything.

Ahead, the jungle began to change—the trees thinned just enough for Shayne to spot a carved totem, its surface etched with symbols he didn't recognize.

Avara glanced back over her shoulder. "Stay close," she warned. "From here on, the eyes that watch you... belong to my people."

The words struck Shayne harder than he expected. He glanced at the canopy, half-expecting to see shadows moving, arrows nocked. His mouth went dry. But when he looked back at Avara, he couldn't help but notice the calm way she carried herself—as if danger and safety were the same thing in her hands.

Shayne swallowed, nodding—but when she looked away, he couldn't help the way his eyes stayed on her for just a moment longer.

* * *

The thick jungle, heavier air in this location— every breath felt like swallowing warm water.

Adam pushed a low branch aside for Megan, letting it snap back after she passed. She stepped gingerly across roots and stone, muttering to herself, "ruined pedicure" with just enough sass to make Adam smile.

"Gonna have to charge you for all this bodyguard work," he teased, ducking under a vine.

Megan smirked, brushing sweat from her forehead. "Bodyguard? Isn't that what boyfriends are supposed to be?"

Adam grinned, glancing back at her. "I suppose it is."

For a moment, the banter cut through the oppressive green, a reminder of what it was like before the crash—before the island felt like it was closing in around him.

But Grent killed that mood like a shadow crossing the sun.

He walked behind them, cigarette clamped between his fingers, his scar catching a beam of weak light. His gaze wandered, always wandering—and too often landing on Megan.

Adam saw it.

Every. Single. Time.

Megan didn't, or maybe she pretended not to. She was busy plucking burrs from the hem of her dress, laughing softly at her own clumsiness.

Grent took a slow drag, then said, almost conversationally, "You two keep joking like that, people might think this island's not dangerous."

Adam looked over his shoulder. "Maybe we just don't feel like being miserable every second."

Grent's eyes met his. Calm. Unblinking.

"Misery keeps us alive," Grent said, flicking the cigarette ash to the ground. "People who laugh too much? They don't see it coming."

The words weren't loud, but they hung in the air like a warning.

Megan's smile faltered, but she forced a little laugh. "Cheery guy, huh?" she muttered to Adam, clearly trying to shake off the chill in Grent's voice.

Adam didn't answer. He couldn't stop watching Grent, his gut twisting.

He didn't know what Grent was planning—but he knew he was planning *something*.

Adam's hand brushed the pocketknife clipped to his belt. For the first time, he wondered if he'd need it—not for the jungle, but for the man walking with them.

* * *

By the time the sun dipped low, the jungle had opened just enough to reveal a small clearing.

Not the full village—Shayne could tell that much—but an outpost, maybe a watch point. A few huts, smoke rising from a modest fire, and a scattering of Vokari warriors who stood like statues, eyes locked on every movement Shayne and Cartwright made.

Avara spoke quietly to the warriors, her voice firm but calm. Whatever she said, it was enough to keep spears lowered, though not enough to make the tension go away.

Shayne sat cross-legged near the fire, trying not to look as nervous as he felt. He reached for a stick, idly tracing circles in the dirt, then glanced at the little girl watching him from across the clearing.

She couldn't have been more than ten— Luma, Avara had called her.

She stared at Shayne like he was a strange animal, head tilted, dark eyes curious.

Shayne gave her a small wave. "Uh... hi?"

Luma blinked, then said something in the Vokari tongue.

Shayne hesitated, then tried to mimic it— clumsy, awkward syllables tumbling out of his mouth.

The girl's eyes widened. Then she burst into laughter.

Her laughter was sharp and bright, ringing through the tense air.

Shayne groaned. "Great. First impression ruined."

This time, Avara *did* smile, a small one, but real. "At least you tried."

Shayne scratched at the back of his neck, feeling heat rise in his face. "Guess I'm not fluent in... goat-scent language."

Avara finally looked at him, the firelight catching in her dark eyes. "Your accent is bad," she said, her tone flat out teasing, "but you listen. Most outsiders don't."

Shayne held her gaze a second too long, then grinned to cover it. "Guess I'm full of surprises."

Cartwright, sitting off to the side sharpening his knife, muttered, "God help us," without looking up.

Shayne ignored him. He kept his focus on Avara, who had turned back to her herbs, but he noticed—just barely—the way she hadn't quite hidden her smile.

The sound of Luma's giggles still lingered in the clearing, softening the edge of fear. For the first time since they'd washed up on this dared to: the beginning of trust.

* * *

The jungle had grown darker as evening fell, the light slipping away until everything was tinted in shades of green and gray.

Adam walked close to Megan, close enough that their shoulders brushed every now and then.
She didn't seem to notice—she was focused on her bare feet, muttering under her breath as she plucked a thorn from her heel.

Behind them, Grent had gone quiet. Too quiet.
Adam glanced back.

Grent was a few paces behind, a cigarette glowing faintly between his fingers. The smoke curled upward, thin and lazy.

He wasn't looking at the path.

He wasn't looking at Adam.

He was looking at Megan.

Adam's stomach knotted.

Grent took a long drag, the ember flaring, and then he murmured something under his breath. Too low for Adam to catch the words, but the tone was wrong—like a whisper meant only for himself.

Adam slowed, letting Megan step ahead so he could fall back, just enough to be closer to Grent.

"What did you say?" he asked, keeping his voice even.

Grent's eyes shifted to him, calm, flat, unreadable.

"Almost there," Grent said, flicking the cigarette butt into the brush.

Adam frowned. "Almost where?"

Grent's lips curved into the faintest smile. "You'll see."

He started walking again, the smoke still lingering in the air behind him like a warning.

Adam's chest felt tight. He didn't know what Grent meant. He didn't know what Grent wanted.

But he knew one thing for certain.

He didn't trust him.

And for the first time, Adam felt something colder than fear: certainty. Grent wasn't just dangerous. He was waiting for his moment.

* * *

Matthew felt it in his bones before he saw it—the way the trees seemed to space out, the ground firming under his boots, the smell of smoke threading faintly through the humid air.

Ahead of him, the Vokari warriors marched in silence, Kaia's limp body carried carefully between two of them. Her head lolled with each step, auburn curls slipping into her face.

Matthew kept close, every instinct screaming at him to snatch her back, to run—but he knew better. He saw shadows along the trail, and heard whispers. "Tala shatai..."

Every glance from the warriors told him one thing: he wasn't in control here.

Beside him, Dr. Varn walked quietly, her eyes scanning every totem, every feather hanging from the trees, every painted symbol etched into the bark. She said nothing, but her expression spoke volumes—this was deeper than anthropology now.

Matthew's gaze locked on the faint gray plume ahead.

Smoke.

And then, just for a moment, the jungle broke.

He could see it—rooftops of thatched huts, a tall carved post rising in the center, figures moving between firelight and shadow.

The Vokari village.

Matthew's breath caught.

This was it.

Whatever happened next would decide everything—Kaia's life, his group's survival, maybe even whether they ever left this island alive.

A low chant drifted through the trees now, rhythmic and unyielding. It carried with it a promise—or perhaps a warning—that judgment waited beyond the firelight.

* * *

*The trees were thinning, the ground turning to packed earth—and for the first time, Matthew saw the smoke of the village rising ahead like a promise, or a warning.*

# Chapter 24  The Village of the Vokari

One moment, Matthew was pushing through ferns and vines, Kaia's breath barely warm against his chest—and the next, the trees gave way to open earth.

The Vokari village stretched out before them like something from a lost world.

Thatched huts clustered around smoky cooking fires. Tall poles carved with spirals and beastlike faces stood like guardians along the perimeter.
Animal skins dried on racks. Bundles of herbs hung from rafters. Children peeked out from behind low fences, wide-eyed. Warriors stood still as stone.

And all of it went silent the moment Matthew stepped out of the trees.

He didn't stop walking.

Kaia was limp in his arms, her skin pale, lips parted.

Dr. Varn trailed just behind him, her eyes scanning everything with the sharpness of someone trying to memorize what might be her final surroundings.

They passed the first ring of huts. Villagers murmured. Some stepped back, clutching their children. Others pointed at Kaia and whispered to one another in a language Matthew didn't know.

Then someone spat on the ground near his feet.

Matthew flinched, but didn't look up. He kept walking.

Kaia needed help. That was the only thing that mattered.

Two warriors stepped forward—the same ones who'd carried her before—and gently took her from his arms. He wanted to resist, to shout. *No, I'll take her,* but he knew better now.

They carried her toward the center of the village, where smoke curled up into the sky from a large communal fire. The carved pole beside it stretched nearly twenty feet high, its surface etched with images: animals, storm clouds, a man with fire in his hand.

Matthew stopped walking.

The air here was heavier—not with heat, but with history.

And judgment.

From all sides, the Vokari were watching him.

He wasn't sure if he was a guest, a threat... or a prisoner.

The warriors led them into the heart of the village, past long lines of woven mat, drying fruit, and low fires where elders sat with folded legs and narrowed eyes.

At the far end stood a raised platform shaded by a wide, sloping canopy of palm and bark. A carved wooden seat rested at its center, worn smooth by years of use.

Upon it sat a man—Chief Nukapana

He was broad-shouldered, his bare chest painted with streaks of white and black. His hair was mostly gray, bound back in strips of cloth, with threads of black still woven through. Every line in his face seemed earned. His hands were clasped calmly in his lap, but there was no mistaking the weight of his gaze.

To his right stood Shia, the shaman—thin and wiry, with feathers and beads in her hair, her face partially painted in deep red markings. Her expression was harder to read.

The crowd behind Matthew grew still as the warriors brought him and Varn forward.

Chief Nukapana studied them for a long moment before he spoke.

His voice was low, gravelly—and in broken, deliberate English:

"Outsiders... come again. Why?"

Matthew opened his mouth, the question hitting him harder than expected.

Varn stepped forward first. "She is poisoned," she said, gesturing toward the direction Kaia had been taken. "A snakebite. She'll die without help."

Nukapana's eyes shifted slightly, his face unreadable.

He turned his gaze to Matthew. "You carry her... long way."

"I would've carried her to the ends of the island if I had to," Matthew said, his voice steadier than he felt.

Something flickered in Nukapana's eyes. Not warmth—but recognition.

The chief lifted a hand slowly. At his signal, a warrior stepped forward and said something in Vokari. Shia replied in a tone that was half warning, half observation.

Nukapana looked back to Matthew.

"You say... you come to help?"

Matthew hesitated. "I didn't come here to hurt anyone."

The chief leaned forward slightly. "Others came. Before. Said same."

That landed like a stone in Matthew's gut. "Others?"

Varn glanced at him, her brow creasing. "He's not talking about us..." she said under her breath.

Nukapana's gaze lingered on Matthew "Outsider man. Silver hair. Eyes like ice. He come. Long ago."

Matthew's heart skipped. That description... it couldn't be—

"Clark?" he whispered aloud before he could stop himself.

Varn turned to him. "You think it's—"

"I don't know," Matthew said, eyes locked on the chief. "But someone they remember did something bad here."

Nukapana sat back, eyes still locked on him.

"He say he help. He lie."

Matthew's throat was dry. "I'm not him."

The chief studied him long and hard. Then he sat back. His next words were quieter.

"We see."

A low murmur spread through the gathered villagers. More were arriving now, emerging from huts and behind smoke-wreathed fences, drawn by the presence of outsiders standing before the chief.

Shia the Shaman stepped forward, speaking rapidly in the Vokari tongue. Her gestures were sharp, directed at Matthew and Varn, then toward the path Kaia had been carried down.

Whatever she was saying, it stirred the crowd.

Koro, the scarred warrior who had first confronted them, stepped up beside Shia, voice like gravel as he pointed at Matthew. He spat words that needed no translation—his posture said it all: he wanted them gone.

Matthew tensed but didn't move.

"Let me guess," he said under his breath. "He's the welcoming committee."

Varn's eyes didn't leave Koro. "He's probably the reason there's a spear pointed at your spine."

A few elders on the opposite side of the gathering began arguing back—gentler tones, hands open, one even gesturing toward the healer's hut. Their voices were quickly swallowed by the louder ones.

The debate rippled outward like waves. Voices rose; arms flew. One woman cried out and threw a small bone totem at the ground in frustration.

Matthew stood still, trying to understand without words.

They were divided.

Not just about him—about Kaia. About what her presence meant. About what *they* represented.

A sudden sharp whistle cut through the noise.

Chief Nukapana had not moved—but he had raised one hand, fingers splayed, palm outward.

Silence returned.

He looked at Matthew again. Then to Varn. Then back to the people.

His voice, though quiet, carried over the crowd.

"Outsiders come. Say peace. Say help. Last time..." He paused, pointing to the fire pit between them. "...they bring flame. Death. Take people. Leave nothing."

Matthew felt a cold twist in his gut.

Nukapana's gaze fell back on him.

"This girl... she different?"

Matthew nodded, throat tight. "Yes."

The chief studied him, then turned to his people and said something in Vokari—slower this time. The crowd didn't cheer. They didn't protest either. They only listened.

When he finished, Shia stepped back with a faint nod.

The decision, it seemed, had been made.

Two warriors broke away from the circle, disappearing down a narrow path between huts. Moments later, they returned—not with weapons, but with a long, woven stretcher.

They walked past Matthew without a word and disappeared again toward the healer's hut.

Shia the Shaman turned without waiting for a signal, her long feathers trailing behind her as she followed.

Matthew took a step forward instinctively, but a spear crossed in front of his chest.

Koro.

His face said everything his silence didn't.

"You've made your decision," Matthew said, his hands half-raised. "At least let me be there."

Koro didn't speak. He only shook his head once.

Matthew's jaw clenched. "She's all I care about. I'm not here to spy. I'm not here to steal from you. I just want her to live."

Varn stepped beside him and spoke softly. "Don't push them. They're helping—for now. That's all we can ask."

From across the fire, Chief Nukapana finally spoke again.

"You stay. Here."

Matthew turned to him, his frustration barely held back. "Why?"

The chief stood slowly, descending from the platform with a deliberate slowness that commanded silence from the watching tribe. He stepped toward Matthew until they stood just a few feet apart.

His gaze was heavy, but not unkind.

"If you true..." he said, pointing toward the healer's hut, "...you wait."

Then he tapped two fingers against Matthew's chest.

"If not... no words help her."

Matthew swallowed hard, stepping back as Nukapana returned to his seat.

From the far side of the village, Matthew could see Shia entering a hut—the one they had taken Kaia to. Smoke began curling from its small chimney, carrying the scent of something pungent and herbal.

The door flap closed behind her.

Kaia was in their hands now.

The fire in the center of the village burned low, its smoke curling into the dusky sky. Matthew stood near it, fists clenched at his sides, staring at the healer's hut as if sheer willpower could keep Kaia breathing.

Footsteps approached.

When he turned, Chief Nukapana was there, moving with the steady, unhurried gait of a man who knew every eye in the village followed his steps.

Two warriors flanked him, but they didn't raise their weapons.

The chief stopped a few feet from Matthew, his gaze hard but not without depth. "She... strong," Nukapana said in his careful English. "Maybe live. If we choose."

Matthew's breath caught. "If you choose?"

The chief nodded once. "Not free."

Matthew frowned. "What do you want?"

Nukapana tilted his head, eyes narrowing. "Not what I want. What you show."

"I don't understand."

The chief's voice dropped, quiet but firm. "Others... outsiders, before you. They take. Lie. Bring fire." His gaze locked on Matthew's, sharp and unblinking. "You same... or you not?"

Matthew shook his head, his voice fierce. "I'm not like them. Whoever they were—I'm not."

Nukapana studied him for a moment, as though searching for cracks in the words.

Finally, he spoke again. "You prove."

Matthew's chest tightened. "Prove what?"

The chief gestured toward the villagers watching from the edges of the firelight, then toward the jungle beyond. "You walk. You fight. You face what we face. Then... maybe we help your woman."

Matthew felt the words like stones in his stomach.

"I don't get a choice, do I?"

Nukapana's face was unreadable. "Choice? Choice is always. But not always good."

Matthew looked past him, to the healer's hut, where Kaia's life now hung on strangers' hands and the outcome of a test he didn't understand.

The smell of smoke and herbs thickened in the air, drifting from the healer's hut like a promise or a warning. Every beat of the drum, every whisper from the crowd pressed against Matthew's chest until it felt hard to breathe.

* * *

*Matthew looked at the healer's hut, where Kaia's life now hung by the work of strangers, and then at the chief, whose dark, steady eyes made it clear—saving her would mean proving himself first.*

# Chapter 25  Between Firelight and Shadows

Back in the jungle where it opened into a long, sloping stretch of mossy earth, shafts of sunlight broke through the canopy like golden ladders. The air smelled faintly of damp leaves and something sweet—flowers hidden high above.

Shayne slowed his pace just enough to walk alongside Avara, though he was careful not to make it too obvious.

Cartwright walked a few paces behind them, ever watchful but giving them space—the kind of space a soldier recognizes when two people are trying not to admit they enjoy being near each other.

"So," Shayne said, brushing a low vine aside, "you're really not going to tell me what all the symbols mean?"

Avara glanced at him, her expression unreadable. "You would not understand."

"Try me."

She sighed but pointed to a nearby tree where strips of cloth and bones had been tied into a hanging spiral. "That means safe path. Others use colors or feathers. That one is for warriors."

Shayne studied it. "And what about the double ring I saw back there? Two loops tied with string?"

She paused, a little surprised. "You see that?"

"Of course. I've got eyes like a hawk. A really sweaty, very tired hawk."

She rolled her eyes—but there was a faint smile trying to hide in the corners. "Double loop is a place of listening. A place spirits visit."

Shayne arched a brow. "We walked *right through* that."

Avara shrugged. "Maybe the spirits are listening to you now."

Shayne smirked. "If they are, I hope they speak sarcasm."

They continued on, ducking beneath a cluster of thick vines. Avara reached up to brush one aside, but Shayne stepped in and did it for her—his hand brushing against her wrist.

She looked at him. Not annoyed. Just still.

Their eyes met.

"I meant what I said earlier," Shayne said. "Back when you saved us. I'm not like the others. I've studied tribes—cultures, languages, belief systems. Not like this... not this close, but I've always wanted to understand, not take."

Avara watched him for a long second. Then she spoke softly: "You listen better than you speak."

"Hey now," he said, placing a hand on his chest in mock offense. "That's practically a compliment."

She reached up—slowly—and brushed a small leaf from his hair, her fingers pausing for just a moment too long.

"It is," she said.

For the first time since the crash, Shayne's chest felt light, like the weight of the jungle wasn't pressing in but parting for them.

* * *

The fire was small—just enough to cast flickering light on the three faces gathered around it.

Adam sat with his back against a thick tree root, poking gently at the flames with a stick. His eyes kept drifting toward Megan, who was stretched out nearby, her bare feet propped up on her pack, legs streaked with dirt and scratches.

She groaned softly and turned over onto her side. "My entire body hurts. My feet feel like I stepped on a porcupine made of lava."

Adam chuckled under his breath. "You're lucky I didn't let you bring those stilettos. You'd be crawling right now."

She opened one eye at him. "Oh, *that's* what this is? You are saving me from myself?"

"Yup. I'm your jungle-appointed life coach now."

Megan gave him a tired smirk. "Then you seriously need a new wardrobe."

Adam smiled—a genuine one—and handed her his water bottle. She took it, gulped, then wiped her mouth on her sleeve.

Across from them, Grent crouched in silence, his back to the fire, staring into the dark like he was waiting for something to emerge from it.

Megan whispered, "Is it just me, or does he get creepier the quieter he is?"

Adam didn't answer right away. His eyes had been locked on Grent for most of the evening.

Grent hadn't said a word since they stopped. Not one.

Megan curled up under the thin blanket they'd salvaged, nestling closer to Adam's side without hesitation. "Don't let me roll into a snake's mouth while I'm sleeping."

"I'll keep an eye out," Adam said softly, not smiling this time.

His gaze flicked to Grent again.

The man hadn't moved. Still hunched there, a human shadow outlined in orange light, smoke curling from the cigarette that burned low between his fingers.

Something about the way he watched the fire— not with reflection, but calculation—made Adam's skin crawl.

It was as though Grent was waiting for the night itself to give him permission.

The fire had burned low, casting long, twisted shadows that flickered across the trees like restless ghosts.

Adam was asleep, one arm loosely draped over his pack, his body turned toward Megan, who slept curled on her side beside him. Her breathing was soft, steady. The kind of sleep earned through exhaustion, not comfort.

And there was Grent.

He sat with his back against a tree, knees bent, hands resting loosely in his lap. Eyes open. Awake.

Watching.

The last ember of his cigarette faded out between his fingers, and he flicked it into the dirt. For a long moment, he didn't move.

Then—slowly, silently—he did.

He rose from his crouch without making a sound and stepped over the remains of the fire, each footfall deliberate and measured.

He stood over them.

Adam stirred faintly, shifting onto his back. His mouth parted slightly as he exhaled. But he didn't wake.

Grent's gaze lingered on him for only a second... before turning to Megan.

She lay facing the opposite direction, one hand tucked under her cheek, the other arm draped loosely across her stomach.

Grent crouched beside her.

Watched her.

Then—almost casually—he reached out and brushed his hand across her hip.

She twitched.

Grent froze.

Megan mumbled something incoherent, her face scrunching slightly, but she didn't wake.

Grent's hand moved again. Lower.

He touched her butt cheek.

It was brief. Just a lingering graze—but intentional.

Megan shifted again, turning slightly in her sleep. Her shoulder bumped into Adam's arm.

Grent pulled back immediately, his eyes flicking toward Adam.

Still asleep.

Grent's jaw tightened, and for a split second his mask of calm cracked—an ugly hunger flashing across his face before it was gone.

Grent stood, slow and silent, and stepped back into the shadows, face unreadable.

He lit another cigarette and took a long drag, the tip glowing faint orange in the dark.

He muttered, barely audible—almost to himself: "Soon."

The jungle mist clung low over the forest floor the next morning, hanging in the air like a held breath.

Adam was already awake—had been for over an hour. He hadn't slept much after the fire went out.

He kept glancing at Grent, who sat just a few feet away, legs stretched out, a whetstone in his hand, slowly sharpening a long hunting knife with methodical, scraping strokes.

The sound was soft... but it cut through the silence.

Across from them, Megan yawned and sat up, stretching her arms above her head. Her hair was tangled, her tank top loose around one shoulder.

She blinked at Grent, then at the blade in his hands. "Okay, I'm just gonna say it. That is, like, the creepiest wake-up I've ever had."

Grent didn't look up. Another scrape of steel.

"I mean," she continued, trying to smile, "you're just missing a horror movie soundtrack and a ski mask."

Grent finally looked at her. His face was calm— too calm.

He sheathed the knife. "It's not the knife you should worry about."

Megan blinked, unsure how to respond.

Adam stood up. "Alright, enough edgycrap for one morning."

Grent smirked faintly. "Relax, kid. Just keeping it sharp."

He slid the knife into his belt and picked up his pack. "Never know what we'll run into next."

Adam's gaze didn't leave him.

Megan grabbed her things, casting a slightly nervous glance between them. "Okay. So, uh... shall we hit the road before the vibe here gets any weirder?"

Grent gave her a long look. Then smiled.

"Ladies first."

Adam stepped between them. "I'll go first."

Grent's smile didn't fade—but it didn't reach his eyes.

* * *

*The jungle was quiet, but Adam's thoughts weren't. He hadn't truly slept—not with Grent so close, not with the way he had looked at Megan. A knot had formed in his gut, and it wasn't going away.*

# Chapter 26  The Trial of Worthiness

The dawn mist clung to the jungle trees like breath on glass.

Matthew sat beside Kaia's still form, one hand gently resting on hers, the other cradling his forehead. Her breathing was shallow, but steady—a fragile thread anchoring her to this world.

Dr. Varn sat nearby, organizing leaves and herbs they'd been given, her movements careful, quiet. The tension between hope and dread hung over them both like a storm that hadn't yet broken.

A rustle of feet in the dirt pulled Matthew from his thoughts.

Chief Nukapana approached, flanked by two warriors. His expression was carved of stone and time, but his eyes held something older—not cruelty, but caution.

Matthew stood slowly.

The chief looked him over. "You care for her," he said, the words slow, shaped with effort. "You say... she must live."

Matthew nodded. "I'll do anything."

Nukapana studied him. "Then... you must show. Not just speak. Show heart."

Matthew glanced at Kaia. "What do I have to do?"

The chief took a step forward. "Outsiders... many come. Most bring lies. But one—before you—he bring worst thing."

Matthew's brow furrowed. "Who?"

The chief's eyes hardened. "Helix." The name left his mouth like venom. "He smile. Promise peace. Bring pain. Take our people. Use them."

Matthew froze. "Helix... You knew him?"

Nukapana nodded once. "I know devil when I see him."

Varn stepped closer. "I've seen that name before, Helix. I saw it on Clark's desk back at the university. It said confidential."

Nukapana turned his gaze toward her. "That is name. Helix. Do not speak him like friend."

Matthew swallowed. "Is he... here? On the island?"

"You ask wrong question," Nukapana said. He stepped forward and tapped Matthew's chest with two fingers. "Better question: Is he here?"

Matthew looked down, uncertain. "I don't understand."

"You will."

From behind the chief, Shia, the tribe's shaman, stepped forward. Her frame was wiry and weathered, her hair laced with beads and feathers. Her eyes, marked with white paint, felt like they could see through bone. In her hand, she carried a shallow bowl filled with murky, dark liquid.

She spoke calmly. "You drink. Then, you walk inside your shadow. You see what lives behind your eyes."

"I'll do it," Dr. Varn said suddenly, stepping forward. "Let me. I've studied him—I can handle—"

"No," Nukapana said sharply. "You... not heart of her. He is." He looked at Matthew. "Only he can walk this trial."

Matthew looked at Kaia again. Her pale lips. Her stillness.

He turned back to them. "Alright. I'll do it."

Nukapana nodded, then gestured to two warriors who stepped in to guide Matthew away—toward a clearing beyond the huts, where firelight flickered and stone formed a ritual circle.

As they walked, Varn called after him, "Be strong, Fisher! And remember—none of it is real."

But Matthew didn't look back.

Because some part of him already knew... That was the lie.

The drumbeat began—slow, hollow, inevitable—keeping time with Matthew's pulse as the village exhaled in one uneasy breath.

* * *

Matthew sat cross-legged inside the narrow stone chamber; its walls painted with swirling patterns in reds and blacks, the air thick with smoke from burning herbs. The faint hum of chanting voices echoed from outside.

197

Shia stood in front of him, cloaked in feathers and beads, a bone charm swinging gently from her neck.

She held the clay bowl in her hands—the same one she'd mixed the foul-smelling concoction in—and extended it to him.

"Drink," she said, her voice steady, eyes dark as obsidian. "See truth. See self."

Matthew hesitated only a moment before taking the bowl. He thought of Kaia—the way her breath had stuttered as they'd carried her, the way her eyes had fluttered half-shut. He brought the bowl to his lips and drank.

The taste was like rot and ash and dirt. He gagged but forced it down.

The world tilted sideways.

—

The jungle swelled around him, impossibly tall trees curling toward the sky like reaching fingers. Everything glowed in unnatural hues—emerald light, violet shadows. The vines pulsed like arteries. He was inside a living organism.

Then the jungle split open.

A lab corridor now—long-abandoned, cracked glass tubes lining the walls. The Double Helix symbol flickered on a shattered screen. Inside one of the tubes floated a deformed creature—part human, part dinosaur, its eyes shut.

Matthew stumbled backward.

"Too far ahead of its time," came a voice behind him. "Or maybe just... exactly what was needed."

He turned. Professor Clark stood in the hallway, wearing his university blazer—but the jungle bled into his silhouette. His body flickered between that of a man and something taller, more skeletal. Golden light beamed from his irises.

"You've always wanted truth, haven't you?" Clark asked gently. "But truth doesn't wait for permission. It carves through you."

"You're not real," Matthew said, his fists trembling. "You died during the crash."

Clark smiled.

"I'm the part of you that knows what's coming.

The lab corridor flickered and melted away—replaced by images:

•Fisher standing over Bryce's grave, mud on his hands.

•Kaia in his arms, bleeding from the bite.

•A tower of flame in the distance, something massive roaring behind it.

•The tribe, chanting.

•And then—

Megan.

She was laughing, her hair glowing in the sun, then suddenly running—barefoot, terrified—through dark brush. She looked over her shoulder. Screamed.

"Adam! Help me!"

Matthew reached out to grab her, but she passed through him like fog. Behind her came Grent, walking calmly, predator-like.

Megan tripped. Screamed again.

And the scene exploded into static—screaming and snapping bone.

Matthew was alone again.

—

The jungle was gone. Now he stood in front of a mirror.

He looked... older. Tired. Beard thicker. Eyes hardened. Scars across his arms. He wore tribal paint on his chest and a necklace he didn't recognize.

"You'll be someone else when this ends," Clark whispered from behind him. "That's the cost."

Matthew turned, but there was no one there.

Just the sound of Kaia's voice, soft and faint: "Come back to me..."

—

He gasped awake, lungs clawing for air.

The chamber was dim. The fire had burned down to embers. His back was slick with sweat. Shia sat beside him, legs crossed, watching.

"You walk the flame and shadow," she murmured. "You still here. That mean something."

Matthew leaned forward, elbows on knees. "Kaia?"

Shia gave a slow nod. "She live. For now."

His relief was immediate—but incomplete.

Because somewhere, in the echo of the vision, Megan's scream still rang in his ears.

And Grent's face, calm and smiling, was now burned into his mind.

Matthew pressed his palms to the cool stone and closed his eyes—just once—before pushing himself up. "Hold on," he whispered to the woman who wasn't here to hear him. "I'm coming."

* * *

Kaia's skin was pale beneath the flickering light of the healer's hut. Her breaths came in shallow gasps, her body limp atop a woven mat of reeds and fur. The snakebite on her calf was an angry purple, swollen and streaked with red veins trailing up her leg.

Shia moved quickly, her hands sure. The air was thick with the scent of ground herbs, crushed roots, and bitter smoke. Two younger Vokari women assisted her, holding bowls of water and crushed poultices.

"She close to spirit path." Shia muttered in her native tongue, eyes sharp. "But not yet."

Dr. Varn knelt just outside the circle of firelight, nervously wringing her hands. "Can I help?'

Shia looked at her, then nodded once. "Hold her hand. Talk."

Varn crawled forward and gently grasped Kaia's hand. "Kaia? It's Emilia. You're not alone. Matthew's doing something... something risky, to help you. You have to stay with us. You hear me?"

Kaia didn't respond—but a shiver rippled through her body.

Shia dipped a carved bone tool into a thick green salve and began packing it into the wound. Kaia moaned, eyes fluttering open for just a second.

"Shh," Varn whispered, brushing Kaia's hair from her face. "You're okay. We've got you."

Outside, the sound of drums had stopped. The village was hushed—listening, waiting.

Shia placed her hands on either side of Kaia's head and began to chant low and steady, her voice like wind moving through stone. The other women echoed her, creating a rhythm of healing, tradition, and power.

Kaia's body jerked once—then stilled.

She exhaled.

A long, deep breath.

Varn blinked, holding back tears. "She's breathing easier..."

Shia nodded without breaking rhythm. "She come back. Spirit not take her."

As the chanting faded, Kaia's eyelids fluttered again. This time, they opened—just a sliver.

"Matthew..." she whispered, barely audible.

Varn smiled, voice shaking. "He's here. He's fighting for you."

Kaia's eyes closed again, but her breathing remained steady.

The danger had passed.

But the price was still being paid—somewhere, in that dark ceremonial chamber, where Matthew Fisher had been forced to confront something far more terrifying than poison.

Outside, a child's voice—Luma—began a soft counter-chant near the doorway, and one by one the elders answered, the sound like a woven rope tugging Kaia back from a brink only they could see.

* * *

The sun had just begun to rise over the jungle canopy, casting soft orange light over the Vokari village. Smoke drifted lazily from cooking fires. A quiet hush lingered over the huts, as if the entire tribe had been holding its breath.

The ceremonial hut door creaked open.

Matthew stumbled out, his eyes bleary and unfocused, sweat still clinging to his skin. He blinked against the light, heart pounding with remnants of the vision.

He felt different—not just tired. Changed. Marked.

Shia stepped out behind him and placed a steadying hand on his shoulder. "You still here," she said in her low voice. "Spirit not break you."

Matthew swallowed, voice raw. "Kaia?"

Shia didn't answer—she just tilted her head toward the healer's hut across the clearing.

He moved toward it in a half-run, nearly falling to his knees as he reached the doorway. Varn looked up from inside and gave a tiny nod.

Matthew stepped in.

Kaia lay beneath a fur blanket, her face pale, but peaceful. Her breathing was slow and steady. Her cheeks held the faintest trace of color.

He dropped to his knees beside her. "Kaia...?"

Her eyes fluttered. For a moment, nothing—and then they opened.

"Matthew...?" Her voice was hoarse, but real.

"I'm here." His hand found hers, squeezing gently. "I'm here."

Tears welled up in her eyes. "I thought... I wouldn't..."

He smiled, throat tight. "I'm not letting you go. Not now. Not ever."

Kaia squeezed his hand in return. Weakly, but firmly.

Dr. Varn quietly stepped outside, giving them a moment.

Across the village, the guards at the wooden perimeter gates called out in surprise. Shouts of confusion, followed by a few tense moments—and then a familiar voice answered:

"Whoa, Whoa! Not a threat! We come in peace!"

Matthew turned toward the sound, eyes widening. "Shayne?!"

—

Shayne Wood, covered in sweat and jungle dirt, stepped cautiously into the clearing beside Captain Cartwright. Behind them walked a young Vokari woman with beaded braids—Avara. She moved with practiced ease through the guards, clearly known to them.

Cartwright's eyes swept the village. "Well I'll be damned..."

Shayne blinked in disbelief as he spotted Matthew exiting the healer's hut. "Holy sh—Fisher?!"

"Shayne!" Matthew jogged across the clearing.

The two collided in a hug that was part relief, part disbelief. Cartwright clapped him on the back with a gruff smile.

"Didn't think we'd see you again," Shayne said breathlessly. "You look like hell."

"You too," Matthew laughed. "But she's alive. Kaia's okay."

Shayne glanced toward the healer's hut, nodding solemnly. "Then it was worth it."

Avara stepped closer, nodding respectfully to Matthew. "You are the one who sought help. The one they speak of."

"I guess that's me," he said, still catching his breath. "You helped them get here?"

"I did," she said. "But not everyone will be happy they're here."

Matthew turned just as Chief Nukapana emerged from his hut, flanked by Koro and several warriors. The chief's expression was unreadable—a mask of wisdom and warning.

"She live," Nukapana said, gesturing toward the healer's hut. "Because you fight spirit. Because you care. That matter."

Matthew stepped forward. "Thank you. Truly."

Nukapana nodded slowly, then raised one hand to silence the murmurs spreading among the tribe.

"But not over," he said. "You prove to spirit. Now... you prove to us."

Koro stepped forward, his muscular arms crossed, face hard. "A final test," he growled. "To show you not same as the one who hurt us before."

Matthew's shoulders straightened. He felt Kaia's eyes watching from the healer's doorway. Shayne, Cartwright, and Varn stood nearby, silent but steady.

"What kind of test?" Matthew asked.

Nukapana's eyes narrowed. "A fight. Not to kill—unless it must. You face one of us. If you stand tall... we trust."

Matthew's gaze met Koro's—sharp and fierce.

He nodded once. "Then I'll stand."

From behind him, Kaia's voice whispered faintly: "Come back to me again."

As the tribe formed a wide ring, a hush fell—then a single elder struck a drumhead with her palm, once, twice, three times. The circle closed. The test began.

* * *

The fire crackled low in the jungle clearing.

Adam sat with his back against a log, eyes half-closed, the weight of the day pressing down on him. Grent was a few feet away, carving something into the dirt with a stick, eyes hidden beneath the shadows of his brow. Megan lay curled in her sleeping spot, barefoot, using her backpack as a pillow.

Crickets chirped softly in the distance. The jungle, for now, was still.

"I'm going to pee," Megan mumbled groggily, standing and brushing her tangled hair behind her shoulders. She gave Adam a sleepy glance. "Don't let him eat my snacks."

Adam smirked. "Can't make any promises."

Megan smiled and turned, walking barefoot down the narrow trail, the flashlight in her hand flickering slightly. The brush closed behind her.

Grent watched her go.

He waited five slow seconds, then stood.

Adam looked up. "Where are you going?"

Grent didn't answer. He just nodded off toward the trees. "Stretching my legs."

Adam didn't think much of it at first. He leaned his head back and closed his eyes.

—

Megan crouched near a fern, grumbling under her breath. "God, what I wouldn't give for plumbing..."

She set the flickering flashlight on the ground beside her and glanced around nervously. The sounds of the jungle were louder here—leaves rustling, frogs croaking, something distant howling.

Then, a rustle. Close.

She froze. "Adam?"

Silence.

Her heart quickened. She reached for a rock beside her just in case, rising to her slowly.

Branches parted—and Grent stepped through.

She exhaled sharply. "Jesus, don't sneak up on people like that."

Grent didn't smile. He stepped closer.

"W-What are you doing?" she asked, voice suddenly tight.

He tilted his head. "You like Adam, don't you?"

"What?"

"You think he'd stay safe if I walked back without you?" His voice was calm. Too calm.

Megan took a half-step back, clutching the rock. "If you touch him—"

"I won't have to. If you do what I say."

She stared at him, stunned. He pulled a knife— not to strike, but to show her he wasn't bluffing. His other hand reached toward her.

"Strip," he said.

She shook her head, trembling. "No..."

"You want him to live?" Grent's tone turned icy. "Then do it."

Tears filled her eyes. Her body shook.

She slowly pulled off her shirt, sobbing quietly. Her voice cracked. "You're a monster..."

He stepped closer and ran his hand down her side—grabbing her breast, then her hip.

She flinched.

And then—*WHAM*—she kneed him hard in the stomach and bolted, screaming into the trees.

"ADAM!!"

—

Back at the fire, Adam sat up. "Megan?"

He heard it again—faint, but unmistakable.

"Adam! Help me!"

He jumped to his feet, grabbing the flashlight. "MEGAN?!"

He turned toward the trail but didn't know which way to go. The sound had already faded.

"MEGAN!"

—

Megan ran wildly, branches slicing her arms and legs, flashlight long gone. She burst through a patch of ferns—and then something tackled her hard from behind.

They crashed to the ground.

She kicked and screamed, but Grent was stronger, fueled by fury.

"You Bitch!" He growled. "Should've just listened."

She scratched at his face, but he grabbed her neck with both hands.

"Please..." she gasped. "Please don't—"

*SNAP*

Silence.

Megan's body went limp.

Grent panted, his face scraped, sweat beading along his scalp.

He looked down at her, the life gone from her eyes.

A small silver glint caught his eye—**the necklace.** The one she always wore.

He reached down and ripped it from her neck, staring at it.

Then he stood.

—

By the time he returned to camp, Adam was pacing, flashlight in hand, looking toward the trees.

"She's gone," Grent said flatly.

Adam turned. "What?"

"I tried to follow. I saw... one of those tribesmen. They took her. Quiet. Quick."

"No." Adam's voice cracked. "No way. You're sure?"

Grent nodded slowly. "I'm sorry."

Adam looked down at the dirt, face pale. "We head toward the village. We get her back."

Grent nodded slightly. "Lead the way, my highness."

In his closed hand, **Megan's necklace** gleamed. And he smiled.

—

*Elsewhere in the jungle, Megan Truss's body lay still beneath the trees—her voice silenced, her necklace gone. And no one yet knew the devil had just gotten away with murder again.*

# Chapter 27  Trial by Combat

The morning air clung heavy with mist, curling through the narrow alleys of the Vokari village like restless spirits. Fisher sat hunched on the wooden threshold of the healer's hut, elbows on his knees, face in his hands. His knuckles were still raw, dirt crusted into the creases from where he'd clawed at the jungle floor yesterday, desperate to reach help.

Inside, Kaia lay breathing—slowly, but stronger than before. He could hear the subtle rustle of fabric and the occasional cough from within. She was alive, and yet... he'd never felt further from peace.

Footsteps approached—quiet, deliberate. Fisher looked up.

A line of Vokari warriors stood before him, flanking a taller figure draped in a dark ceremonial cloak. Chief Nukapana stepped forward, his expression carved in stone. The warriors behind him held long staves wrapped in sinew and bone beads.

"You come," the chief said, his voice deep and roughened by age. "Time is now."

Fisher stood slowly, his joints aching from another sleepless night. "Time for what?"

Shia emerged from the mist behind them, eyes painted, face solemn. "The balance must return," she said cryptically. "A life was spared. The fire spirits stir. There must be a test."

Cartwright stepped up from behind a hut, arms crossed, sensing tension. "What kind of test?" he asked warily.

The chief turned to him, then back to Fisher. "He fight. Prove heart. Spirit. Not like the one before."

Fisher's stomach turned. *The one before*—Helix.

Dr. Varn appeared behind them, her arms folded tight. "You mean he has to fight one of yours?" she asked cautiously.

Before Nukapana could answer, the crowd parted.

Koro.

He stepped forward with slow, deliberate confidence. His body glistened with oil and streaks of ash-paint, dark eyes locked on Matthew's like a predator stalking prey. In his hand, he held a ceremonial staff—blunted at the ends but wrapped with thick hide.

Koro didn't speak. He simply raised his staff to chest level and let the tip rest against the dirt, planting it firmly in the earth between them.

"I'll do it," Matthew said before anyone could speak.

Kaia stirred from inside the hut. Her voice came, weak but clear. "Matthew—"

"No," he said, his voice stronger than he expected. "If this is what it takes to prove we're not the enemy... then I'll fight."

The gathered villagers began to murmur. A drumbeat echoed from somewhere deeper in the village—low, steady, ancient.

Chief Nukapana gave a single nod. "Then we prepare. Come."

As Fisher stepped forward, Koro's eyes followed him, calm and unreadable.

From the shadows, Shayne whispered to Cartwright,

*"They don't just want to see if he can fight... They want to see what kind of man he is when he bleeds."*

—

The ceremonial grounds had changed.

A circle had been cleared in the center of the village—wide and flat, its edges lined with spears planted in the earth like silent sentinels. Smoke rose from incense burners placed at each corner, mixing with the jungle's humidity to create a thick, humming haze. Tribal villagers gathered in growing numbers, forming a wall of bare chests, woven fabrics, and painted faces. Their voices were quiet, reverent.

Matthew stood just outside the circle, his fists clenched at his sides. His heartbeat thudded louder than the rhythmic drums that now pulsed across the village. Sweat rolled down his back despite the cool morning air.

Across the circle stood Koro, arms crossed over his broad chest. He was motionless—a sculpture of muscle and tension. His face was streaked with fresh red and black paint, forming jagged lines that ran from his temple down to his jaw like the marks of some ancient predator.

He stepped forward, into the ring.

Chief Nukapana raised a gnarled walking stick high above his head. The crowd fell instantly silent.

In the Vokari tongue, Nukapana spoke, his words slow and weighty. Shayne stood at the edge of the circle next to Cartwright and Varn, whispering a rough translation under his breath.

"He says this is the Way of Fire... the Rite of Strength," Shayne murmured. "That this isn't war. It's tradition. One soul standing before the flames to be measured."

Matthew stepped into the ring. His boots crunched softly in the packed earth. Koro's gaze tracked his every step like a lion watching a rival enter its territory.

Koro spoke now, voice deep and unwavering, but not cruel. A ritual tone.

Shayne translated again. "He offers himself as the tribe's hand. Their sword. He says... 'if your spirit is true, you will endure me. If not, the jungle will bury your bones.'"

The villagers did not cheer or jeer. This was not entertainment. It was sacred.

Chief Nukapana turned to Matthew now. "You fight. No kill. Win by strength, not death."

Then, slowly, "You want leave now... you can."

The world seemed to pause. A test. An exit.

Matthew looked down at the ground, his thoughts a storm—but when he looked up again, his eyes were clear.

"No," he said. "I'll earn your respect. Not by running."

Behind him, Kaia had emerged from the healer's hut with the help of one of the younger villagers. Her hand rested on the doorway for support, but her eyes were locked on Matthew.

Dr. Varn turned and saw her. "You shouldn't be up," she whispered.

Kaia didn't look away. "If he's risking himself for us... then I'm not lying in bed."

Inside the circle, Koro bowed his head slightly— not mockery, but acknowledgement.

The chief nodded once, approving. Then he raised his hand and shouted a single word in Vokari.

The crowd responded in unison with a booming, haunting chant—low, rising, rhythmic.

The duel had been accepted.

*The first drum thundered like a heartbeat. A column of smoke rose above the village as the final preparations began.*

———

The air inside the ceremonial hut was thick with the scent of herbs and burning resin. Faint rays of light pierced through the gaps in the woven ceiling, illuminating motes of dust that danced like spirits above the ground.

Matthew sat cross-legged on a fur-covered platform, stripped to the waist. His chest rose and fell steadily, but his hands trembled in his lap.

Two Vokari men entered quietly and knelt beside him. One held a shallow stone bowl filled with a dark green paste, the other a folded cloth soaked in water. Neither spoke. One dipped the cloth and began wiping the dirt and dried blood from Matthew's arms, face, and chest with deliberate care. The other prepared the paint.

Shia stepped through the curtain at the back of the hut and approached like a whisper. Her face was already painted with bone-white lines and spirals, her long hair woven with feathers and shells that rattled softly as she moved. She crouched in front of Matthew, her eyes sharp but distant—as if she were only partially here.

"You feel fear," she said simply.

Matthew nodded. "I'd be stupid not to."

A thin smile tugged at her lips. "Good. Fear is not weakness. It is the fire before the storm."

She dipped two fingers into the green paste and began to draw markings across his body—slow, precise strokes across his biceps, collarbones, and chest.

She murmured softly as she worked, half in Vokari, half in English:

"This... is strength."

A curved line across his right arm.

"This... is renewal."

A broken circle over his left shoulder.

"And this..."

She pressed a flame symbol in the center of his chest, just over his heart.

"This is truth."

Matthew looked down at the marks. They felt less like war paint and more like armor—not of the body, but of the spirit.

"Why truth?" he asked quietly.

Shia tilted her head. "Because truth is what breaks bone and bends fate. You carry it in your heart. Now you show it in your skin."

There was a moment of stillness. The noise outside the hut had faded into a rhythmic thrum of drums and chanting.

From the entry flap, a shadow appeared. Kaia.

She leaned on the support of a young villager, her movements slow, but her eyes burning with intent. Dr. Varn followed just behind, arms folded, trying to dissuade her with quiet warnings. But Kaia stepped inside anyway.

"Matthew..." she said, her voice raspy but strong. "You don't have to do this."

He turned to face her. "I already did."

"I just got you back," she whispered, voice breaking. "Don't make me lose you now."

Matthew stood, paint still wet on his chest, and crossed to her. He gently took her hand.

"I'm not doing this to win anything," he said. "I'm doing this because if we want a chance here—a real chance—then someone has to prove we're not like him."

Kaia's eyes welled, and she pressed her forehead against his.

Dr. Varn gently stepped forward. "If you love him," she said to Kaia, "then trust him to finish what he started."

Kaia didn't answer. She just held Matthew's hand a second longer before letting it go.

Shis stepped forward again, lifting a ceremonial headband woven from bark and beads. She placed it on Matthew's brow, tying it tightly behind his head.

"You are ready," she said. "When the fire calls, you step forward."

Matthew turned toward the flap of the tent.

*Outside, the drumbeat grew louder—not just a sound, but a pulse. Like the island itself was waiting.*

—

The jungle was silent.

Even the birds seemed to sense the weight pressing down over the Vokari village. The chanting had stopped. All that remained was the deep, steady thrum of the ceremonial drums—slow, willful, echoing like thunder through the valley.

Matthew stepped out of the hut, the soft dirt warm beneath his feet. His skin still tingled with the drying paint, the symbols etched into his flesh now feeling less like decoration and more like a vow.

The crowd parted for him in solemn silence.

Ahead, the ritual circle lay open, ringed by spears, fire pits, and watching eyes. Smoke curled into the sky from the corners of the arena, carrying with it a strange mix of sage, bone ash, and something unplaceably ancient.

Koro was already there, bare-chested, standing at the far end of the circle. His muscles were tight with readiness, but his face showed no emotion. Not arrogance. Not anger. Only the calm certainty of a man who had lived his life in battle and never once doubted its necessity.

In his hands, he held two blunted ceremonial staves, both wrapped in animal hide and etched with runic patterns. He set one gently on the ground, keeping the other.

Shia stepped into the circle, her arms raised. In her hands, she held a bundle of dark feathers and a smoldering branch. She circled the arena's edge, chanting softly, casting smoke across the dirt floor. As she passed answering her incantation.

Then she turned and pointed her staff at the center.

Koro stepped in first, his bare feet silent as a cat's. He gave a small bow—precise and formal.

Matthew followed. The heat of the fires licked at his skin. When he entered the ring, he bowed in turn, mimicking Koro's motion. No words. Just respect.

Chief Nukapana stood at the edge of the circle, flanked by elders.

"This is not fight for anger," he said in his rough English. "This is fight for truth. Blood is not price—it is witness."

A silence fell.

Then he raised his hand... and dropped it.

The drums stopped.

Koro moved first—a blur of muscle and fury.

His staff came in low, sweeping Matthew's legs. Matthew jumped—not quite in time. The strike clipped his shin, sending him stumbling backward.

He caught himself, heart pounding.

Koro pressed forward, striking again—this time a downward blow that Matthew barely blocked with his forearm. The impact numbed his wrist instantly.

The crowd remained silent, unmoving, like statues watching gods at war.

Matthew shifted, circling, remembering how Clark once told him to think ahead of a problem—not react, but anticipate. He tried. Looked for openings. But Koro's form was tight, practiced. No wasted movement.

Another strike—this time a feint left before crashing from the right. Matthew took it across the ribs. He gasped, pain blooming hot and sharp.

From the edge of the circle, Shayne muttered, "He's not fighting to win... he's fighting to endure."

Kaia gripped the edge of a woven pole for balance, eyes wide, lips trembling, she didn't blink.

Matthew rolled away from the next hit, landing hard on his shoulder. Sand flew into his mouth. He spat, coughing, rising again—slower now.

Koro waited.

No jeers. No mockery. Only challenge.

The paint on Matthew's chest had begun to run with sweat, the flame symbol smudged but still visible. He steadied his breath. Thought of Kaia. Of Bryce. Of Megan.

*"To lead, you must first endure,"* echoed Clark's voice in his memory.

He stood straight again. Blood ran from his lip. His left arm hung lower. But he raised his staff—and motioned for Koro to come again.

*Somewhere beyond the ring, a hawk cried out—a sharp, echoing sound—as the second round began.*

—

The hawk's cry faded into silence, but its sharpness seemed to echo inside Matthew's chest.

Koro circled him now, more slowly. The warrior's brow furrowed, just slightly—not out of frustration, but curiosity. Matthew was still standing. Bleeding, bruised, trembling—but standing.

The fires surrounding the arena crackled louder now, stirred by a sudden gust of wind that sent smoke curling inward, momentarily obscuring their faces. For a moment, the crowd vanished into shadow. Only the two of them remained, shaped in the haze.

Then Koro moved again—faster this time. He came in with a feint high and a low thrust toward Matthew's gut.

But Matthew had learned.

He spun with the blow, letting it graze past him, and brought his staff around hard into Koro's side. The thud was solid—flesh and bone yielding for the first time.

The crowd murmured.

Koro staggered two steps.

Matthew didn't pause. He pressed forward with a new rhythm—not trying to overpower, but to outmaneuver. He ducked under a swing, jabbed with both ends of the staff in rapid succession—a strike to the thigh, then should, then backpedaled just before Koro could retaliate.

Sweat poured down his face. Every breath burned.

But something had shifted.

Koro's attacks grew less precise. He favored his left leg now—a barely perceptible limp. Matthew caught it, remembered it. An old injury, maybe.

He aimed for it.

Another strike landed, knocking Koro's stance off balance. A ripple of movement passed through the villagers. Shia, at the edge, lowered her head in solemn approval.

Matthew's arms trembled from effort, but he held on, pushing his advantage. With a sudden roar, he swept low—knocking Koro's weakened leg out from under him. The warrior fell hard onto one knee, staff flying from his hands.

A silence dropped like a curtain.

Matthew stood over him now, battered but upright, the ceremonial staff raised in both hands. One more strike, and it would be over.

He looked down.

Koro stared back, chest heaving, lips tight. He didn't plead. He didn't flinch. He waited.

This was the moment the crowd had come to see.

Matthew's grip tightened...

...and then he let the staff fall.

Not as a weapon—but to the dirt.

The clatter rang out like a bell.

Matthew stepped back and extended his hand to Koro.

Gasps rippled through the tribe.
Even Nukapana raised an eyebrow.

Koro looked up at him, sweat running down his painted face. His eyes searched Matthew's—and whatever he found there, it was enough.

Slowly, he reached out... and accepted the hand.

Matthew pulled him to his feet.

The two men stood face to face, breathless, bodies broken but standing.

*Around them, the silence cracked—not applause, but with reverence, as the people began to chant a single word in unison:*

*"Mató... Mató... Mató..."*

—

The chanting grew louder.

**"Mató... Mató... Mató..."**

It reverberated from the trees, from the huts, from the mouths of every Vokari elder, warrior, and child watching the circle. The name had no direct translation— not in English—but the meaning was clear in their voices.

It meant **the one who endures.**

The one who chooses mercy over conquest.

Matthew stood, dizzy with exhaustion, his hand still clasped in Koro's

Then Koro turned to face the crowd, lifted Matthew's arm high in the air, and let out a fierce cry in Vokari.

The tribe erupted into a chorus of howls and claps, not like a crowd celebrating a victor—but like a family welcoming a long-lost son.

Shia stepped forward, her feathers swaying as she entered the circle. She placed a palm gently on Matthew's chest, directly over the smudged flame symbol.

"You burn bright," she whispered.

Then she turned to Chief Nukapana and gave a solemn nod.

The chief stepped into the ring.

He looked first to Koro, who bowed low, fists to the earth—a formal submission. Then he looked at Matthew.

"You fight... not for pride," Nukapana said slowly, his voice carrying across the circle. "Not for blood. You fight for spirit. For truth."

He placed a hand on Matthew's shoulder. "You are now **Friend of Flame.** Tribe see you. Island see you."

The crowd repeated it softly: "Friend of Flame... Friend of Flame..."

Kaia, pale but upright, pushed through the wall of villagers with Cartwright's help. She reached Matthew just as the crowd began to disperse around them.

He turned to her—battered, sweat-drenched, blood trickling from his temple.

"I'm okay," he said softly.

She didn't say anything at first. Just threw her arms around him and buried her face in his chest.

"You didn't just save me," she whispered. "You saved all of us."

Behind them, Avara gently pressed her forehead to Shayne's, whispering, *"He walks in the heart now. He is one of us."*

Cartwright stood off to the side, arms folded, watching the scene with a strange, quiet pride.

Dr. Varn leaned over to him and said, "He's not just a student anymore, is he?"

Cartwright shook his head. "He's something else now."

*As the torches blazed into the night and the tribe began a feast in celebration, Matthew stood at the heart of the fire circle—not as an outside, not as a leader—but as* **one of them.**

—

The celebration roared behind them—drums, laughter, the scent of roasted meat rising with the night breeze—but Matthew had slipped away.

He sat at the edge of the village, near the ceremonial fire pit now glowing low with orange embers. The jungle whispered beyond, thick with the sounds of crickets and distant calls. He leaned back, elbows in the grass, breathing in the quiet.

His body ached in a dozen places, but the pain no longer felt like punishment. It felt... earned.

Kaia appeared beside him, barefoot, moving softly through the dark.

"You always this dramatic?" she asked gently, folding herself beside him.

He smirked without turning. "Only when a girl almost dies and a tribe almost exiles me in the same week."

They sat together for a long moment in silence, watching the embers rise toward the canopy.

Kaia spoke first. "You didn't just survive out there. You changed them."

Matthew turned to her. "I didn't want to. I just... had to."

She looked at him now, her face lit by the fading firelight—soft and full of something she hadn't shown before.

"Back at school, I always knew you had something in you," she said. "Something that wasn't about grades or fieldwork or impressing Clark. Something real. And today... I saw it."

He met her gaze.

"I've wanted to say this since before the crash," she whispered. "I love you, Matthew."

The words were quiet, but they hit harder than any blow he'd taken that day.

He sat upright, heart thudding in a new way now—and leaned closer.

"I love you too," he said, his voice almost a breath. "I think I always have."

Their lips met—not with urgency, but with something deeper. Something earned. The fire crackled beside them as the stars blinked above the canopy.

When they finally pulled apart, she leaned her head on his shoulder, and they simply sat—the sounds of the jungle surrounding them like a lullaby.

*For the first time since the crash, the fire didn't feel like survival—it felt like home.*

# Chapter 28  A Light in the Dark

The first light of morning crept gently over
the Vokari village, bathing the woven huts and jungle trees
in a golden warmth. A soft breeze stirred the smoke trails
from last night's scents of ash, flowers, and something
herbal and sweet.

Matthew stirred, eyes blinking open to a woven
ceiling above him. For a moment, he didn't move—just
laid still, breathing, listening. No screams. No monsters.
No death. Just birds chirping and the rhythmic rustling of
palm fronds.

He turned his head.

Kaia was sitting upright on a mat beside him,
wrapped in a light cloth that the healer had draped over
her shoulders. Her hair was loosely tied back, and she
sipped from a small clay bowl filled with a steaming herbal
concoction. Her skin still looked pale, but there was color
returning to her cheeks—and life in her eyes.

"You're awake," she said with a faint smile.

"You're sitting up," he replied, half-smiling back as he pushed himself up to his elbows.

She leaned toward him, her voice hushed. "And you're still ugly."

He gave a breathy laugh, wincing slightly as the bruises from the fight with Koro
reminded him, they weren't just a bad dream. "Guess I should've ducked more."

"Guess you should've died less," she murmured, setting the bowl down beside her. Then, more seriously: "You didn't have to fight him, you know."

He shook his head. "Yes, I did. For you. For all of us."

They sat in silence for a moment, the intimacy of the stillness settling between them. Kaia reached over and took his hand in hers. Her fingers were warm and trembling slightly—not from fear, but from recovery. From coming back to life.

"I heard your voice," she whispered. "When I was out. I heard you say my name."

Matthew nodded, his eyes softening. "I thought I lost you."

"You almost did," she replied, then smiled faintly. "But you're stubborn. That's why I'm still here."

He brushed a thumb gently across her knuckles. "No. You're still here because you're stronger than anything on this island."

Kaia tilted her head, eyes searching his. "Do you really believe that?"

"I do," he said.

They leaned toward each other, and their lips met again—slower this time, not rushed by panic or survival. It was tender. Sure. Quietly full of everything they didn't yet know how to say.

When they pulled apart, Kaia exhaled and rested her head on his shoulder.

"I don't know how long we'll get this peace," she said. "But I want to hold onto it for as long as we can."

Matthew looked past her toward the rising sun over the treetops. Somewhere out there, danger still waited. But here, for now, she was warm beside him, and the world was still.

"So do I," he whispered.

* * *

The village had changed.

Where once the Vokari watched with narrowed eyes and hands near weapons, now they glanced curiously at Matthew and Kaia as the two emerged from the healer's hut. Morning sunlight filtered through hanging vines and thatched rooftops, casting long shadows that danced across the ground.

Children darted between huts, laughing as they chased each other with wooden carvings of birds and beasts. One small girl, Luma, paused at the sight of Kaia. Her bright eyes widened with delight, and she tiptoed forward, holding out a small charm woven from grass and bone beads.

Kaia knelt with effort, accepting it with both hands. "Is this for me?" she asked gently.

Luma gave a shy nod and whispered, "You came back."

Kaia blinked, touched, and smiled warmly. "Thanks to all of you."

As the child scampered away, Matthew noticed Koro leaning against one of the support beams near the training circle, his arm in a sling and a wide bruise darkening the side of his face. The warrior's expression was unreadable—until Matthew caught his eye.

A beat passed.

Then Koro gave a single, respectful nod before limping away.

Matthew stood there for a moment, unsure what that nod meant—acceptance, perhaps. Or a truce. Either way, it was more than he'd expected.

"You're making friends," Kaia said beside him, smirking.

"I'd prefer the ones who don't want to kill me."

From the side, a voice called out. 'Fisher!"

It was Shayne, seated cross-legged under a shade canopy with Avara beside him. His long hair was tied back with a leather cord, and his Vokari writing, clearly mid-lesson.

"Check it out," he grinned, pointing to his chest where the symbols spelled out what he claimed was his name.

Avara leaned in and whispered something in Vokari, laughing softly. Shayne turned pink. "Okay, maybe not my name. But I'm getting there."

Matthew chuckled and approached them. "Making progress?"

"Learning faster than I did in Spanish class," Shayne said. "Turns out fear of getting skewered really boosts language retention."

Avara stood and gave Matthew a respectful bow. "You fight with heart," she said in careful English. "Koro says... he sees honor in you now."

Matthew raised his brows. "He said that?"

She smirked. "He grunted. But I speak grunt."

Kaia leaned on Matthew's shoulder, chuckling as the lighthearted energy returned to the group. For the first time since the shipwreck, there was laughter that didn't feel forced.

Then the drums sounded.

Not loud. Not a war call—but a steady rhythm that echoed across the village. Tribe members gathered near the central fire where Chief Nukapana stood, his arms crossed over his broad chest, his long, grey-streaked hair flowing in the wind.

Matthew and the others stepped forward as the chief addressed the tribe in Vokari first, his voice steady and commanding.

Shayne translated quietly under his breath, just enough for the group to follow:

"He says the spirits have watched. They've seen outsiders fight for life, not take it. He says... we are not the same as Helix."

Matthew's gaze sharpened at the name.

Nukapana then switched to broken English, looking directly at Matthew.

"You... not like him," he said. "You bleed for others. You choose no power. This... good."

The tribe murmured. Some clapped hands to chests in agreement. A few still looked uncertain.

"You and yours," Nukapana continued, "may stay. But listen: bring no lies. No weapons for power. Or we end what you bring."

Matthew bowed his head. "You have my word."

Nukapana stared for a long moment before giving a solemn nod.

The drums ended.

Peace—fragile and earned—had settled over the village.

But peace, on this island, never stayed for long.

* * *

The late morning sun filtered through the trees at the edge of the Vokari village, where the jungle began again—wild, deep, unknowable. Matthew stood with a spear in hand; one the tribe had given him after the ceremony. He wasn't training with it, just holding it... getting used to the weight. The idea of needing it again was no longer hypothetical.

Behind him, the village hummed with cautious warmth—Kaia resting under the healer's canopy, Shayne still teasing Avara, and children mimicking Koro's training stances with playful grunts and imaginary bruises.

Footsteps approached from behind.

"You look like a man thinking too much," Captain Cartwright muttered, his voice low and gravelly.

Matthew turned. "Probably because I am."

Cartwright folded his arms. His shirt was sweat-streaked, and a crude Vokari blade was now strapped to his belt—a quiet admission of how quickly he'd adapted to survival. "You did good yesterday. Kaia's alive. The tribe isn't sharpening spears at our throats anymore."

Matthew nodded. "Feels like a win. I just don't know how long it'll last."

Cartwright glanced into the trees. "It won't. Not unless we do something about the rest of our people."

Matthew followed his gaze. "You think they're still out there?"

The captain's jaw tightened. "Adam? Maybe. Grent? Unfortunately, I'd bet money he's still breathing.

Jules... Megan..." He trailed off, then shook his head. "I don't like not knowing. And I sure as hell don't like waiting."

Matthew lowered the spear, fingers tightening around it. "Kaia's still recovering. She's better, but not ready to move again. I want to wait at least one more day before heading out."

Cartwright didn't argue—not yet. He just studied the boy in front of him, who had somehow become more of a man since the crash. "You care about her."

"I love her," Matthew said, no hesitation in his voice now.

Cartwright raised a brow, then gave a quiet grunt that might've been approval.

"Then here's the truth," the captain said. "You got maybe twenty-four hours. After that, I'm going into that jungle, with or without you."

Matthew nodded. "You won't go without me."

Cartwright finally allowed himself a small smirk. "Didn't think I would."

A moment of silence passed between them, not awkward—just heavy with mutual respect.

"Listen," Cartwright said more quietly. "What we've got here? This moment of calm? It's not real. It's just the island catching its breath. And when it exhales..." He gestured toward the jungle. "We better be ready to move."

Matthew looked toward the tree line—toward whatever was still out there.

"I will be," he said.

*  *  *

The jungle was a wall of green, thick and unrelenting. Every branch seemed to claw at their arms, every root eager to trip them. The heat was heavier here, pressing down on Adam's shoulders like a warning.

They hadn't spoken in over an hour.

Grent led the way, hunting knife in hand, hacking at the undergrowth with short, brutal swings. His shirt clung to his back with sweat, and his breathing was steady—too steady for someone who'd been walking this long.

Adam followed behind, less certain, constantly glancing over his shoulder as if Megan might suddenly appear.

But she wouldn't.

His stomach twisted at the memory of her scream—distant, panicked, and gone too quickly. He hadn't said it aloud, but he knew something wasn't right. He'd questioned Grent three times. Gotten vague, evasive answers every time.

And still, he followed.

"We're close," Grent muttered without turning around.

Adam wiped sweat from his brow. "You keep saying that."

"This time I mean it," Grent said. "Smokes in the air. You smell it?"

Adam sniffed—and he did. Faint, but there. A thin trace of campfires carried on the breeze.

His heart jumped. Maybe it was the others. Maybe Kaia was okay. Maybe they had found shelter. Maybe—

A rustle.

Adam's head snapped left. He stopped walking.

"Grent—"

Grent had already raised his knife, eyes scanning the foliage.

The jungle around them went silent. No birds. No insects. Nothing.

Then—movement.

A blur shot from the trees. Adam cried out as a figure tackled him from the side, knocking him flat on his back. Another dropped down from the canopy, landing on Grent like a shadow with a spear in hand.

"AMBUSH!" Grent roared, swinging wildly. His blade caught one attacker in the shoulder, but it didn't stop them—not completely. More emerged.
Silent. Coordinated.

Vokari scouts.

Adam's arms were pinned. A sharp point pressed against his throat. He shouted, "WAIT! We're not enemies! Please!"

Grent fought like a beast, snarling, fists bloody— but it was useless. There were too many. One scout clubbed him hard across the temple. He hit the ground with a grunt and didn't get up.

Adam twisted to look at him—chest rising, unconscious but alive.

The scouts spoke to each other in clipped, urgent Vokari. One bound Adam's wrists. Another checked Grent for weapons and pulled the knife and pistol away.

Adam didn't resist. Not now.

"We were just trying to find our friends," he muttered, mostly to himself. "We didn't mean harm..."

But no one responded.

They were lifted roughly to their feet—Grent slumped between two warriors—and forced into a quick march.

Adam caught glimpses as they moved: faded symbols carved into trees, woven charms hanging from branches, the smell of smoke growing stronger.

They were being taken somewhere.

Somewhere important.

And if they were lucky... maybe familiar.

* * *

The midday sun hung high over the Vokari village when the scouts returned—and they did not come alone.

Matthew and Kaia were seated near the central fire pit when the first voices echoed through the trees. The warriors standing watch gave a shout. Moments later, the gates parted.

A line of Vokari scouts marched into the village clearing, weapons raised.

Between them were two men—Adam Nolan, wrists bound but walking upright, face bruised and wide-eyed with disbelief. And behind him, slumped between two warriors, blood drying on the side of his head, was Silas Grent.

Kaia stood abruptly. "Adam?"

Matthew was already moving.

Adam's eyes locked onto to hers. "Kaia!" Relief flooded his voice. "You're—You're alive!"

He barely had time to take a step before Koro stormed into the square, pushing past others with a snarl.

"No!" Koro barked. "Not him! That one—" he jabbed a finger toward Grent "—stinks of the other. Of Helix."

The gathered villagers murmured. Weapons were raised. A few shouts followed in Vokari. Fear and fury surged around them like fire catching dry grass.

The scouts dropped Grent to the ground. He groaned and blinked, then smiled through cracked lips as he looked up at the crowd.

"Home sweet home," he muttered.

Chief Nukapana stepped forward, his expression stone.

Kaia grabbed Matthew's arm, her voice urgent. "You have to do something. They'll kill them."

Matthew stepped between Koro and the bound men.

"Wait!" he shouted, hands up. "They're with us. Adam is one of us—he's, my cousin. And Grent..." He hesitated.

Gent met his gaze, bloody and calm. Waiting.

Matthew exhaled. "Grent may not be a good man. But he helped us survive after the crash. If you punish him, you punish us too."

"You trust his one?" Nukapana asked in his broken English, eyes narrowing.

"No," Matthew said plainly. "But I take responsibility for him. Both of them."

The chief studied him. Behind him, Koro was shaking his head, fists clenched.

"You speak for this danger?" Nukapana asked again.

Matthew swallowed, feeling the weight settle in his chest. "I do."

A long silence followed. Finally, Nukapana raised his hand.

"Then you carry his burden," the chief said. "If he brings harm, it is your word that will burn with it."

Matthew nodded solemnly.

The chief gestured, and two warriors lifted Grent, dragging him toward a guarded hut on the far edge of the village. Grent laughed softly as they pulled him away.

Adam stepped forward shakily, his group rushed to his side. They all embraced.

We thought you were dead," Matthew whispered.

"Is M-Megan here?" Adam asked quietly.

"No we are it, was she with you?" Matthew muttered.

"She was but Grent said the tribe took her." Adam murmured.

As the villagers dispersed, Koro lingered by the fire pit, staring at him.

"You vouch for devils now," the warrior said, quiet but sharp.

Matthew looked back at him. "I vouch for family."

Koro walked away without a word.

*As Grent was dragged into the shadows, his crooked smile still stretched across his face, Matthew felt the weight of every decision pressing down—and wondered if trusting a monster, even out of necessity, would come back to devour them all.*

# Chapter 29  Buried Truths

The fire crackled low in the heart of the Vokari village, its light casting flickers across Adam's face as he sat hunched forward, elbows on his knees, staring into the flames.

Around him, the tribe moved with quiet purpose—children gathering water, warriors sharpening spears, villagers preparing food in woven baskets. But to Adam, it all blurred into static. Just motion. Just noise.

She was gone.

He clenched his jaw.

Megan should've been here—complaining about the heat, making sarcastic remarks about the food, or asking Kaia if she had a signal bar just for the hell of it. Instead, there was just this... emptiness.

He hadn't told anyone what he saw that night. Not the scream. Not Grent's cold reaction. Not the growing feeling in his chest that something was terribly wrong.

A soft voice broke the silence. "Adam?"

He turned. Kaia stood a few feet away, hair tied loosely back, still pale but recovering steadily. She wore a concerned look, eyes already reading too much.

"Can I sit?" she asked gently.

He nodded, and she lowered herself beside him, wrapping her arms around her knees.

"You haven't said much since you got here," she said after a pause.

"I haven't had much to say."

Kaia watched the fire with him. "I heard you three got separated after the attack."

Adam nodded. "Yeah. Me and Megan ran into Grent afterwards."

She waited, giving him space.

"We were looking for shelter," he said, voice low. "It got dark fast. We were so exhausted. Megan... she started complaining. Said she needed to pee. Walked off into the trees. Then I heard her scream."

Kaia's head turned sharply toward him. "What happened?"

"I ran after her. I yelled her name... but she was gone." His voice cracked slightly. "Grent said she must've been taken. But..."

He trailed off.

"But what?"

Adam shook his head. "It doesn't make sense. There was no sign of a struggle. No blood. No footprints. Just... silence. And the way Grent looked at me after..."

He didn't finish the sentence.

Kaia placed a hand gently on his knee. "Do you think he lied?"

Adam's jaw tensed again. "I don't know what I think. I just know something's wrong."

She nodded slowly.

"When you're ready... we'll help you find out."

Adam looked over at her, grateful—but still hollow inside. He wasn't ready to accuse Grent.

Not yet.

Not until he knew.

*　*　*

Dr, Emilia Varn sat just outside her hut, notebook open across her lap, pen tapping rhythmically against her knee. Her eyes weren't on the page though—they were fixed on Silas Grent.

He sat near the edge of the village under guard, wrists still loosely bound, a spear planted in the dirt beside him. The two Vokari warriors watching him never looked away—but Grent didn't seem to mind. He sat calmly, almost serenely, as if resting in a garden instead of being detained in the heart of an unforgiving jungle.

Emilia scribbled a note:

*Calm under duress. No visible anxiety. No efforts to negotiate or manipulate. Yet carries a presence that suggests control, not submission. Classic signs of sociopathic conditioning—possibly trauma-adapted.*

She looked up again.

He caught her staring.

Grent smiled. Just slightly. Just enough.

She didn't flinch—but her pen paused.

There had always been something off about him. She had dismissed it back on the yacht as military rigidity. Quiet type. Watchful. Stern. But she remembered the way he stood near Clark... no, Helix—always slightly behind, always silent, but always aware.

Another note:

*No one watches that closely unless they've been trained to. Or unless they're part of something deeper.*

Her mind flashed back to the yacht—a quick moment. Clark had been speaking to the group during the first dinner, raising his glass in a toast. Emilia had turned just slightly and caught Grent looking at Clark. Not with admiration. Not even subordination.

With understanding.

It wasn't a glance between a professor and hired security. It was a look between co-conspirators.

She hadn't questioned it then. But now...

Grent looked away, as if bored, and leaned back against the post behind him. One of the Vokari guards nudged him with a spear and barked something. Grent raised both hands in mock surrender, smirking again. The gesture was relaxed—almost friendly.

It unsettled her more than any outburst would have.

Emilia flipped to a new page and wrote slowly:

*Grent and Helix were connected before this trip. Unclear if he was executor, protector, or handler—but he's not just a mercenary. He's something else. And if Clark is truly Helix... this entire trip was engineered long before it began.*

She set the notebook aside, eyes narrowing.

She didn't know what Helix wanted. Not yet. But she was certain of one thing now.

Grent wasn't just a threat. He was part of the foundation the danger was built on.

* * *

The sun had begun its slow descent behind the jungle canopy, turning the sky shades of gold and violet as Shayne Wood followed Avara up a narrow trail that overlooked the village. She moved with quiet purpose, each step light and deliberate, as if she knew every rock, every branch, every shift in the wind.

Shayne, ever the outsider, stumbled a little but kept pace.

They reached a small ridge dotted with moss-covered stones and sat in silence for a moment, overlooking the valley below.

"It's beautiful," Shayne said softly.

Avara didn't respond right away. Her eyes were distant, watching smoke trails rise from the village hearths.

"You asked about Helix," she said at last.

Shayne turned toward her, nodding. "You don't have to talk about him if it hurts."

"No" she replied, gaze still forward. "You should know."

She took a breath, her voice steady but low.

"When I was younger... he came to us. Not him at first—his people. They wore white. They spoke in strange tongues. They said they brought peace. Gifts. Medicine."

Her fingers traced the edge of a carved stone beside her, the motion slow and absent.

"They took my father, my brother, and me. We were separated. I didn't know why. I didn't understand the machines, the lights, the pain."

Shayne's breath hitched. "They experimented on you?"

She nodded. "They wanted to know what made us different. Why we survived this island. Why the jungle didn't kill us." Her lips tightened. "But it wasn't about knowledge. It was control. Curiosity without heart."

Shayne leaned closer. "How did you escape?"

"My father and I fought. We escaped through the tunnels when the fire broke out. My brother…" Her voice caught. "He was too weak. They had done too much to him. He died inside that place."

Silence stretched between them like a taut wire.

"I'm so sorry, Avara," Shayne said, reaching out. His hand found hers, and she didn't pull away.

"You didn't do it," she whispered.

"No," he said. "But I'm part of the world that did."

Avara turned toward him finally, her dark eyes soft but strong. "You're not like them. You ask. You listen. You care."

Shayne swallowed the lump in his throat. "You're the strongest person I've ever met."

A moment passed. Then she leaned in and kissed him—not rushed, not desperate, but firm and certain.

When they parted, she touched her forehead to his.

"Stay," she whispered.

Shayne closed his eyes and held her hand tighter. "I'm not going anywhere."

* * *

With the jungle quieting down. Dusk painted the sky in smoky blues and burnt oranges, and the rhythmic sounds of village life gave way to the low crackle of fire and the occasional snap of branches far off in the trees.

Matthew Fisher sat near the outer fire pit with Captain Lee Cartwright, a small flickering flame between them. Around them, the village prepared for nightfall   but the air held a sense of calm that felt more like a pause than peace.

Cartwright leaned forward, poking the fire with a stick. "You ever think you'd end up here, kid?"

Matthew cracked a dry smile. "Not once. Not even in the weirdest dreams."

Cartwright grunted. "Funny thing is, I think you were always meant to."

Matthew glanced at him. "What do you mean?"

"You've held this group together longer than I thought possible. You earned the tribe's respect. You've made choices—hard ones—and you're still standing. You've got that look now... the one people follow."

Matthew didn't respond. He just stared into the flames.

After a long pause, Cartwright said, "We need to start thinking about the next move. Can't stay in one place too long—not with that bastard Helix still out there."

Matthew nodded slowly. "There's someone else we still haven't found. Jules."

Cartwright grimaced. "Yeah... him."

"I don't know if he's alive," Matthew admitted. "But if he is, we owe it to him to try."

Cartwright tossed the stick into the fire. "And if he's not, we still need to know. One way or the other,"

Matthew looked up. "Helix has to have a base here. A lab, a bunker, something. There's too much control, too much intent behind this island. He didn't build this overnight."

Cartwright leaned back, hands on his knees. "You said you saw his symbol after the crash."

Matthew nodded. "The double helix. Half-buried on a crate near the wreck. It's real. His work is here—and I think the answers are, too."

The captain's eyes narrowed. "You think he's still watching us?"

"I think he's been watching all along," Matthew replied. "Testing us. Testing me."

Cartwright shook his head. "Then we go to him. Find out what the hell he wants. And we end it."

Matthew looked toward the darkening jungle.

"Tomorrow," he said. "We rest tonight. But tomorrow... we begin again."

*  *  *

The fire had died down, casting long shadows across the village as the Vokari slipped into sleep. Only a few guards remained at their posts, spears in hand, eyes glowing in the dark like stone statues.

Inside one of the huts, Matthew Fisher slept fitfully.

His brow twitched. His fingers curled.

And then, the jungle faded.

—

He was standing in a long, dim corridor—metallic, humming, and impossibly clean. The floors gleamed under his feet. Rows of sealed glass tanks lined the walls; each filled with a pale green fluid. Shapes floated inside— some animal, some... not.

A footstep echoed behind him.

Matthew turned.

At the end of the hall stood Professor Clark, dressed sharply in a white, hands folded behind his back. The smile on his face was warm, almost fatherly.

"Matthew," Clark said, stepping toward him. "You're finally starting to see it, aren't you?"

Matthew looked around warily. "What is this place?

Clark gestured to the tanks. "This is possibility. Legacy. The future that others were too frightened to embrace."

A tank beside them flickered to life—a floating form inside, humanoid but not human. Its limbs were too long, its eyes glowing faintly red.

"You're not just surviving anymore," Clark continued. "You're becoming something more. A leader. A force. Just like I hoped."

Matthew took a cautious step forward. "Why are you showing me this?"

Clark's voice softened. "Because I need you to understand. The island isn't chaos, Matthew. It's order. It's evolution, set free from the small-minded hands of politicians and fearful fools. But not everyone deserves to shape it."

Suddenly, the corridor shifted—swallowed by a rush of wind and vines. The jungle returned, but twisted, dreamlike. At its center, on the moss-covered ground, lay Megan.

Still.

Broken.

Her necklace missing.

Matthew's breath caught. He staggered forward but couldn't move fast enough. His voice cracked. "No... no, that can't be—"

Clark appeared beside him again, calm as ever. "She was a variable. An unplanned one."

Matthew turned on him. "You said this was about possibility. About purpose."

Clark's smile faded. "Possibility comes with sacrifice. Purpose demands it."

And then—behind them—a massive vault door sealed shut with a deep metallic clang. Embossed on its surface: a symbol. Two twisting strands of a double helix. No name. Just the mark.

Matthew stepped toward it, instinctively drawn to what was hidden beyond. But vines erupted from the ground, pulling everything into blackness.

—

He awoke with a sharp breath, heart pounding in his chest. The shadows in the hut loomed larger than they had the night before. He sat up, wiping sweat from his brow, his mind spinning.

Professor Clark's voice still echoed in his skull.

*"Possibility comes with sacrifice."*

And somewhere in that dream—in the space between memory and madness—he had seen a truth he couldn't unsee.

*Somewhere out there, something was waiting—and Matthew knew that whatever was behind the Helixis symbol, it wasn't done with them yet.*

# Chapter 30  Love and Loss

The morning sun rose slowly over the Vokari village, casting long golden streaks through the towering trees. Smoke drifted lazily from a cooking fire, the smell of roasted roots and jungle herbs wafting gently through the air. Birds called overhead, but their song felt too cheerful for what weighed on Adam Nolan's chest.

He stood near the edge of the village, arms crossed, staring toward the tree line. His jaw was tight. Eyes bloodshot. He hadn't slept.

Behind him, villagers moved about their daily tasks—cleaning hides, sharpening spears, tending to woven baskets—but Adam couldn't hear any of it. His mind was replaying her scream. Over and over.

Finally, he turned and walked with purpose across the clearing.

He found Matthew Fisher kneeling beside a pile of supplies, repacking their dwindling rations. Captain

Cartwright stood nearby, speaking quietly to a young warrior about repairing the spears they'd borrowed. When Adam approached, both men looked up.

Matthew's expression shifted immediately. "You okay?"

Adam's voice was low. "We need to talk. Now. Somewhere quiet."

Cartwright nodded, already reading the tension. "Come on. Let's take a walk."

—

They moved down a short path just beyond the huts, far enough that the villagers couldn't overhear. A few steps into the shaded trail, Adam stopped and turned.

"I need to say this out loud, and I don't want anyone else hearing it."

Matthew and Cartwright waited.

Adam glanced behind them, then took a breath. "Grent's lying. About what happened to Megan."

Cartwright stiffened. Matthew's brows pulled together. "What do you mean?"

"I told you she screamed and disappeared. But that's not all." Adam's voice cracked. "I heard her scream *twice*. I went looking for her. I thought it was the tribe. That maybe they grabbed her. But now... I know that's not it."

He ran a hand through his hair. "Grent came back alone. Said she was taken. But his clothes weren't dirty. He wasn't scratched. He didn't have a damn mark on him."

Matthew stared at him. "Are you saying...?"

"I'm saying I don't know what he did, but I *know* it wasn't the tribe. And I think Megan's dead."

Silence.

Cartwright looked to Matthew, then back to Adam. "You think he killed her."

Adam nodded slowly. "And I need to know for sure."

Matthew's voice was steady but cold. "So what do you want to do?"

"I want to find her body," Adam said. "If we find it... we'll be able to see how and if she was killed."

Cartwright exhaled through his nose. "All right. I'm in."

Matthew gave a sharp nod. "Let's get our gear. We head out now, just the three of us—no one else needs to know where we're going."

Adam started to turn, but Matthew's voice stopped him. "Adam... if we do find her body, and it's clear she was murdered... we can't just accuse Grent without proof."

Adam's eyes hardened. "Even if we both know it was him?"

Matthew hesitated, jaw tightening. "Especially then. He's tied up now, but the tribe isn't going to keep him there forever. Without solid evidence, we risk dividing the group—and if that happens, we all lose."

Adam didn't respond, but the set of his shoulders said everything. He'd go along with it—for now.

* * *

The jungle here was softer than the wild edges Shayne had grown used to—less snarling green, more dappled gold. Sunlight spilled through the canopy in bright patches, painting the moss-covered stones with shifting patterns. The air was warm and damp, scented with flowers that bloomed in tight clusters along the trail.

Shayne followed Avara up a gentle rise, her bare feet silent against the earth. She glanced back at him with a teasing smile.

"You walk loud," she said, almost whispering.

"Loud? I'm just letting the predators know I'm coming so they don't get startled," Shayne said, grinning. "It's a safety tactic."

Avara rolled her eyes, but her smile lingered. She pushed through a curtain of leaves—and the world opened.

Before them stretched a small, perfect lake. Sunlight shimmered across its surface, scattering diamonds of light into the air. The water was so clear Shayne could see smooth river stones on the bottom, shifting as tiny fish darted past. At the far edge, a thin waterfall slid down black rock into the lake, the sound a constant, soothing whisper.

Shayne took a slow breath. "This place is... wow."

Avara's voice softened. "When I was young, my father would bring me here. It was safe. Quiet. A place the world could not reach."

She stepped closer to the water and, without warning began slipping off her tunic. Shayne froze.

"You coming in?" she asked, glancing over her shoulder, her dark eyes challenging him.

Shayne's mind went blank. "Uh... yeah. Yeah, I... just didn't bring my swim trunks."

Avara smirked, then let her tunic fall to the grass, followed by the wrap around her waist. She waded into the lake, water climbing over her legs, her hips, her back, until she dove under in a flash of silver. She surfaced a few feet away, hair slick against her skin, water beads glinting in the sun.

"Well?" she called.

Shayne laughed, shaking his head, and began stripping down. "If I drown, you're giving the eulogy."

He splashed in after her, the cool water sending a shiver up his spine. They swam for a while, circling, diving, and teasing one another until Shayne floated beside her near the center.

Avara's expression shifted, her tone quieter. "I did not think I would ever feel this again."

Shayne tilted his head. "Feel what?"

"Hope," she said simply.

He reached for her hand beneath the water, their fingers locking. They drifted in silence for a long moment before he leaned in. Their lips met—soft at first, then with the pent-up intensity of two people who had been circling each other for days. The kiss deepened, water rippling gently around them.

They swam back to shore, pulling themselves onto the warm grass. Avara's hand stayed in his. He brushed damp hair from her face.

"You're something else, you know that?" Shayne said.

She smiled faintly. "And you talk too much."

She kissed him again, pulling him down with her. The jungle around them faded to nothing but the sound of the waterfall and their hearts, quick and certain. The moment was tender, but unguarded—two people choosing closeness in a world that had given them little but danger.

When they finally lay still, Avara rested her head against his chest, her eyes closed. Shayne stared at the shifting leaves above them, thinking for the first time in weeks that maybe—just maybe—there was something worth staying for.

* * *

The jungle here was different—tighter, darker. The canopy above pressed in, blotting out most of the light. Every step seemed to sink into damp soil, muffled under layers of leaves and rot.

Matthew, Cartwright, and Adam moved in silence, their eyes sweeping the undergrowth. Adam led the way, his pace sharp, almost impatient.

"We're close," Adam muttered, glancing toward a gap in the trees.

Matthew's gaze stayed forward, but he caught Cartwright's look—the silent warning to be ready for whatever they were about to find.

The deeper they went, the heavier the air became. A faint smell began to creep in, sour and unmistakable.

Adam froze.

Matthew stepped up beside him, following his stare.

There, half-hidden behind a tangle of roots and ferns, was Megan.

Her body lay twisted on the ground, eyes open but lifeless, staring at nothing. Her hair was matted, her clothes torn. Dirt streaked her skin.

Adam dropped to his knees so fast it startled Matthew. His hand trembled as he reached toward her, stopping just shy of touching her face. "Oh... God." His voice broke.

Cartwright's jaw clenched, his eyes narrowing on the space just above her collarbone. The skin there was raw, the chain gone—yanked from her neck—her necklace missing.

Matthew swallowed hard, the image colliding with the memory of his **vision**—her lying in the dirt, that same empty stare, the echo of her scream in his head.

He hesitated, then said quietly, "Adam... there's something I need to tell you."

Adam looked up, eyes red. "What?"

"I... saw this," Matthew said. "Not here exactly, but... in a dream. A vision. Megan screaming, and then—" He stopped, shaking his head. "I didn't know if it was real until now."

Adam's expression shifted from grief to shock to fury in an instant. He surged to his feet, grabbing Matthew by the collar and shoving him against a tree.

"You *knew!* You saw this and you didn't stop it?!" His voice was raw, spitting each word like it hurt to say them. "She's dead because you didn't say anything!"

Matthew's hands went up defensively. "I didn't know it would happen! I didn't even know if it *could* happen—"

Adam shoved him again. "You should have told me! I could have—"

"Enough!" Cartwright's voice cut through the jungle like a rifle shot. He stepped between them, prying Adam's hands off Matthew's shirt with a soldier's grip.

"Fighting each other won't bring her back," Cartwright said, locking eyes with Adam. "And a vision doesn't give us all the answers. We need proof if we're going to deal with Grent—*real* proof, or the others will never believe it."

Adam's breathing was ragged, his fists still clenched. For a moment, Matthew thought he'd lunge again. But slowly, Adam stepped back, jaw tight, eyes still burning.

"Fine," Adam said. "Then we get proof. And when we do, I'll be the one to finish him."

Cartwright nodded once. "Help me lift her. We're not leaving her here."

They worked in tense silence, Matthew and Cartwright carefully easing Megan into their arms while Adam brushed dirt from her hair.

As they turned back toward the village, the jungle felt heavier than before, the shadows thicker.

*There had been joy today. There had been love. And now, there was only loss.*

# Chapter 31  Breaking the Circle

The sun was sliding low when Matthew, Cartwright, and Adam emerged from the jungle.

Between them, they carried Megan. Her body was wrapped in a woven mat the Vokari had given them earlier in the week—a mat that should have been for sleeping, not for this.

The village went still. Conversations stopped, tools were set down, and eyes followed the three men as they stepped into the open clearing. The crackle of the main fire seemed louder in the silence that spread.

Shayne and Avara had just returned from the far side of the village, smiles fading as soon as they saw what Matthew carried. Kaia was kneeling near one of the cooking pits, but the moment her gaze found him, she stood quickly and came toward them.

Matthew avoided her eyes, walking straight past to a shaded spot near the healer's hut. They lowered Megan gently to the ground.

Adam's face was unreadable, but his hands were clenched so tight his knuckles blanched. His eyes never left the hut where Grent sat bound under guard.

Kaia knelt beside Matthew, touching his arm. "Matt..."

He shook his head slightly. "Not now." His voice was low, the kind that didn't invite argument.

Across the clearing, Grent shifted in his seat inside the hut, the faintest smirk touching his mouth.

The air felt heavier than the humidity, thick with the unspoken truth that everyone seemed to feel but no one dared voice.

—

The Vokari elders gathered quickly once Chief Nukapana understood what had happened. Without question, they agreed to give Megan a place of rest just beyond the village walls—a patch of soft earth beneath a wide, flowering tree that the tribe reserved for their honored dead.

The sky had dimmed to a deep amber by the time the grave was dug. The villagers stood in a ring, their torches swaying in the warm evening breeze. The only sounds were the crackle of the flames and quiet hush of the jungle beyond.

Matthew, Adam, Cartwright, Shayne, Kaia, Avara, and Dr. Varn stood together on one side, facing Nukapana and several warriors.

Nukapana stepped forward, his weathered face solemn. He raised both hands to the sky, then lowered them toward the grave. His deep voice carried across the gathering:

*"Keta*

*mora vunakai, shta talo kenai, hura vona shatai Ken'varu... ken'vo malakai Sharo'hai, shta tola yenavai."*

Shayne's voice was low beside Matthew, translating for the outsiders. "She walks now in the eternal river, where pain is no more. The spirits guide her to the firelight of her ancestors. The Sky Death will not find her, nor the Death Bird. She is not lost. She is returned."

Adam stood stiffly, his hands balled into fists, staring down at the wrapped shape before them. His jaw worked as though he wanted to speak, but no words came.

Kaia stepped forward, kneeling to place a small white flower atop the wrapped mat before it was lowered into the ground. Her voice was soft but steady. "We'll remember you."

One by one, others stepped forward, laying small tokens—a bead, a carved feather, a folded scrap of cloth— onto the mat before it disappeared into the earth.

When the grave was filled, Adam didn't move. He stood there long after the others began drifting away, the firelight from the torches throwing sharp shadows across his face. Finally, he crouched down, pressing a hand to the mound of fresh soil. His voice was barely above a whisper, but Matthew, standing nearby, heard him clearly:

"I'll make him pay for what he did."

Across the clearing, Grent shifted inside his hut, eyes locked on Adam. The faint, mocking curve of his lips made Matthrew's stomach knot.

—

The burial had left the village quieter than usual. Even the children seemed to sense the heaviness in the air, playing in small, subdued groups near the huts. Smoke from the funeral torches still hung faintly in the clearing, curling upward toward the darkening sky.

Matthew sat on a low bench near the outer fire pit, absently turning a strip of woven grass in his fingers. Across from him, Cartwright lowered himself onto an overturned basket, the weight in his expression mirroring Matthew's own.

Adam wasn't with them. After the burial, he'd gone to sharpen a spear, each stroke of stone against wood ringing with a restless energy.

Cartwright kept his voice low. "We both know it was him."

Matthew didn't look up. "Knowing it isn't enough. Not here."

Cartwright's gaze flicked toward the guarded hut where Grent sat bound in the shadows. "So how do we get proof?"

"The necklace," Matthew said. "If we find it, there's no arguing. Adam said Megan wore it that day. Actually, said she would never take it off. If Grent's got it, he's finished."

Cartwright leaned forward, elbows on his knees. "And where exactly do you think he's keeping it? He's tied up in there—doesn't have a pocket to his name."

Before Matthew could answer, a shadow fell over them. Dr. Varn stepped into the firelight, brushing a strand of hair from her face.

"I couldn't help overhearing," she said. "You're right about needing proof. But I think you're looking in the wrong place."

Matthew frowned. "And where should we be looking?"

She glanced toward Grent's hut, then back at Matthew. "When the Vokari brought him in, they searched him. Anything they found—his knife, scraps of food, bits of cloth—they tossed into the supply hut with the other confiscated gear."

Cartwright's brows rose. "You saw this?"

"I was there when they dragged him in," Varn said. "I saw something small and silver drop from him before they shoved him inside. One of the warriors picked it up and threw it in with the rest."

Matthew's heart gave a slow, heavy beat. "The necklace."

Varn didn't confirm, but her eyes said enough. "If it's still there, that's your proof. But if you're caught going through their supplies, you'll lose whatever trust you've built with this tribe."

She started to turn away, then paused. Her voice softened. "And Matthew... I don't think you know Professor Clark as well as you believe."

Then she walked off into the shadows, leaving the two men staring after her, the firelight flickering between them.

—

The night air was thick with the smell of damp earth and smoke from the village fires. Most of the Vokari had retreated into their huts, but the faint murmur of conversation still carried in pockets from around the clearing.

Adam walked with his head low, the wooden spear in his hand tapping against the dirt as he crossed to the far side of the village. The guarded hut loomed ahead—the one where Grent sat tied inside, a warrior stationed at the door.

The guard eyed Adam but didn't stop him when he approached. Instead, he stepped aside with a slow, deliberate motion, as if curious to see what would happen next.

Through the bars, Adam could see him—Silas Grent, sitting with his back to the wall, ankles and wrists bound with thick rope. The firelight from the nearest torch painted half his face in gold, the other half in shadow.

"You enjoying yourself in there?" Adam's voice was low, sharp.

Grent lifted his head slowly, the corner of his mouth twitching upward. "Better than Megan, I suppose."

Adam's grip on the spear tightened. "Say her name again."

Grent leaned forward just enough that the light caught the scar running across his cheek. "Megan."

The spear shaft cracked against the bars with a sharp *thwack*, rattling the whole frame.
Grent didn't flinch—he just smiled, that slow, taunting smile.

"She was weak," he said. "And weakness gets eaten here. Sooner you learn that the longer you'll last."

Adam's pulse roared in his ears. He reached for the door latch, ready to step inside, ready to end this right now.

"Adam!"

The voice snapped him back—Avara, standing a few paces away, her dark eyes fixed on him. She walked forward, her tone measured but firm. "If you kill him now, without proof, you dishonor her memory. And you give the jungle nothing to judge."

Adam's chest heaved, his knuckles white on the spears shaft.

Grent tilted his head, eyes narrowing in something that might have been amusement.

Avara stepped between Adam and the door. "You said you wanted justice. Justice waits. Revenge wastes itself."

Adam's jaw clenched so tight it hurt, but he forced himself to step back. He turned without another word and stalked off into the darkness.

Grent leaned his head against the wall again, his smile lingering long after Adam's footsteps faded.

—

Night settled heavy over the Vokari village. The fires burned low, casting long shadows that swayed across the huts. The air was thick with the scent of ash and damp earth, and the jungle beyond the walls hummed with the restless chorus of unseen creatures.

Matthew lay on his side in the small guest hut, eyes half-closed but mind wide awake. Every time he blinked, he saw Megan's face again, the soil falling over her grave.

The quiet was broken only by the distant pop of the main fire and the soft breathing of Kaia, asleep a few feet away.

And then—

The firelight dimmed, swallowed by a creeping darkness. When Matthew opened his eyes again, he was no longer in the hut.

He stood in a void lit only by a single lantern on a wooden desk. Seated at that desk was Professor Clark, his hands folded neatly, a faint smile curling his lips.

"You're troubled," Clark said, voice warm and patient. "You've seen what happens when truth and proof don't match."

Matthew tried to speak, but no sound came out.

Clark rose slowly, stepping around the desk until he was standing just a foot away. His eyes caught the dim light, glinting in a way that felt almost... predatory.

"Some truths," Clark said, "can't be proven... only enforced."

The shadows around them began to shift, swallowing the lantern's glow until Matthew could barely see him. The last thing he heard before the darkness took everything was Clark's voice—softer, but sharper.

"You'll understand soon."

Matthew jolted awake, his heart hammering. The fire outside had burned low to embers. Kaia stirred slightly, murmuring something in her sleep.

He lay back down, staring at the ceiling of the hut, the echo of Clark's words gnawing at him long into the night.

Across the village, in the guarded hut, Grent sat in the dark, his eyes glinting faintly in the firelight—and the faintest of smiles playing at his lips.

# Chapter 32  Proof in the Shadows

The morning mist still clung to the village, curling in thin ribbons around the huts and drifting across the open clearing. The air was cool, damp with the promise of rain later in the day.

Matthew moved quietly, slipping between huts until he spotted Cartwright leaning against the outer palisade. Adam was already there, pacing in short, sharp strides, the restless energy rolling off him almost palpable.

"You're late," Adam muttered.

"I didn't want to draw eyes," Matthew said, glancing around to make sure no one was close enough to overhear. "This stays between us."

Cartwright straightened, his voice low and steady. "Varn said the tribe dumped everything they took from

Grent into the supply hut after they brought him in—
weapons, scraps of food, anything on him.”

Adam stopped pacing, his eyes locking on
Matthew. “Including Megan's necklace.”

“That's the idea,” Cartwright said. “Hunting party
leaves soon. Half the warriors will be gone for
hours. It's the only window we'll get.”

Adam gripped the shaft of his spear like he
wanted to snap it in half. “We find it, we drag him out, and
I end this.”

Matthew stepped closer, his voice low but firm.
“No. We find it, we hold it, and we use it when the time is
right. If you kill him without the tribe on our
side, we'll lose everything—their trust, their protection,
and maybe our lives.”

Adam's jaw tightened. “I don't care
about their trust.”

“I do,” Matthew said. “And you should,
too.  Grent's tied up now, but he won't be forever. We do
this clean, and we do it smart.”

The distant blast of a horn cut through the
morning air—the signal for the hunting party to gather.
Warriors began to move toward the gates, spears in hand,
their voices low.

Cartwright gave a silent nod toward
the supply huts. “That's our cue.”

—

The hunting party moved through the village gates
in a quiet line, their spears and bows glinting in the pale
morning light. The heavy wooden doors swung behind
them, leaving the clearing noticeably emptier.

Matthew led the way toward the far side of the village, keeping his pace casual. To anyone watching, they were just three outsiders crossing from one end of the clearing to the other.

The supply hut sat low to the ground, its walls woven tightly from thick reeds, the doorframe bound with leather strips. The air near it smelled faintly of dried meat and smoke.

Cartwright went in first, ducking under the low lintel. Inside, the light was dim, filtered and netting hung from the rafters, baskets of roots and smoked fish stacked along the floor. A rack of clay jars lined one wall.

Adam slipped in last, his shoulders tense. "Where do we start?"

Matthew pointed to a row of baskets pushed into the back corner. "Anything small would be tucked away. We check everything."

They moved quietly, sifting through supplies. Matthew worked methodically, lifting bundles of cloth and checking under them. Cartwright checked the clay jars, tapping each lid back into place with care. Adam pulled baskets forward one by one, his movements sharper, less patient.

"This is a waste of—" Adam stopped mid-sentence, crouching over a half-buried bundle behind a coil of rope. His fingers worked it loose, pulling out a small leather pouch, worn and stained from use.

He untied the string with shaking hands. Something metallic clinked softly inside.

Adam tipped the pouch into his palm.

**Megan's necklace slid out,** the silver chain dulled and bent, the small pendant caked with a thin crust of dirt.

Adam's breath caught. For a moment, no one spoke.

Cartwright broke the silence, his voice low. "There it is. Proof."

Adam closed his fist around it so tight his knuckles whitened. "It's more than proof. It's my permission."

Matthew's tone hardened. "Don't. Not yet. We need the tribe with us before we move on him."

Adam didn't answer. His eyes stayed on the necklace, jaw clenched like a vice.

Cartwright glanced toward the doorway. "We should get out of here before—"

A sound outside—a faint crunch of footsteps.

The three froze.

Matthew crept to the doorway, peering out into the bright clearing. No one was there... but across the way, near the edge of the tree line, **a figure stood watching**. Too far to make out clearly, but close enough to know they'd seen.

By the time Matthew blinked, the figure had vanished into the jungle.

They slipped out of the supply hut one at a time, careful to keep their movements unhurried. The clearing felt different now—heavier, like the air itself was holding its breath.

Matthew led them to a shaded corner near the palisade wall, away from the main path. Cartwright scanned the village, his hand resting near the hilt of his knife. Adam stood a few feet away, still holding the necklace in his fist.

"Alright," Cartwright said, his voice low. "We have it. No doubt now."

Adam looked down at his hand, slowly uncoiling his fingers to reveal the pendant. Even dulled by dirt, it seemed to glint in the weak morning light. His jaw worked, the muscle in his cheek jumping. "He wore this around her neck like a trophy," he said, voice tight. "Now it mine— and so is what comes next."

Matthew stepped closer, keeping his voice calm but firm. "Listen to me. If you walk in there and kill him now, the tribe will see it as murder.
They won't care what's in your hand."

Adam shot him a glare.
"It's not murder. It's justice."

"Not to them," Matthew said. "To them, you're just an outsider spilling blood in their village. And if that happens, they'll stop protecting us. All of us."

Cartwright nodded. "He's right. We need to make the Vokari see the proof. Make them want him gone as much as we do."

Adam closed his fist again, his breathing heavy. For a moment, Matthew thought he might still push past them and head for the guarded hut. But instead, Adam shoved the necklace into his pocket.

"Fine," he said. "But when it's time... I'm the one who does it."

Matthew didn't argue. "When it's time."

A shadow of movement caught Cartwright's eye. "We need to be careful. Someone saw us in there.
I don't know who, but they were watching."

Matthew's gaze went to the tree line, where the figure had stood earlier. The jungle loomed quiet now, but the feeling of eyes in the shadows lingered.

"We keep this between us," Matthew said. "No one else knows until we decide how to use it."

Adam gave a short nod, but the set of his jaw said the decision was already made in his mind.

* * *

The village began to stir again as more Vokari emerged from their huts, the sound of conversation drifting back into the morning air. Somewhere across the clearing, someone laughed—a sharp, sudden sound that felt out of place.

Matthew, Cartwright, and Adam kept their distance from each other, blending back into the normal flow of the day. But every time Matthew's gaze drifted toward the tree line, he saw nothing but the thick curtain of leaves and vines.

He knew what he'd seen.

In the dim light beneath the canopy, a shape shifted. Just enough for the faintest glint of eyes to catch the morning sun before disappearing again.

The jungle swallowed the figure whole, leaving only the quiet rustle of leaves.

Matthew forced himself to look away and keep moving, but the sensation stayed with him—that someone out there now knew they had proof... and was deciding what to do about it.

# Chapter 33 The Confrontation

The day had been slow, the air heavy with the wet heat of the jungle pressing down on the village. The necklace burned a hole in Adam's pocket from the moment they found it, each step making the chain shift and clink softly like it was whispering at him to act.

By late afternoon, he couldn't stand it anymore.

Matthew was on the far side of the village helping Kaia with a water jug when Adam stalked past, spear in hand, his shoulders set like stone. Cartwright noticed first.

"Adam—" Cartwright's voice was low, warning, but Adam didn't slow.

The hut that held Grent was dim, guarded by a lone Vokari warrior. Adam didn't bother asking for entry—he pushed past, ducking inside. The smell hit first—sweat, damp rope, and something faintly metallic.

Grent sat against the back wall, ankles and wrists bound, head tilted lazily as Adam stepped in. His eyes flicked to the spear, then to Adam's face.

"You look like a man about to do something stupid," Grent said, voice calm, almost amused.

Adam didn't answer. He pulled the necklace from his pocket and tossed it so it landed between them, the pendant clinking against the dirt floor.

Grent glanced at it, then back up at Adam. "And?"

Adam's jaw flexed. "You took it from her."

Grent's smirk deepened. "I took a lot of things."

That was all it took.

Adam lunged, driving the butt of the spear into Grent's chest and knocking him back into the wall. Grent grunted, but his smile didn't fade. Adam struck again, the wood cracking against bone this time.

Outside, the guard shouted something in Vokari, but before he could act, Matthew was there, shoving past him into the hut.

"Adam! Stop!"

Adam didn't stop. He hit Grent again, the ropes creaking as Grent's body jerked with the impact.

Matthew grabbed the spear, yanking it back. "This isn't what we do!"

Adam spun on him, eyes wild. "He murdered her! And you want me to just let him breathe?"

Matthew's voice was sharp, every word clipped. "We have proof now. Let the tribe see it. Let them turn the jungle loose on him—not you."

Adam's chest heaved, sweat dripping from his brow. For a moment, Matthew thought he'd have to physically fight him off. Then, slowly, Adam's grip loosened.

Matthew stepped between them; his gaze locked on Grent. "You're not worth dying over. Let the jungle finish you."

Grent chuckled low, blood trickling from the corner of his mouth. "You think the jungle's the worst thing out there?"

Matthew ignored him, pulling Adam toward the door. Cartwright was waiting outside, tense, watching the villagers who had begun to gather.

As they walked away, Matthew didn't see Grent push himself up against the wall, a faint, knowing smile curling his lips.

The air outside the hut was tense, charged with a kind of quiet that wasn't really silence at all. A cluster of Vokari had gathered, their murmured words in the native tongue rolling through the clearing like low thunder. Spears rested loosely in their hands, but their eyes were sharp, following every movement.

Matthew stepped out first, Adam right behind him, the necklace now clutched tight in Matthew's hand. Cartwright closed the gap quickly, keeping his voice low. "They saw enough to know something happened in there."

Chief Nukapana approached from the far side of the clearing, his steps measured, his gaze unblinking. The villagers parted for him without a word. He stopped in front of Matthew, his eyes dropping briefly to the silver pendant in his palm.

Matthew held it out. "She wore this the day she died. We found it among Grent's things."

Nukapana's expression didn't change. He reached out and took the necklace, turning it once between his fingers before looking back at Matthew. "You are certain?"

Matthew nodded. "We are."

For a long moment, Nukapana said nothing. The only sound was the faint crackle of the village fire. Then the chief closed his hand around the necklace and looked to the guards by the hut.

"Ken'vo sharo," Nukapana ordered.

Shayne, who had been watching from nearby, stepped forward to translate quietly for Matthew and Cartwright. "He says, 'Return death to the jungle.'"

The guards nodded, and Nukapana turned back to Matthew. "At dawn, he goes. The jungle will decide his fate."

Adam took a step forward. "And if it doesn't?"

Nukapana's gaze shifted to him, steady and unyielding. "Then perhaps the jungle has other plans. But you will not act while you are under my protection."

Adam's teeth clenched, but he said nothing.

As the chief walked away, Matthew caught Adam's arm. "Don't do anything tonight."

Adam pulled free. "If the jungle doesn't get him... I will."

He stalked off into the shadows, leaving Matthew staring after him, the weight of both the tribe's decree and Adam's promise pressing down like a stone.

Night draped the village in a thick, humid darkness. The jungle beyond the palisade pulsed with the steady rhythm of insects and distant cries of unseen creatures. The air smelled of damp leaves and woodsmoke, and somewhere high in the canopy, something shifted with a heavy, deliberate weight.

Grent sat in the corner of a small, low hut near the village edge—not the one he'd been held in before, but a temporary holding space until dawn. The ropes around his wrists and ankles were looser now, more symbolic than secure. The guards outside had grown bored, their low voices fading into the occasional laugh.

He tested the bindings. They gave with a slow, deliberate twist of his wrists. The skin beneath was raw, but the pain barely registered.

One of the guards coughed. The other muttered something in Vokari, his tone lazy.

Then their footsteps drifted a few paces away, leaving only the low burn of a torch by the hut's door.

Grent moved.

He slipped out into the night, sticking to the shadowed side of the hut until he was clear of the firelight. His legs trembled under his own weight, the bruises from Adam's attack blooming dark across his ribs.

He staggered toward the palisade. No one stopped him.

The village gates were shut, but there was a gap near the wall where the wood met the roots of a massive tree. Grent dropped to his knees, crawling through, the bark scraping his back.

On the other side, the jungle waited—a living, breathing wall of heat and shadow.

He moved slowly at first, one hand braced against a tree as he forced himself deeper into the undergrowth. His breathing grew ragged, each step stirring the scents of wet soil and rot.

"Let the jungle finish me..." Grent muttered under his breath, a dry chuckle escaping. "We'll see about that."

# Chapter 34  The Vision of Truth

The Vokari village was quiet in that deep, heavy way the jungle sometimes allowed—as if every living thing had agreed to hold its breath for the night. The firepits burned low, their glow casting long shadows across the packed-earth paths. From somewhere beyond the palisade walls came the faint, distant cry of a night bird.

Matthew sat near one of the smaller fires, his hands wrapped around a wooden bowl of warm water that Kaia had brought him earlier. She sat beside him now, silent, her gaze fixed on the flames.

The soft thump of a walking staff broke the stillness. Chief Nukapana emerged from the darkness, his broad frame outlined by the firelight. The painted markings on his weathered face made his eyes seem even sharper than usual.

"It is time," Nukapana said, his deep voice carrying weight like a stone dropped into still water.

Matthew glanced at Kaia. "Time for what?"

The chief stepped closer, looking down at him. "To see what the *morakai* saw," he said in his halting English. "To see what I saw... when Helix came before."

The name hit Matthew like a jolt. He almost asked the chief to repeat it, but something in Nukapana's face stopped him.

Nukapana gestured toward the far side of the village, where a faint orange glow flickered through the gaps in the huts. "Come."

Kaia started to rise with him, but the chief's staff blocked her path. "No," he said firmly. "This journey is his alone."

Her mouth tightened in protest, but she stayed seated, her eyes following Matthew as he stood.

Nukapana led the way through the village, the two of them moving in near silence. The air grew heavier as they approached a low, round hut set apart from the others. The scent of burning herbs drifted from the doorway, mingling with the smoke curling into the night.

Inside, the firelight was dim and golden, reflecting off the strings of beads and feathers that hung from the ceiling. Shia, the tribe's shaman, waited beside the central fire, her face painted in symmetrical lines of black and white. She did not speak, only studied Matthew as if measuring his worth.

Nukapana placed a hand on Matthew's shoulder. "You will drink. You will see. And when you wake... you will know."

Shia's gaze didn't waver as Matthew stepped inside. The shaman moved with deliberate slowness, circling him once before stopping at the fire. The air was thick with the scent of crushed leaves and bitter roots, each breath leaving a faint sting in his throat.

Nukapana closed the hut's woven door flap behind them. "*Morakai,*" he said quietly, gesturing to himself, 'is more than chief. It is protector. Witness. Chosen by the *shatai*—our ancestors." He met Matthew's eyes. "Tonight, you will see through the eyes of the *morakai* before you. Through my eyes. Through the day Helix walked among our people."

Matthew's pulse kicked up. "Why me?"

Shia answered in Vokari, her voice low and melodic:

**"Vren shatai yenavai... shava tala vokari."**

Nukapana joined her, his deeper voice merging with hers.

Shia turned to a carved wooden vessel simmering over the fire. Steam rose from the dark liquid inside, carrying a sharp, earthy bitterness. She poured a portion into a smaller cup and offered it to Matthew with both hands.

"Drink," Nukapana instructed.

The liquid was thick and hot, tasting of soil, smoke, and something sharp enough to make his eyes water. It burned on the way down, spreading heat through his chest and belly.

The firelight swelled. Shadows along the hut walls seemed to ripple and twist, no longer matching the movements of the people who cast them. The chants grew louder, echoing from places that weren't in the hut at all.

Matthew's knees buckled. His surroundings blurred—the feathers, the beads, the fire—all melting into a wash of gold and black.

The last thing he saw before the world gave way was Nukapana's face, solemn and still, and the whisper of his voice: "See what I saw... and understand."

The firelight vanished.

Matthew opened his eyes to a sterile corridor that stretched in both directions, walls gleaming with brushed steel. The air smelled of antiseptic and machine oil, humming with the low pulse of unseen generators. His own reflection flickered faintly in the polished floor—except it wasn't his reflection.

Dark skin weathered by sun. Grey-streaked hair tied back with a strip of leather. The face of Chief Nukapana.

*I'm in his body.*

Harsh voices echoed ahead. Matthew—or rather, Nukapana—turned the corner and froze. Two men in pale lab coats shoved Vokari tribespeople, wrists bound, toward a reinforced glass chamber. Among them, younger faces Matthew recognized even through the distortion of memory: Avara, barely more than a teenager, clutching the arm of a broad-shouldered man with the same eyes—her father.

"They're scared," a man in a black security vest muttered in English. "Don't see the point in keeping them here. They're just slowing us down."

A familiar voice answered, smooth and commanding. "That's because you're thinking too small."

From the far end of the hall, a figure emerged. Dark hair with silver starting to show, swept back with precision. Sharp, charismatic features. The faintest smile playing at his lips. He wore a dark lab coat that moved like a tailored suit jacket, the Helixis insignia stitched into the breast.

Matthew's stomach turned cold. "*Clark...*

Except it wasn't Clark. It never had been.

"Dr. Ardan Helix," one of the lab coats greeted.

Helix stepped closer, eyes sweeping the captives as though examining specimens rather than people. His gaze lingered on Avara's father, then shifted to the hybrids pacing in nearby enclosures—long-necked, scaled creatures with serrated teeth, and farther down, a hulking saber-tooth raptor hybrid wearing a steel collar that pulsed faintly with blue light.

"Dispose of the failed specimens," Helix said casually, as if ordering coffee.

"Yes, sir," the security man replied.

And then Helix stopped. Turned. Looked directly into Matthew's eyes—through the vision—as if aware of his presence.

"Matthew..." His smile widened. "I was wondering when you'd see me for who I am."

The walls warped. The lights flared white.

Matthew gasped awake in the ceremonial hut, chest heaving, the firelight flickering across Shia's calm, unreadable face.

Matthew sat forward, still struggling to catch his breath. The taste of the bitter brew clung to his tongue, the images from the vision burned into his mind.

Chief Nukapana stepped closer, his face drawn and solemn. "You saw it," he said, voice low.

Matthew swallowed. "Clark... it was him. He— he's not Clark at all. He's... Helix."

Nukapana's jaw tightened. "Ardan Helix," he said, pronouncing the name like a curse. "The false morakai. The one who came from the sky with promises of life but brought only cages and death."

Matthew shook his head, trying to force the pieces together. "He—he was experimenting on your people. On the animals. I saw Avara... I saw her father—" His voice caught. "And those things...those hybrids—"

Nukapana's gaze held his. "I was there, Matthew Fisher. It was my eyes you saw through. I watched my people taken. I watched my son die in his hands."

Matthew's chest tightened. "Why didn't you tell me sooner?"

"Because truth is heavy," Nukapana replied. "Too heavy for a man not yet ready to carry it. Now you are ready—and you must carry it, or it will crush you."

Matthew's mind reeled. His mentor, the man who had invited him onto that yacht, the man he thought he could trust... was the architect of all of this.

Nukapana stepped closer, his voice sharpening. "Helix will not let you leave this place alive unless you kneel to him. If you choose to fight him, you will need more than courage. You will need to know every shadow he hides in."

Matthew clenched his fists, the weight of the revelation settling into something cold and unshakable in his gut. "Then I'll find those shadows. And I'll burn them out."

* * *

The jungle was a wall of black and silver, moonlight breaking in fractured beams through the canopy. Every step was an effort—mud clinging to his boots, blood dried in a crust across his shirt from Adam's fists.

Grent stumbled forward, leaning against a tree for support. His breath rasped in his throat. Somewhere far off, something called—low, guttural, and too big to be anything natural.

He chuckled bitterly under his breath. "You think the jungle's the worst thing out there..."

The words tasted like mockery now. He pushed off the tree, taking two more steps before a soft crunch in the undergrowth made him freeze.

A figure stepped out from the shadows, his silhouette crisp even in the dim light. Clean clothes. Controlled posture. Eyes that cut right through him.

"Helix..." Grent rasped, straightening as much as his battered body would allow. "So glad to see you."

Helix stopped a few paces away, tilting his head with a faint smile. "You had one job," he said, his voice smooth and almost disappointed. "And you failed."

Grent smirked, hiding the flicker of unease crawling up his spine. "You going to finish me yourself?"

Helix glanced down at the small device in his hand—a sleek black remote with a single recessed button. "No," he said quietly. "She will."

The undergrowth behind him shifted, then parted.

It stepped into view—a nightmare on two legs. The body of a raptor, long and low, with the coiled strength of a cat in its muscles. Saber-length fangs jutted from its curved jaw, glistening with saliva. Its eyes burned gold in the moonlight. Around its thick neck, a reinforced collar pulsed with a faint blue light.

Helix gestured toward it with quiet pride. "Raptoryx. Engineered for precision hunting. Smarter than a wolf... faster than a cheetah... loyal only to the hand that holds the key."

Grent's smirk faltered. "You're kidding me."

Helix's thumb pressed the button. The collar's lights flared—and the Raptoryx let out a shriek that rattled the leaves. It lunged.

Grent barely had time to bring up his arms before it hit him, driving him into the mud. The fangs found his throat, tearing through flesh in a spray of crimson. His scream was cut short.

Helix watched without blinking. When it was over, the Raptoryx stood over the body, blood soaking its muzzle. Helix clicked the remote again. The beast turned, padding obediently to his side.

Without a backward glance, Helix stepped into the shadows, the predator following silently at his heel.

* * *

The village was quiet, the fires burned low. Most of the Vokari had retreated into their huts, leaving only the soft crackle of embers and the hum of insects in the night.

Matthew sat alone near the edge of the open square, elbows on his knees, staring into the dark beyond the torches. Kaia slept a few feet away, her breathing steady at last.

But his mind wasn't calm.

The vision clung to him like smoke—the metallic corridors, the screams of the Vokari captives, the rows of hybrid creatures. And most of all, the face of Ardan Helix staring directly at him, speaking his name like it had been carved into him since the day they met.

He could still hear that voice, smooth and certain: *"I was wondering when you'd see me for who I am."*

Matthew's fists tightened. He had trusted Clark. Believed in him. And now he knew—the man who brought them here was the very one they should have feared most.

Beyond the reach of the torches, the jungle swayed in a lazy breeze. Somewhere out there, Helix was moving, closing in.

The night seemed to breathe with it—a slow, patient inhale before the strike.

# Chapter 35  The Vision of Truth

The world was smoke and shadow.

Matthew's lungs felt heavy, his chest rising and falling like he'd been running for hours. The low, rhythmic chant of Shia's voice pulsed through the air—not from her mouth now, but from everywhere at once, vibrating in his bones.

Shapes began to take form in the swirling dark. A horizon. Palm fronds swaying in warm light. Then, with the sudden clarity of a memory not his own, the scene sharpened into a village—the Vokari village, but younger. The huts were freshly woven, smoke rising from cooking fires, children racing barefoot through the sand. Laughter. Peace.

A shout cut through it.

Figures appeared at the edge of the clearing—men in black tactical gear, rifles slung across their chests, strange insignias stitched to their shoulders. Matthew's

eyes locked on the patch: the double helix logo.
He didn't need Shayne to translate it. He knew.

The soldiers moved with precision, surrounding the village. Behind them came scientists in white coats, tablets in hand, jotting notes even as their escorts shoved people to their knees. Among them, taller than the rest, walked a man with silver at his temples and an expression as sharp as a blade. Not "Clark." Not the friendly professor with the easy smile.

Dr. Ardan Helix.

He was younger here, but unmistakable—his voice commanding without raising volume, every word a quiet order.

"Take the strong ones," Helix said. "Separate them. We'll begin trials immediately."

Matthew felt himself pulled forward, like he was walking through the memory. He saw the moment they seized a young man with Avara's eyes—her father—and a broad-shouldered man who could only be Chief Nukapana in his youth. Nets were thrown, bindings tightened.

At the far end of the village, a caged truck idled. Inside were... things. Shapes shifting in the dark, scales scraping against metal. One low growl carried across the clearing, and Matthew's blood ran cold.

Helix didn't look at the tribe members as people. He looked at them like specimens. Assets.

And the Vokari looked back with a kind of fear Matthew had never seen in any living thing.

The smoke swirled again, the image starting to dissolve—but not before Helix turned his head. His gaze locked directly on Matthew, as if he could see him there in the vision.

"You were always meant to see this," Helix said, his voice impossibly clear.

The village dissolved like ash in the wind.

For a heartbeat there was only blackness—then sound rushed in, deafening. Screams. Gunfire. The air was thick with the stink of burning wood and something far worse, a chemical bite that clawed at Matthew's throat.

He stood now inside the heart of the Helixis compound. It was larger than he had imagined—steel walkways, glass enclosures, massive, reinforced pens housing shapes that shifted and slammed against the walls. Lights strobed red as sirens wailed overhead.

The creatures were escaping.

A pair of raptors burst from a shattered pen; talons wet with blood. A scientist tried to run; one leapt, dragging him down in a spray of white coat and flesh.

Helix moved through the chaos like it was a controlled experiment. No panic, no hesitation—just cold assessment. He barked orders to armed security: "Contain what you can. Destroy the rest. No evidence leaves this island."

Matthew's eyes tracked a younger Silas Grent in the crowd, the jagged scar across his cheek catching the red flash of the alarms. Even younger, he moved with the same cold precision, dragging a screaming man toward the edge of the dock. Without hesitation, Grent shoved him into the sea and turned away as if taking out the trash.

A massive roar shook the air. Matthew turned to see something worse than a dinosaur—a hybrid, plated in thick, black scales with saber fangs jutting past its lower jaw. It barreled through a steel fence like paper, sending armed guards scattering.

Helix didn't run. He simply watched as tranquilizers failed, bullets bounced off its armor, and the beast tore through a vehicle. Then, almost bored, he said: "Initiate the lockdown. Seal the wormhole. No one leaves."

From above, a shimmering light spread—not sunlight, but a rippling distortion in the sky. The wormhole was closing. Around them, the remaining workers and scientists scrambled for boats, for radios, for anything. The ocean swallowed more than it spared.

Chief Nukapana—younger, bloodied—was among the prisoners dragged out during the chaos. He fought like a man possessed, freeing himself and a handful of his people. The others... Matthew didn't want to look.

The fire spread faster. Glass shattered overhead as another hybrid creature fell through the skylight. Matthew's vision tilted, the edges of the world pulling inward, drawing him back.

But before the smoke took everything, Helix looked toward him again. His voice carried as clear if they stood in the same room.

"This was only the beginning. And you... you'll finish what I started."

The smoke thickened until Matthew couldn't see the compound anymore.

Through it, a single figure remained—Helix. The flames didn't seem to touch him, the alarms didn't seem to exist for him. He stood in that strange calm he'd worn since the first moment Matthew saw him in the vision.

"You've seen enough," Helix said.

The words weren't shouted, but they cut through the noise all the same.

The ground dissolved beneath Matthew's feet, and suddenly he was nowhere—a vast, empty black space. No jungle. No sea. Just Helix, stepping forward, each footfall echoing like it was in his head.

"You think these dreams were gifts from your precious spirits?" Helix asked, his tone almost amused. "No. Every word, every image, every moment you thought came from some benevolent guide... it was me."

Matthew's stomach turned. "You—"

"I wanted to see what you would do," Helix continued, circling him slowly. "If you could lead. If you could make the hard choices. And you've done better than I hoped. You're stronger now. Smarter. Closer to what I need."

"What you *need?*" Matthew spat. "You tore apart a village. You made monsters. You killed people who—"

"I created life," Helix interrupted sharply, his voice cutting like glass. "And sometimes, Matthew, to build something extraordinary, you burn
away what's ordinary. That is leadership."

Matthew's hands curled into fists, but the air felt thick, sluggish, like he was moving underwater.

Helix leaned closer, voice low and almost fatherly. "When the time comes, you'll see I was right. This island isn't your prison. It's your inheritance."

The black space began to splinter—cracks of light tearing through it. The chant of Shia's voice rose again, urgent now, pulling him back.

Helix's final words chased him as the vision shattered:

"You're not here to escape, Matthew. You're here to take my place."

Matthew's eyes snapped open to firelight and the thick scent of herbs. His breath came fast, chest
rising like he'd surfaced from deep water. The walls of

Shia's hut wavered in the flickering glow, shadows stretching and twisting.

Shia was crouched beside him, her painted face unreadable. She murmured a final line in Vokari, pressing a hand to his chest before pulling away.

Chief Nukapana stood in the doorway, broad shoulders blocking most of the night beyond. His eyes locked on Matthew's, and for the first time, there was no hint of skepticism—only a grim certainty.

"Now you know," Nukapana said, his voice low, each word deliberate. "The truth of the false god."

Matthew swallowed hard, still feeling the echo of Helix's words in his head. *You're here to take my place.*

"Why didn't you tell me sooner?" he asked, his voice rasping.

"It is not told," Nukapana replied. "It is earned. Only then can you see what must be done."

A movement at the edge of the firelight drew Matthew's gaze. Kaia was at the hut's entrance, leaning on the frame for balance. She looked pale but awake, wrapped in a woven blanket.

"You're up," Matthew said, his voice softening.

"Couldn't just lie there forever," she said with a faint smile, though her eyes searched his face. "You okay?"

Matthew hesitated. He could tell her everything— about Helix, the experiments, the manipulation. But instead, he forced a nod.

"We can't trust him," was all he said.

Kaia didn't press, but she stepped closer, her hand brushing his before she left with one of the healers.

Nukapana's voice drew his attention back. "What you saw... it is not finished. The false god still moves against us. And now, you must decide how you will move against him."

Matthew looked past the chief, into the darkness beyond the hut, the jungle swaying under the moonlight. His heart pounded with something heavier than fear.

It was purpose.

The cool night air hit Matthew as he stepped out of Shia's hut, the firelit heart of the Vokari village spreading out before him. Warriors sharpened spears in the glow, their eyes flicking toward him as if they already sensed the shift in him.

Shayne was the first to spot him. He was crouched near the fire with Avara, working a knife over a strip of cured meat. "Hey," Shayne said, standing. "You look like you just wrestled a storm cloud. Everything alright?"

Matthew gave him a long look. "We're going to need everyone ready. Helix... he's not just a problem. He's *the* problem. And if we don't move soon, we'll lose any chance to stop him."

Adam rose from where he sat by Cartwright, his hands flexing unconsciously. "Then say the word. I'm ready to go now."

Kaia emerged from the healer's hut with one of the tribe's woven cloaks around her shoulders. She moved slower than usual, but there was no hesitation in her voice. "I'm coming with you. Don't even try to leave me behind."

Cartwright adjusted the strap on his rifle which he was given from a warrior from the supply hut, glanced toward the shadowy tree line. "You're talking about hitting the compound?"

Matthew nodded. "The longer we wait, the stronger his position gets. We go in with the tribe's help, end this before it spreads beyond this island."

From the edge of the group, Koro stepped forward, his expression unreadable. "If you go, we go. Our debt to the false god can only be paid in his blood."

A ripple of assent passed through the other Vokari warriors nearby. Avara stood beside Shayne, her hand resting briefly on his arm—a silent promise that she would see this through with him.

Matthew scanned the faces around him—allies from two worlds that should never have met, united now by survival and vengeance. The weight of what came next pressed on him, but for the first time since the crash, the path forward felt clear.

He looked toward the dark jungle that hid Helix's domain.

"We finish this."

# Chapter 36  Gathering Allies

The night air in the Vokari village still carried the fading scent of the fire from Nukapana's council hut. Matthew stood in the open space between the roundhouses, his voice from moments ago—*We finish this*—still ringing in his own head. The words had been for the others, but they had anchored something in him, too.

Around him, the small war council was forming. Shayne leaned against a spear haft, arms crossed, eyes bright with the thrill of movement after too many days of waiting. Adam stood on the opposite side, rolling his shoulders like a fighter itching for a match. Cartwright's posture was all military readiness, hands clasped behind his back, scanning the faces like a commander measuring his unit's morale. Avara stood beside him, silent but with the coiled grace of someone already halfway in battle.

Chief Nukapana stepped into the center, the torchlight deepening the lines on his face. "You will not reach the false god's den alone," he said, his Vokari words slow and deliberate, with the occasional broken-English syllable slipping through. "Our enemy... is not only him. His land has teeth."

Matthew nodded. "Then we take those teeth out. But we can't do it with just the five of us. We'll need your best."

Shayne straightened. "The warriors who fought in Varro's Challenge—they'll follow you now."

Adam smirked faintly, though the impatience in his voice bled through. "Good. Because every second we waste is a second Helix has to dig in."

Matthew let Adam's words hang before replying. "We move soon—but we move right. Survivors and Vokari, together. That's the only way we make it there... and back."

Cartwright gave a short nod. "We plan it like an assault. Fast, tight, no wasted movement."

Avara spoke for the first time, her tone flat but certain. "Then we choose the ones who will not break."

Nukapana's gaze lingered on Matthew for a long, silent moment, as if weighing whether the young outsider truly understood what he was asking for. Finally, he gave a slow nod. "Tomorrow... the morakai will stand with you."

Matthew exhaled, feeling the night grow heavier. Tomorrow, they would walk into Helix's shadow—and none of them could pretend the odds were in their favor.

The next morning broke with the steady drum of preparation. The Vokari village was alive in a way Matthew hadn't seen before—not with festival cheer, but with the measured rhythm of warriors readying for war.

Nukapana led Matthew to the central training ground, where half-circle of the tribe's finest stood waiting.

Each was armed with spears, bows, or the curved obsidian blades the Vokari favored in close combat. Their bodies were painted in sharp black and white patterns, the designs jagged and fierce.

At their head stood Koro.

The tall warrior gave Matthew a slow once-over, his jaw tight, his eyes steady. He stepped forward until they were only a pace apart. "You think you can walk into the false god's nest and live?" he asked in heavily accented English, his voice low and dangerous.

Matthew didn't flinch. "I know I can't do it without you."

Koro's stare lingered a moment longer, then—almost imperceptibly—his mouth curved into the faintest hint of a grin. "Good. I do not fight for those who think they are gods themselves." He turned, barking a command in Vokari, and the warriors thumped their spear hafts into the earth in unison.

Shayne muttered under his breath, "I think that's the closest thing to a handshake you're going to get."

From there, the camp fell into motion. Warriors sharpened blades with rhythmic strokes of stone. Bowstrings were replaced; arrows tipped with fresh obsidian. Bundles of dried meat and water gourds were packed for the march.

At the far side of the grounds, Shia moved among the warriors, brushing each with a handful of crushed herbs, murmuring words Matthew couldn't quite catch—the cadence more like a chant than a blessing. She caught his eye as she passed and gave him a small nod.

Koro returned, now armored in boiled leather reinforced with bone plates. "We leave at first shadow," he said. "The jungle is quieter then. Even the false god's beasts sleep."

Matthew felt the weight of the moment settle on him. The alliance was no longer talk—it was a living thing, forged in mutual necessity. Tomorrow, they would set foot in Helix's domain together.

As the day wore on, the clamor of preparation softened into smaller, more deliberate movements. Warriors finished binding their gear, checking every knot twice. Survivors adjusted their packs, cinched straps, and found small corners of the village for quiet moments before the march.

Matthew found Kaia sitting outside the healer's hut, sunlight catching in her auburn curls. She was wrapping a bundle of herbs with slow, thoughtful care, but her eyes locked on him the moment he approached.

"I'm coming with you," she said before he could speak.

He crouched down beside her, resting his forearms on his knees. "You're still recovering. If something goes wrong here, they'll need someone they can trust."

Her lips tightened. "You think I can't fight?"

"I think you're one of the strongest people here," he said softly, brushing a loose curl back from her face. "Which is why your strength belongs here right now— making sure this place is still standing when we get back."

Her protest faltered, replaced by the quiet weight of what he was asking. "You'd better come back to me, Matthew Fisher," she whispered.

"I will." He leaned in, and their kiss lingered longer than either meant it to—not their first, but the most serious, charged with the unspoken truth that there was no guarantee of another. When he pulled back, he pressed his palm lightly to her cheek before standing.

A short distance away, Avara sat cross-legged, sharpening the edge of her spear. Shayne walked up, trying—and failing—to keep his usual smirk in place. "You know, we could always just tell them we're lost. Head in the opposite direction. Start a nice little farm."

She didn't look up from her work. "You would grow nothing but weeds."

He chuckled, then let the smile fade. "Just... watch yourself out there, alright?"

This time she did meet his eyes, her expression unreadable for a heartbeat. Then, in her own language, she said softly, "Return to me." Shayne didn't need the translation.

Near the supply pile, Cartwright was checking the weight and balance of a rifle while Adam cinched the straps of his pack tight. They didn't talk much, but there was a mutual acknowledgement in the short nod they exchanged.

"You've proven yourself out here, kid," Cartwright said at last.

Adam smirked faintly. "We're not done yet."

"No," Cartwright agreed, slinging the rifle over his shoulder. "We're not."

By the time the sun dipped low, the entire village had gathered near the edge of the jungle. The air was heavy with the scent of burning resin, the smoke curling into shapes that seemed to twist like living things before vanishing into the dusk.

The chosen Vokari warriors stood in a line, weapons at their sides, painted for war. Survivors took their places among them—a strange, patchwork unit bound together by need and circumstance.

Shia approached Matthew with a small object cupped in both hands. It was a talisman—a carved piece of bone threaded with a thin strip of leather, etched in patterns he didn't recognize. She pressed it into his palm and closed his fingers over it. "It carries the strength of those who came before," she said. "When you feel fear... remember they walk with you."

Matthew nodded, the weight of it far heavier than the bone itself.

Nukapana raised a hand and spoke in his language, his voice carrying across the clearing. The words were short, rhythmic, almost like drumbeats—a send-off that needed no translation. Around them, villagers echoed the final line in unison, a low chant that seemed to vibrate in the earth.

Kaia stood at the front of the crowd, her arms crossed, eyes locked on Matthew. She didn't smile, but she didn't look away either.

He glanced at his allies—Shayne, Adam, Cartwright, Avara, Koro, and the Vokari warriors—and felt the full weight of what lay ahead. They turned toward the wall of green that would lead them to Helix's compound.

Matthew tightened his grip on the talisman, "We finish this," he said, his voice cutting through the evening air.

Without another word, the war party stepped into the jungle, the shadows swallowing them whole.

Behind the healer's hut, a shadow moved. Dr. Emilia Varn stepped into the open, her satchel slung tight across her shoulder. She glanced toward the departing group, her face unreadable, then turned and slipped into the forest in the opposite direction.

Her pace quickened as the sounds of the village faded. She pushed through ferns and low-hanging vines, eyes darting ahead as if fixed on some unseen destination.

A whisper cut through the undergrowth. "Now."

Figures burst from the shadows—men in ragged clothing, their faces streaked with dirt and sweat. The shapes of them were familiar, though the torchlight was too dim to be sure. Hands seized her arms, dragging her into the green.

She started to shout, but a rough hand clamped over her mouth. Through the blur of leaves, she caught the glint of a weapon—and the faint smell of saltwater.

Varn's muffled cry vanished into the jungle, leaving only the fading sound of her feet retreating deeper into the dark.

# Chapter 37  Into Helix's Domain

The first light of dawn spilled through the canopy, catching in thin threads of mist that clung to the jungle floor. Matthew stood at the edge of the Vokari village, the damp earth cool beneath his boots, watching the horizon brighten. The war party gathered behind him—survivors and Vokari warriors alike—their breath misting in the crisp morning air.

Koro was already there, towering over the others, his spear point glinting in the pale sun. The elite warriors moved with quiet discipline, their dark eyes scanning the jungle as if they could sense the dangers waiting ahead.

Adam adjusted the straps of his pack, restless, glancing at the warriors with a mix of curiosity and respect. Cartwright, beside him, gave the weapons one last inspection, his rifle slung over his shoulder. Avara stood with her spear in one hand, the other resting lightly against Shayne's arm—a brief, silent exchange before stepping forward.

Matthew noted one absence immediately. *Varn.* She wasn't among the survivors, nor was she with the villagers seeing them off. He scanned the crowd once more, but there was no trace of her. "Guess she's staying behind," Adam muttered. Cartwright's jaw clenched, but he said nothing. Matthew caught the look, a flicker of unease in the captain's eyes, and filed it away.

The forest beyond the village was still, yet it hummed with that low, ever-present tension the island seemed to breathe. Every sound—a rustle in the leaves, a distant birdcall—felt sharpened, amplified.

As they moved, life stirred around them. A *Protoceratops* herd emerged from the undergrowth to their left, small but muscular, their frilled heads bobbing warily. The Vokari warriors slowed, giving the animals space as they shuffled past, snorting softly before vanishing into the ferns.

Farther on, a shadow darted overhead—a massive *Terror Bird* leaping between branches with shocking speed before disappearing into the canopy. Shayne muttered under his breath, "Glad it's not hungry," but kept his hand near the handle of his blade.

The trail dipped into a marshy hollow, where a *Titanoboa* lay coiled in the shallows, its scales glistening like wet stone. The warriors moved in a wide arc to avoid disturbing it, the snake's golden eyes following them until they were gone.

Every creature they passed was a reminder—this was not their land. It was Helix's creation, a patchwork of resurrected beasts and unnatural hybrids, and the jungle itself seemed to watch their progress.

Matthew took one step forward, then another, the rest falling in behind him. This wasn't a hike. This was a march into enemy ground.

The jungle began to change. The deeper they went, the more it felt... wrong.

The air grew heavier, the calls of birds thinning until silence pressed against their ears. The ground underfoot was churned into wide, uneven trenches, roots torn up and scattered like snapped bones.

Koro crouched beside a tree and touched the deep gouges running along its trunk. The marks were fresh—sap still oozed in slow, sticky beads. "*Thova varu*," he said darkly, glancing at Matthew. "Cursed blood-beast."

Adam stepped closer, curiosity warring with caution. "What's that supposed to mean?" Koro didn't answer—he only pointed ahead, where a mound of fur and torn flesh lay in the clearing.

It had once been a *Megaloceros*—one of the giant elk the Vokari hunted for food. Now, its antlers were snapped clean in half, its belly ripped open so violently the ribs jutted through the skin. Flies swarmed thick over the carcass, but even they seemed hesitant, lifting off in jittery clouds whenever a breeze passed.

Cartwright's gaze moved from the elk to the ground beyond. Among the trampled ferns and massive claw prints, another pattern stood out—smaller, sharper... and unmistakably human. Boot prints.

He didn't say it aloud, but his gut tightened. He recognized the tread. Navy-issue. The kind the missing crew from the *Sea Hawk* had worn.

The party moved on, quieter now. They crossed a narrow ravine where water trickled between moss-slick stones. A tree beside the stream had been split nearly in half, as if something had rammed through it at full speed.

Every sign told the same story—something in this part of the jungle was hunting, and it wasn't hunting for food alone.

Matthew glanced over his shoulder, catching the wary looks between the warriors. They were trained, fearless men—but even they walked as if every step might draw attention from whatever ruled this ground.

Somewhere ahead, a branch cracked, slow and predatory.

The war party froze as one. Every set of eyes searched the shadowed green, ears straining for another sound. The silence that followed was worse than the noise—heavy, watchful.

Then the jungle exploded.

The *thova varu* burst from the foliage in a blur of muscle and armored hide, a nightmare fusion of raptor and saber-tooth—the creature Helix had named Raptoryx. Plated scales lined its spine like jagged stone, but its forelimbs were all raptor—hooked claws meant for tearing. The head was broad, with saber-like fangs jutting from a mouth that bellowed a guttural roar.

It hit the ground running, the impact shaking loose leaves from the trees.

"Scatter!" Matthew shouted.

Warriors dove aside as the beast barreled into the clearing, snapping its jaws at the closest Vokari. Spears struck its flanks but skidded off the armored plating. Cartwright fired in short, controlled bursts, the rifle crack echoing through the trees, but the rounds only staggered it for seconds before it charged again.

One of the warriors—Tanu, young but fierce—
planted his feet and thrust his spear upward at the
oncoming monster. For a heartbeat it looked
like he'd braced perfectly... until the beast veered, snapping
its jaws around his torso.

The sound was wet and final. Tanu screamed
once, blood spraying the leaves, before the beast shook
him like a rag and hurled him aside. He landed crumpled
and still, his spear splintered in half beside him.

The sight ignited a fury in the remaining warriors,
but their attacks only made the creature pivot faster,
swiping its claws at anything in reach.

Adam's boot slipped in the churned mud, and he
went down hard. Before he could scramble up, a fallen log
rolled against his legs, pinning him. His hands scrabbled at
the bark, panic flooding his eyes as the Raptoryx fixed on
him.

It lowered its head, growling—a deep, vibrating
sound that felt more like a warning to everything else to
stay away from its prey.

Koro charged, bellowing in Vokari, and drove his
spear into the beast's shoulder. The impact was enough to
stop the swipe of its claws. One raked across Koro's side,
tearing a deep gash before the warrior rolled clear.

Blood hit the ground. The Raptoryx's attention
shifted again, snapping between Koro and Adam like a
pendulum deciding who would die next.

"Keep it busy!" Matthew's voice cut through the
chaos. He had already spotted it—the vulnerable gap
beneath the plated scales at its throat.

The Raptoryx lunged again, its claws gouging deep
trenches into the mud as it charged. Koro staggered
to his feet, one hand pressed to the wound in his side, but
he was too far to intercept.

Matthew didn't think. He broke into a sprint, weaving through the chaos as the warriors hurled spears to draw the beast's focus. The Raptoryx twisted away from most of the strikes, moving with an awful, predatory grace despite its size.

"Hold it!" Matthew shouted.

Two warriors obeyed without hesitation, planting themselves at either flank, jabbing at its armored ribs. The Raptoryx roared, swiping one aside with enough force to send him skidding across the clearing, but the momentary distraction gave Matthew the opening he needed.

He darted to the side, circling until he was behind the beast. His eyes locked on the vulnerable gap beneath its plated throat—unarmored flesh, exposed when the creature reared back to strike.

Matthew gripped the spear tighter, feeling the rough wood bite into his palms. He could hear his own breathing over the chaos.

"*NOW!*"

He drove the spear upward with every ounce of strength, the tip punching through the soft flesh just behind the jaw. The Raptoryx's roar cut short into a choked, guttural rasp. Its claws flailed, raking the air, but the warriors surged in to keep it from turning on him.

Blood poured down the shaft, hot against Matthew's hands. The beast's movements faltered, then slowed, its massive body shuddering before it collapsed onto its side with a final, rattling hiss.

Silence pressed in again, broken only by the labored breathing of the survivors. Matthew stepped back, chest heaving, the spear still jutting from the Raptoryx's throat.

Koro, pale but standing, met his gaze. The warrior touched two fingers to his own forehead, then extended them toward Matthew—the Vokari salute reserved for those who had earned full respect in battle.

One by one, the other warriors mirrored the gesture.

Matthew glanced down at the fallen beast. "One less nightmare to follow us," he said, though he knew Helix had plenty more waiting.

The body of the Raptoryx lay still, its plated spine catching the fading sunlight like jagged bronze. Flies were already beginning to gather around its slack jaws.

Matthew wiped his hands on the damp grass, his chest still heaving from the fight. The warriors retrieved their spears, murmuring to each other in Vokari—words Shayne didn't bother to translate; the meaning was obvious.

Koro knelt briefly beside Tanu's body, closing the fallen warrior's eyes before rising again, his expression like carved stone. No one spoke of leaving him here— the Vokari would return for their dead.

Cartwright had moved a short distance from the group, his rifle at the ready, eyes scanning the tree line.

That was when he froze.

In the dim light beneath the canopy, shapes began to emerge—not animals this time, but people. Half a dozen of them.

They moved in tight formation, each holding a rifle or machete, clothing torn but boots intact. Faces gaunt, eyes shadowed with something darker than exhaustion.

Matthew's breath caught as Cartwright muttered, almost to himself, "No... it can't be."

Adam glanced over. "What?"

Cartwright's voice was barely a whisper. "That's... that's my crew. The ones we lost."

The figures stopped just beyond the clearing's edge, watching in silence. None of them called out. None smiled. Their expressions were empty—unreadable.

Matthew took a cautious step forward, but before he could speak, the lead figure—a tall man with a weathered face—made a short, precise hand signal. The entire group melted back into the foliage without a sound.

By the time the Vokari warriors pushed forward to give chase, the forest had swallowed them completely.

Koro turned to Matthew, his voice low. "They walk with the false god now."

Matthew's jaw tightened. He didn't have to ask who the false god was.

The war party pressed on in silence, the jungle swallowing the last echoes of the Raptoryx fight. The air felt heavier now, as though the island itself had shifted to watch their every step.

The sun bled low through the canopy, its light turning the mist into thin streams of gold. By the time they reached the ridge, the day was already collapsing into twilight.

Below them, carved out of the jungle like a wound, lay the Helixis compound.

Chain-link fences crowned with curling wire surrounded several squat, angular buildings. A dull industrial hum rolled up the slope, mingling with the faint flicker of lights. Here and there, metallic glints marked the patrol paths of armed guards.

In the center rose the tallest structure—a steel-and-glass tower that caught the last of the sunlight and turned it into a burning reflection.

Avara stared at it, her knuckles white around her spear. "The false god is home," she said quietly, almost to herself.

Matthew didn't answer. His eyes stayed locked on that tower, the place where all of this began—and where he knew it would have to end.

# Chapter 38  The False God's Lair

The jungle swallowed them as they descended from the ridge, the faint glow of the Helixis compound pulsing between the trees like the heartbeat of something sick.

Up close, it looked even worse than Matthew had imagined. Sections of the perimeter fence sagged inward, twisted by fallen trees. Whole walls had collapsed, exposing hollow rooms to the night air. Jungle roots pried apart concrete seams, drinking the damp like veins in stone. Yet here and there, pockets of light still burned— square windows bleeding a tired yellow, a hum that never quite went silent. Not abandoned. Not yet.

Koro raised a hand, and the party folded into the shadows. The nearest gate squatted under a dead floodlight. Two men in mismatched fatigues paced opposite routes, rifles slung, boots leaving dull scruffs on wet asphalt. Cartwright motioned to Avara—two fingers, then a downward chop. Wait.

On the far side of the fence, a night bird gave a throaty call. The nearer guard paused, glanced that way, and kept moving.

Cartwright stepped out of the brush like he'd been part of it all along. One arm snaked around the guard's throat, the other sealed over his mouth. Breath wheezed, boots scraped. Then stillness. Cartwright lowered the body into high grass and gave a curt signal.

The second guard pivoted at the squeak of metal. A spear whispered through the gate gap and took him just beneath the collarbone. He folded in a graceless sprawl. The Vokari warrior who'd thrown it padded forward, retrieved the shaft, and wiped it with a handful of ferns.

"Move," Cartwright murmured.

They slipped through a torn seam where the fence bowed like a mouth pried open. Inside, Helix's kingdom smelled of mold and oil and faint decay—the compounded stink of a place that should be dead but refuses to admit it.

The path beyond the gate had been a neat service road once. Now it was a creek of mud and leaf rot, reflectiing the dim, flickering lamps that clung to poles like feverish stars. Shadows shifted at every step, layers of jungle ripple laid over the rigid bones of the facility. A door banged somewhere in the wind. Farther off, something metallic fell, clattered, and didn't move again.

"Eyes," Matthew whispered.

They moved in pairs. Cartwright and Avara took point, reading the ground with the calm efficiency of hunters who trusted each other's pace. Adam stayed a step behind Matthew, jaw set, the silence around him loud with things unsaid. Shayne kept close to Koro, mirroring the warrior's hand signals with careful attention. The other Vokari slipped from cover to cover, bodies painted and quiet, each movement deliberate.

At the first corner they froze. A beam of white cut a horizontal line across the darkness—someone sweeping a flashlight down a connecting corridor. Boots followed, crisp, not hurried. The light passed, vanished. Another set approached, slower, uncertain, like the walker was listening to something Matthew couldn't hear.

They waited, listening to the walker breathe.

The light clicked off.

Cartwright's hand rose: hold.

The steps receded. When they moved again, their feet made no noise at all.

They found a service door canted crooked in its frame, paint blistered and furred with moss. Avara eased it inward. The smell hit first—rust and mildew, the sour bite of ancient chemicals. Lights flickered overhead, bucking, throwing the hallway into jittering pale and shadow.

On the nearest wall, a red sign sagged on one bent screw. BIOHAZARD. A smear of something brown edged one corner of it like a fingerprint.

They passed a room that had been a holding area. Cages lined the walls—domed, reinforced, bars bent where something had tried hard to leave. The floor was scored with gouges and scuffs, lines that never ran straight like the thing making them didn't move the way a man moved. Stains spread in spattered circles. A Vokari warrior spat on the threshold and touched the doorframe with two fingers, then his chest.

"Ken'vo sharo," Avara said under her breath. Return death to the jungle.

Another hallway sloped downward. Jungle roots punched through the ceiling panels, drooping like the intestines of the building. A flicker overhead caught and steadied. Somewhere beneath them, a low, steady thrum pulsed. Generators. Life support.

They crossed into a wing that had once been a museum for Helix's theft. Glass cases lined both walls, inside them Vokari artifacts pried from graves and hearths—masks, bone flutes, carved shields, baskets, a spear with a notch worn by a thousand hands. A child's anklet lay beside a cracked ceremonial bowl. Beneath one display card, a bullet hole popped the glass into a spiderweb.

Avara stopped. Her reflection wavered over a funerary mask painted in soot and chalk. She didn't speak. She didn't need to. The tension in her jaw said everything. Then she lifted her spear and drove the butt through the case. The shatter rang down the hall like a chime, crisp and final.

"Easy," Cartwright said, not unkindly. He didn't reprimand her. He didn't have the right.

They found a workbench two rooms later, the table littered with what should never have been collected: personal things, sorted, tagged. A strip of green satin that had once been Kaia's graduation sash, now frayed filthy. Shayne's field journal with his own handwriting on the margins, a smear of dried mud across the word "river." A dented metal bottle with MF scratched into one side.

Adam froze, staring at a small, elastic loop of red fabric tangled among the items. A hair tie. He didn't pick it up. He didn't move at all.

"They've been watching us since the crash," he said, voice flat.

Matthew's stomach went cold. Helix didn't see people. He saw assets. He saw variables. Catalogs were just another way to call a life an experiment.

Footfalls whispered ahead. Not many. The gait was unsteady, the rhythm off, like hunger had chewed the walker down to bone.

Cartwright was moving before the sound reached the corner. He slipped behind a jut of wall, counted the breaths, and took the man by the collar as he staggered into reach. A knife kissed ribs. The guard's eyes flared, then softened, the fight gone as quickly as it had sparked.

"Hold," Matthew said. "He can talk."

Cartwright pressed the man against the wall without cruelty. Avara took the rifle.

"Where is he?" Matthew asked.

The man licked cracked lips. "Waiting," he rasped. His eyes blinked slow, disbelieving. "Thought we'd hear the angels first. He said... he said you'd come."

"Who?"

The man's mouth twitched into something like a smile that had forgotten how. "The doctor. The one with the silver hair."

His knees buckled. Cartwright eased him down. The man's breath rattled, shallow and quick. Matthew crouched, but whatever had kept the guard upright for this long went out like a candle.

They moved on.

The farther in they went, the fewer the cobwebs. Footprints scuffed the dust in fresh arcs. A door stood open with a chair dragged behind it, one leg leaving an arc on the tile. On a desk in a side room, a ceramic mug sat in a ring of its warmth. No steam. But not cold. Matthew trailed a finger through the condensation print and wiped it on his jeans.

"Someone's still here," Shayne said. "Recently."

"More than one," Cartwright replied, eyeing two chairs angled toward each other, not quite aligned with the desk. A notebook lay corner-open to a page neat, compact handwriting—columns, times, illegible codes. None of it looked like Helix's quick, aggressive scrawl. Whoever kept these notes had patience and the habit of gathering evidence.

They crossed a balcony that ran above a cavernous lab. Below, tables lay overturned, glass clinging to frames in jagged teeth. A tank the size of a truck sat spider-webbed with cracks, its floor dark with whatever had been inside it when it failed. Vines threaded the ceiling grid. Something moved in the ducts with a dry, scraping slither and gone. The Vokari warriors tilted their heads in the same instant, listening with the attention of prey that has learned to survive by hearing what is not meant to be heard.

Koro touched the railing, then withdrew his hand as if the metal itself were unclean. "Thova varu," he murmured. Cursed blood-beasts.

"Keep moving," Matthew said. "We're close."

They descended into a corridor whose walls gleamed with a fine film of moisture, as if the building were sweating. The hum grew louder here, layered— generators, server fans, something much deeper that thrummed through the soles of their feet. The air felt cooler, conditioned. Maintenance had been here, recently enough that the smell of solvent still bit the back of Matthew's throat.

The survivors fell silent without being told. Even Adam's grief-sharpened focus narrowed to a razor. Avara glanced at the ceiling cameras—dead eyes with no red LEDs, no little blinks. Either the power to them had been cut or someone wanted them to believe that.

The corridor kinked left, then right, then opened into a long hall that ended at a door built to stop things a building should never have to stop. Thick steel. Reinforced bolts sitting proud on their housings. A faded symbol flaked across the face—two strands twined into a helix that had lost half its paint but none of its arrogance.

Matthew stopped. His chest tightened as if a hand had found his sternum and pressed. This was the artery of the place. On the near wall, a keypad smeared with fingerprints shone from regular use. Above it, a security badge reader blinked a steady green as if it had never known a day of failure.

He swallowed. There was a smear of coffee on the floor near the hinge, dark and recent enough to glisten. Two heel prints overlapped there, one on the edge of the puddle, turned outward, as if two people had stood close together and then stepped away in different directions.

"Here," Cartwright said quietly. No triumph. Just acknowledgement.

The others fanned to either side of the hall, taking positions behind crates and dead consoles. Koro's warriors split, two at the rear watching the way they'd come, four forward with spears leveled low. Avara laid a palm against the wall, closed her eyes a heartbeat, and withdrew her hand.

Adam looked at Matthew. "If he's behind that—"

"I know," Matthew said.

He stepped to the door and laid his fingers on the wheel. Cold metal bit his skin. Beyond it, he could feel thunder through a window long before the sound reaches you.

For a moment he let himself think of Kaia, of the yellow light the healer kept beside her mat, of the way she had smiled when he promised he'd come back. Of Megan's necklace in Adam's fist and the line Adam had spoken over the grave. Of Nukapana's voice naming Helix a false god, and the way the warriors had saluted when the Raptoryx fell, and the silence that came after any victory that costs more than it returns.

He took a breath and looked back at the others. Cartwright's eyes met his and nodded once. Shayne's jaw worked, a joke swallowed. Avara's grip tightened on her spear until tendons shone. Adam's mouth was a thin, bloodless line.

Matthew turned the wheel.

The seal released with a hiss like an exhale.

He didn't open it yet. He let the sound fade into the hum and the breath of the building. Then he leaned forward until his forehead touched the cool steel and said, very quietly, "No more."

He straightened, set his hand to the latch, and moved.

# Chapter 39  Alone with the Devil

The corridor leading to the control room felt longer than it had any right to be—every step a drumbeat in Matthew's chest. Behind him, the rest of the group waited in tense silence. Cartwright's eyes followed him until the last possible moment, the older man giving a slow nod that said, *Come back, kid.*

Matthew placed a hand on the steel door's handle. "Stay here." he told them. "This is something I have to do alone."

No one argued. Adam looked ready to protest, his jaw tight, but Avara's hand landed firmly on his shoulder, keeping him back. Koro shifted his spear, standing just enough in Adam's way to make the point clear.

Matthew stepped through and closed the door.

The seal locked behind him with a hiss, the sound final, cutting away the jungle's humid breath and the faint murmur of his companions. The air here was cold, sterile—an entirely different world. The faint hum of machinery filled the silence, low and constant, like a heartbeat that wasn't his.

Banks of dead monitors lined the walls, each a black mirror catching fractured reflections of him and the single figure standing under the central light. A broad table dominated the middle of the room, a massive map encased under glass, its surface dotted with pins, notes, and cryptic markings.

Helix stood at its far side, his posture relaxed but precise, the way a predator rests while watching its prey. He wore no coat now, just a crisp shirt rolled neatly to the elbows, silvering hair combed back from his face. He turned as Matthew approached, and the smile he offered was warm—disarmingly so.

"Matthew," he said, his voice smooth, unhurried. "You've made it. I wasn't sure if you'd walk through that door... or leave me to my fate."

Matthew stopped just short of the map table, boots heavy on the grated floor. His gaze moved around the room, searching—not for exits, but for signs. And there were signs. Two chairs pulled up, not one. A second coffee cup, still faintly steaming. A data pad on the far end with neat handwriting in a style he didn't recognize.

"You're alone?" Matthew asked, tone sharp.

Helix's smile didn't falter. "For now."

He gestured to the opposite chair. "Please. Sit. We have so much to discuss."

Matthew didn't move. "Say what you have to say."

Helix studied him for a beat longer, the smile thinning as if he'd decided on a particular strategy. "Very well. But understand—what I'm about to tell you... it's not persuasion, Matthew. It's illumination. Once you see the truth of this place, of me, of *you*... the path forward will be obvious."

The hum of the unseen machinery seemed to grow louder in the pause that followed. Somewhere beyond the walls, a faint metallic clang echoed, followed by silence.

Matthew didn't blink. "Then start talking."

Helix's smile deepened, like a man stepping onto a stage he'd been waiting his whole life to stand on.

"Do you know what the world is, Matthew?" he began, his voice low but confident. "A cage. A beautiful one, but a cage nonetheless. And cages are meant to be escaped."

He reached for the map's glass surface, tracing a fingertip over an unmarked patch of ocean. "Years ago, I wasn't looking for this place. I was searching for something else entirely—a stable micro-wormhole that could act as a transport channel for matter without annihilating it. Most experiments fail in the first microsecond. But... mine didn't."

He glanced up, studying Matthew's face before continuing.

"I was running a series of tests in the South Pacific. A remote island chain, uninhabited—or so I thought. Instruments began picking up gravitational distortions... minute at first, then growing. And then, one day, I saw it: a tear in the fabric of space-time. Like a curtain pulling back, just for a moment."

Matthew's fingers tightened on the map table's edge.

"You went in," Matthew said. Not a question.

Helix nodded. "Of course. Wouldn't you?" he leaned forward, his eyes bright with the memory. "Inside... was Helixandra. Untouched by man. A world where creatures long dead still walked. A place where evolution had been... interrupted. And I saw potential immediately."

His tone shifted, warmer, almost conspiratorial. "We established Helixis Corporation under the guise of genetic engineering for medicine, agriculture, life extension. The investors thought the wormhole was just a remote research site. But in reality, I was building something far greater. A sanctuary. A laboratory. An ark."

He turned the map toward Matthew, revealing for the first time its true form—a detailed rendering of the island, drawn with precision, every mountain, river, and valley labeled. At the top of the page, in bold ink, was the name:

**HELIXANDRA**

Matthew's brow furrowed.

Helix then moved from the map table to a long glass cabinet. His fingers lingered on the glass cabinet as if it were an altar. The hydraulic seal hissed, and the doors folded away, revealing row after row of tall jars and smaller containers. The light inside was cold and clinical, reflecting off cloudy preservative fluid and warped, dead eyes staring out from the depths.

"Every great leap in history," Helix began, "was built on the corpses of what didn't work."

He stepped aside, letting Matthew see the horror in full—several limbs, hybrid skulls, mutated organs.

Helix's hand closed around a jar holding something the size of a human head, its face a twisted blend of feathers and fangs. "Raptoryx," he said softly.

"Part Velociraptor, part Smilodon, with avian neurology to sharpen hunting reflexes. The first batches were unstable—skull structure collapsed after high-speed lunges. But the later generations... well, you've met them."

He replaced the jar and gestured toward a massive coil of preserved muscle inside a tall tube. Two curved fangs jutted out from its center. "Boavorex. Titanoboa and Komodo dragon. The venom output exceeded projections. They'd kill prey within seconds—but they had no tolerance for their own kind. Entire breeding pools wiped out from territorial fights."

Helix moved on, picking up a smaller container with something that looked like a bird's talon, only covered in scales and ending in serrated claws. "Ravenghast. Raven intellect, Deinonychus predatory instinct. They coordinated mid-air ambushes, striking from the canopy. Too effective—they emptied whole sectors of prey within weeks. I had to cull them myself."

Matthew's eyes moved to a jar holding a discolored, bloated fish head with glowing, translucent teeth.

"Ah," Helix said, noting his gaze. "Sawmaw. Anglerfish and saltwater crocodile. A perfect oceanic trapper. One bite, and the prey's blood clouded the water so badly they couldn't see to flee."

He crossed to a diagram pinned beside the jars— an armored quadruped with a long, spear-like tail. "Ironback Mauler," Helix continued. "Stegosaurus plating with bull gorilla musculature. Near impossible to bring down... unless you knew about the unarmored spot under the jaw."

He smiled faintly, as though sharing an inside joke. "Most predators never did."

Then he opened another cabinet, this one containing skeletal remains that seemed to shimmer faintly. "Raptoryx Prime. The apex strain. Bone density perfect, reflexes unmatched, but too intelligent for control measures. They learned the location of my supply routes and began... sabotaging them."

Matthew stayed silent, his knuckles whitening on the edge of the table.

Helix's tone shifted, almost proud. "Do you see, Matthew? The island is more than a home for these creatures. It's a proving ground. I don't simply breed survival—I *design* it."

Matthew's voice cut through the air, sharp and low. "And the Vokari? Did you create them too?"

Helix paused—just for a second—then smiled thinly. "No. They were here before me. At first, they were an inconvenience. Territorial. Obstinate. But... then I realized they were an opportunity. A rare, isolated gene pool. Humans untainted by industrial toxins, urban immunity collapses... perfect for testing human adaptation under extreme conditions."

Matthew's jaw tightened. "You used them as lab rats."

'I pushed them," Helix said, stepping closer. "Predator exposure. Scarcity trials. Venom testing. Disease resilience. And they adapted. They *always* adapted. Tell me, Matthew—wouldn't you want to know what humanity could become if given the right... encouragement?"

Helix's hand drifted over the last jar before letting the cabinet seal itself with a quiet hiss. The hum of the room seemed louder now, every machine a background heartbeat.

He stepped toward a covered shape at the far end of the control room. "Everything I've built here—every creature, every trial—was leading to this."

With a single motion, he pulled away the tarp. Underneath stood a tall, circular frame threaded with cables and alloy struts, its center filled with a shimmering distortion like heat haze. The air around it bent subtly, as if reality itself strained against the edges.

Matthew took an instinctive step closer. "What is that?"

"The Threshold Array," Helix said. "The key to passing through the wormhole at will—without the... unpredictable affects you experienced coming in."

He circled the device like a priest at an altar, gesturing to its layered rings and pulsing conduits. "A wormhole, Matthew, is not just a door. It's a needle through fabric. Every time we pass through without control, we risk tearing the weave itself. But with this array... we step between worlds cleanly. Safely."

Matthew's gaze narrowed. "So, you can leave any time you want."

"I could," Helix agreed. "But why would I? Out there, the world is constrained by politics, fear, the small-minded grasp of lesser men. Here, I am unbound."

He tapped another console, bringing a new machine to life—a towering cylinder filled with faint blue light. Inside, three suspended humanoid shapes slowly rotated. The outlines were hazy, half-formed, like ghosts in water.

"This," Helix said softly, "is the Genesis Chamber. DNA reclamation, structural restoration, cellular reactivation. In short... resurrection."

Matthew stared, the hum of the chamber crawling up his spine.

"Not for everyone," Helix continued. "Cell degradation must be minimal. The subject must not have been killed by the island's more... aggressive elements. But given a viable sample?" He turned, eyes gleaming. "They return. Whole."

Matthew's thoughts snapped instantly to Megan. Adam's haunted face.

Helix's voice dropped, coaxing. "You've lost people here. Friends. I could give them back to you. To *all* of us."

Matthew's jaw tightened. "At what cost?"

"No cost," Helix said, almost gently. "Only vision. You think this island is a trap. It's a crucible. It tempers the worthy. And you, Matthew, have proven yourself. Time and again."

He moved closer, lowering his voice to an almost paternal murmur. "You could lead this place when I'm gone. You could shape the next age of life. Imagine an army of Raptoryx under your command. Imagine what we could build, together."

For a long moment, Matthew said nothing. His eyes scanned the array, the chamber, the gleaming instruments—all the pieces of a god's workshop.

Finally, he spoke. "You called it a crucible. You gave it a name."

Helix smiled faintly. "Yes. Helixandra."

Matthew froze. The syllables rolled in his mind, breaking apart, reassembling. His eyes hardened. "Helixandra... Ardan Helix."

Helix didn't flinch. "You're quick. Quicker than I was at your age."

Matthew shook his head slowly. "All this time... Clark was a lie."

"Clark was an introduction," Helix said, his tone never wavering. "Helix is the truth."

Matthew took a slow breath, trying to steady the pulse hammering in his ears. "You've spent years playing god," he said quietly. "Killing people. Using them. And you think I'd just... take your place?"

Helix didn't move, didn't blink. "I think you understand the difference between sentiment and survival. You've seen what happens when the weak try to lead. You've *felt* it—every time someone died because they weren't fast enough, strong enough, ruthless enough."

"Ruthless," Matthew echoed. His tone was flat, but his hand had drifted near the back of his belt—to the weight of Grent's pistol, retrieved from the Vokari supply room before they left.

Before Helix could respond, a voice came from the shadows.

"He's right, Matthew."

Matthew's head snapped toward the far corner. Dr. Emilia Varn stepped into the light, her eyes steady on him. "You've been fighting this place since the moment you arrived. But you could master it. We could."

The betrayal hit like a physical blow. "You've been with him... this whole time?"

Her expression didn't change. "I saw the truth before any of you. This island isn't a curse—it's the next step. And he's the only one who can guide it."

Helix stepped forward, spreading his hands like a man offering a gift. "Join us, Matthew. Take the array. Take the chamber. Take *everything*. You'll never have to bury another friend again."

The room felt suddenly smaller, the air heavier. The hum of the machines seemed to press against

Matthew's skull. For a moment, he imagined it—Megan alive again, Kaia safe forever, the tribe armed against any threat.

Then he saw the other side. The hybrids tearing through the jungle. The Vokari shackled in Helix's labs. Grent's smirk over Megan's broken body.

Matthew stepped forward slowly, placing the pistol on the table between them. "Two bullets," he said. "One for each of you, if you choose."

Helix's brow furrowed, but before he could speak, Matthew stepped back toward the door. "You'll stay here. Both of you. And you'll never hurt anyone again."

He moved quickly, yanking the heavy soundproof door shut. The lock engaged with a deep metallic clunk.

Inside, Helix's voice was muffled but clear enough to carry. "You can't cage what you don't understand, Matthew. This island *needs* us."

Matthew stared at the sealed door for a long moment, his throat tight. Then he spoke, voice low and steady. "No. It needs to survive you."

He turned and walked away, the corridor swallowing him in shadow as the machines hummed on behind steel and silence.

# Chapter 40  The Last Path Home

The door to the control room thudded shut, the sound echoing through the hollow corridors like the last beat of a dying heart. Matthew turned the wheel lock until it ground against the frame, then stepped back. His reflection stared back at him in the steel—sweat streaked, eyes hard, jaw clenched. Somewhere inside that room, Helix was likely already plotting his next move. Varn too. But not today. Not on his watch.

Cartwright was waiting at the end of the corridor, rifle cradled, eyes scanning for movement. "It's done?"

Matthew walked toward him, forcing his voice to stay even. "It's done."

The older man's gaze flickered over Matthew's expression, searching for something—regret, doubt, maybe. Whatever he found, he kept it to himself. He just gave a sharp nod and fell in beside him.

The air in the compound was thick with the acrid tang of gunpowder and the copper bite of blood. The hallways were quieter now, the chaos of minutes ago replaced by the soft, unsettling hum of the generators. Outside, the sharp pops of gunfire came sporadically— Vokari warriors and the remaining survivors finishing off Helix's loyalists.

As they stepped into the open, the jungle pressed against the outer fences, green and wild, reclaiming the edges of the false kingdom. Avara stood near the courtyard gates with two of her warriors, their spears slick with rain and something darker. She gave Matthew a single nod, a silent acknowledgement that the fight here was almost over.

Adam emerged from behind a collapsed wall, wiping sweat and grime from his face. His eyes searched Matthew's like a man checking the weather before a long voyage. "Well?"

Matthew didn't answer right away. He didn't need to. The way he strode toward the gate, past Adam, past the bodies cooling in the mud, said enough. "We're done here," he said at last.

The group began moving toward the jungle path, their footsteps muted in the damp soil. Behind them, the compound loomed—silent, waiting. Somewhere deep inside, behind layers of steel and silence, Helix waited too.

The jungle greeted them with the familiar, restless chorus of chirps, trills, and distant roars. Even after everything, the sounds of Helixandra had a way of reminding them that the island was still alive... and still dangerous.

Cartwright took point, scanning the path with the calm precision of a man who'd spent half his life moving through hostile terrain. Avara moved at his flank, speaking in low bursts of Vokari to the two warriors shadowing them. Adam stayed close to Matthew, his steps quick, like if he lingered too long, he might start thinking about the compound they'd left behind—or the people they hadn't brought out.

"I hate this part," Adam muttered.

Matthew glanced at him. "The walking?"

"The waiting," Adam said. "Knowing Kaia's back there, not knowing what's happened while we've been gone..." His voice trailed off, heavy with something unspoken.

Matthew didn't answer. He knew the feeling too well—Kaia's absence had been a knot in his chest the entire time they'd been inside the compound. Every step toward the Vokari village was a step toward untying it.

They moved in near silence, save for the wet slap of mud under boots and sandals. At one point, the brush ahead rustled with heavy movement, but when a shadow flickered across the trail, it melted back into the green without showing itself. A reminder that, even without Helix's loyalists, the jungle would never be theirs.

The rain started halfway through the trek, a slow drizzle that clung to their hair and clothes, cooling them but making the ground slick. Avara didn't slow—if anything, she moved faster, as though the rain was a blessing that pushed them homeward.

By the time the treetop spires of the Vokari village came into view, the knot in Matthew's chest had pulled tighter. Somewhere up there, Kaia was either safe... or she wasn't.

The moment they stepped into the village clearing, the air shifted. Vokari eyes followed them from the woven platforms above, from shadowed doorways and half-hidden walkways in the trees. Then, movement—a figure breaking from the cluster of huts.

Kaia.

She was down the ramp before anyone could call her name, rain-dark curls plastered against her face. Matthew didn't care who was watching—he caught her as she hit the ground, arms closing around her like if he let go, the island might take her too.

"You're late," she murmured into his shoulder, voice thick but teasing.

"Got caught up," Matthew said, pulling back just enough to look her over. "You're okay?"

She smiled faintly. "I am now."

Behind them, Avara had moved to meet Shayne, their hands brushing before she pulled him into a hug that lasted too long to be casual. He grinned in that crooked way he always did when he was trying not to say something sappy.

Cartwright clasped Chief Nukapana's forearm in the way warriors do, their eyes locking in a mutual respect forged by battles survived together.

It didn't take long for word to spread—by the time the warriors had set their spears aside, the entire village seemed to know the outsiders were leaving. A fire was lit, and the farewell began.

The Vokari gathered in a wide circle, voices rising in a low chant that carried like the hum of the earth itself. Shayne stood beside Matthew until Avara stepped forward, her gaze fixed on him.

"I stay," she said softly.

Matthew blinked. "What?"

Shayne's eyes didn't leave hers. "I'm not going back, Matt." He hesitated, then smiled faintly. "I've been searching for a place that made sense. I found it."

Avara's hand slid into his, her fingers lacing with his like they'd been doing it for years. The look between them said more than any speech could.

Matthew didn't argue. He just pulled Shayne into a quick, rough hug. "Don't get yourself killed."

"No promises," Shayne said, smirking through the emotion in his voice.

Adam stood off to the side, silent, his thumb absently rubbing the smooth surface of Megan's necklace. His eyes were fixed on the fire, but his mind was somewhere far away.

The chanting rose, the voices weaving words Matthew didn't understand but somehow felt. A blessing. A promise. A goodbye.

When the embers began to dim, the moment to leave could no longer be pushed back. The rain had stopped by morning, leaving the jungle steaming in the first heat of the day. Warriors walked ahead and behind them, spears in hand, their presence more escort than guard now.

The path to the coast felt different this time—less like a place trying to swallow them whole, more like a living corridor guiding them toward an ending.

Cartwright's voice was low when he leaned toward Matthew. "You really think that stabilizer will still work after sitting in a ruin this long?"

"It has to," Matthew said. He didn't add the other thought—the one where it didn't work and they were stuck here for good.

Kaia stayed close, her hand brushing his now and then. Adam trailed behind them, quiet, the necklace glinting against his palm whenever the sunlight broke through the canopy.

Hours later, the tree line broke to reveal the old Helixis hangar—half-collapsed, metal ribs jutting into the air like the carcass of some giant machine. The smell of saltwater drifted from beyond it, faint but tantalizing.

The warriors fanned out, scanning the perimeter before giving a short call of "Shava," their word for *clear*.

Inside, the stabilizer stood where Helix must have left it—tall, skeletal, and humming faintly, like it was breathing. Beside it, a sleek boat sat cradled in the remains of a launch bay, its hull untouched by rust.

Matthew stepped forward, running his hand along the stabilizer's frame. "This is it," he said quietly. "Our way out."

Kaia gave him a faint smile. "Then let's go home."

They began checking the boat, untying lines, and prepping supplies. Outside, distant roars echoed from somewhere deep in the jungle—reminders that the island wasn't going to give them an easy send-off.

By the time the sun dipped low, the boat was ready. The survivors stood at the water's edge, the stabilizer's frame glowing faintly in the twilight like a doorway to somewhere impossible.

Chief Nukapana approached first, carrying a small carved talisman of bone and shell. He pressed it into Matthew's hand. "For protection," he said in halting English. "From the kenai... and from the thova."

Shia, the shaman, stepped forward next. She dipped her fingers in ash and drew a line across each of their foreheads, chanting in Vokari:

*Keta*
*mora vunakai, shta talo kenai, hura vona shatai... ken'vo malakai,*
*shta tola yenavai.*

Shayne translated quietly from where he stood beside Avara: *She walks now in the eternal river, where pain is no more. The spirits guide her to the firelight of her ancestors. She is not lost. She is returned.*

It wasn't just for them—it was for every friend the island had claimed.

When the blessing was over, Matthew and Shayne clasped forearms, then pulled each other into a rough hug.

"You sure about this?" Matthew asked.

Shayne grinned faintly. "I've never been more sure of anything. You'll be fine without me."

"Not the point," Matthew muttered, but he let go.

Avara took Shayne's hand, and together they stepped back into the crowd of warriors.

Kaia squeezed Matthew's hand as they boarded the boat, Adam following without a word, eyes still shadowed with thoughts of Megan. Cartwright started the engine—a low, steady rumble filling the air.

The stabilizer flared to life, light bending and folding in on itself until a swirling portal of mist and color bloomed in the air before them. The wormhole.

As they crossed the threshold, the air changed— denser, colder, alive with static. Matthew kept his gaze forward, the island fading into a mirage behind them.

Wind roared around them as the wormhole flickered like a dying star, its shimmering edges collapsing inward. The four remaining survivors huddled together in the small escape vessel — scraped, bruised, sunburned, but alive.

Matthew gripped the railing as the boat surged forward, pulled by a force none of them could understand. Kaia leaned against him, trembling, her breath uneven but warm against his shoulder. Cartwright steered with white-knuckled hands, jaw clenched against pain and exhaustion.

Adam sat alone near the stern, elbows on his knees, staring hollow-eyed at the unraveling tear in reality. He hadn't spoken since they'd boarded. He hadn't cried. He just… existed. The grief wrapped around him like a second skin.

The island glowed through the shrinking rift — Helixandra's mountains rising like the ribs of some great, sleeping colossus… the jungle canopy rolling in slow, restless waves… the dome of the lab barely visible through the mist.

Matthew swallowed.
Part of him expected something to burst from the trees — a roar, a shadow, claws — some final nightmare refusing to let them go.

But the island stayed still.
Watching.
Always watching.
Kaia squeezed his arm.
"You did it," she whispered. "You got us home."

Matthew didn't answer.
Because he didn't feel like a hero.

He felt changed. Marked. Like the island hadn't just tested him — it had chosen him.

As the wormhole shrank to a glowing thread, he caught one last glimpse of the treeline… and for a heartbeat, he thought he saw a figure step forward — raising something to the sky.

Then the rift snapped shut like a blinking eye.
Silence.

Ocean. Wind. The world they once knew.

Matthew exhaled for the first time in what felt like days.

Kaia released a shaking breath.

Cartwright steadied the wheel, muttering, "Hold together… just a little longer…"

Adam didn't move.

Didn't blink.

Just stared at the empty horizon where Megan would never stand again.

"They're safe," Kaia whispered, trying to convince herself. "Shayne is safe. He chose to stay with her."

Matthew nodded softly. Avara's face flashed in his mind — fierce, steady, loyal.

"He's where he needs to be."

But they all knew the truth:

Shayne wouldn't have stayed unless he believed the island needed him.

Unless someone needed him.

Matthew lifted his eyes toward the horizon, jaw tightening.

Kaia looked up at him.

"What are you thinking?"

Matthew forced a breath.

Forced a smile, he didn't feel.

"Just… that it's over."

Kaia accepted the lie, resting her head against him.

But Matthew knew better.

Helixandra wasn't done.

Not with them.

Not with the world.

And neither was Helix.

The boat cut across the open sea, carrying the four survivors toward a future forever marked by the island they left behind — and the shadow still rising beneath it.

Fade to black...

# Epilogue  The Rebuilding

Somewhere deep inside the Helixis compound, the sealed control room door creaked open.
A heavy lock dropped with a metallic chunk.

Jules Fenwick slipped into the room, his flashlight beam cutting through smoke and dust. Emergency lights pulsed faintly, barely illuminating the wreckage of consoles and shattered glass.

Two figures sat against the far wall, silhouettes framed by the faint glow of a damaged monitor:
Helix and Varn. Bruised. Exhausted. Alive.

"You're late," Helix said, rising smoothly to his feet.

Jules smirked and tossed him a keycard.
"Had to make sure the others were gone for good."

Helix looked toward the empty doorway, as if he could still hear the faint echo of the survivors leaving.
"We have work to do."

Varn stood beside him, brushing dust from her sleeves, her expression tight but steady.
She wasn't bound. She wasn't resisting.
She had made her choice — for now.

She looked at Helix carefully.
"Do you think they'll come back?"

Helix's thin smile sharpened.

"I'm counting on it," he said.
"And if not… we give them a reason to come back."

A low hum rolled through the floor as battered machinery rumbled awake.
Jules flinched as a shadow drifted across the hallway — one of the surviving hybrids limping past the open door, its yellow eyes glowing in the dark.

Helix turned toward the central console. The cracked screens flickered to life under his touch — genome charts, hybrid behavior logs, island schematics.
One line blinked steadily:
**WORMHOLE GATE —**
**REINITIALIZING… 18%**

Varn watched with a mixture of dread and inevitability.

Jules tilted his head. "Where do we start?"

Helix kept his gaze on the screen.
"With everything they left behind."

Jules flicked off the flashlight. The room fell into darkness again — but not silence.
Deep beneath them, the island shifted… awakening.

The false god had been freed,
and Helixandra's second age had begun.

## ABOUT THE AUTHOR

**Jason M. Bucklew** is an American thriller and speculative
fiction author known for blending cinematic adventure
with emotional character-driven storytelling. A lifelong
lover of mysterious worlds, prehistoric creatures, and high-
stakes survival tales, he writes with a focus on atmosphere,
tension, and the resilience of the human spirit.

When he isn't writing, Jason enjoys exploring the
outdoors, studying folklore, and developing the worlds of
his future novels. *Helixandra* is his debut work and the first
entry in a planned series.

To learn more about upcoming books, artwork, and
behind-the-scenes content, visit:

**JasonBucklew.com**